Ancient Blood

A Kayne Sorenson Mystery

Thomas Paul Severino

Ancient Blood

A Kayne Sorenson Mystery

Thomas Paul Severino

Copyright 2019

Pollywog Pond Communications, Ft. Lauderdale

tomseverino.com

tomseverino100@gmail.com

Cover painting: Joseph Lycett, ca.1817, *Aborigines Resting by a Camp Fire near the Mouth of the Hunter River, Newcastle, NSW*, courtesy National Library of Australia, nla.obj-138500420

ISBN: 979-1-7322278-7-3

Ancient Blood

Also by Thomas Paul Severino

The Kayne Sorenson Mysteries: The Quartet of Blood

Seed Blood

Tribal Blood

Stage Blood

Ancient Blood

The Kayne Sorenson Mysteries: The Quartet of Evil

The Evil Genius

The Shadow of Evil

The Pearl of Great Evil

The Evil League

The Kayne Sorenson Mysteries: The New Adventures

The Crystal Orb

The Flower of Gold

The Amazing Adventures of Rebecca Quinto

The Frozen Diva

The Lost Museum

The Last Maya

Thomas Paul Severino

Ancient Blood

For James, Janet, Mary, and John

We were meant to be joined by blood,

but we chose to be united by love.

We live outside the touch of time.

Love makes a family.

Thomas Paul Severino

Ancient Blood

Acknowledgment of Country

Today, we stand in footsteps millennia old.

May we acknowledge the traditional owners

whose cultures and customs have nurtured,

and continue to nurture this land,

since men and women

awoke from the great dream.

We honour the presence of these ancestors

who reside in the imagination of this land

and whose irrepressible spirituality

flows through all creation.

Jonathan Hill, poet

We are all visitors to this time, this place. We are just passing through. Our purpose here is to observe, to learn, to grow, to love... and then to return home.

Aboriginal Proverb

Thomas Paul Severino

Prologue

"What I need you both to know is that this is a very dangerous pregnancy. Multiple births are always risky. With triplets, and given the dimensions of your pelvis, there is an increased possibility of complications."

The woman looked away from both her husband and her obstetrician and absently ran a hand over her abdomen. Her husband called to the toddler, investigating the doctor's office, pulling a small box of medical supplies to the floor.

"Mitchell Andrew, get over here to your Da, lad, and stop being a bloody nuisance."

The handsome boy gamboled across the office floor, giggling and with arms raised. He jumped and was pulled into the arms of his father. He squirmed a bit and reached for his mother. She tempted him with a teddy bear, and the boy took it into his arms.

The young Marine said, "Speak plainly, Doctor. What are we looking at here?"

The doctor explained. "Your wife's pelvic area is narrow, to begin with. This tends to bring on intrauterine growth restriction. The babies will be small, with low fetal weight. IUGR can cause congenital disabilities or, in some cases, chromosomal abnormalities.

"It is likely that the boys will be born prematurely. We are looking at 37 weeks as opposed to 40. The longer your babies are in the womb, the better the chance they will be healthy. Babies born prematurely are at higher risk of brain and other neurological complications, as well as breathing and digestive problems. The earlier in a pregnancy a baby is born, the more health problems are likely to develop."

The man grunted, "Not good, Mate. We needs 'em strong in the Outback."

"What will happen to me, Doctor?"

"Our biggest fear for you, ma'am, is a condition known as Preeclampsia or Pregnancy Induced Hypertension. While you are in fairly good health now, the risks are considerable because you are young, a first-time mom, and you are carrying identical triplets. Without treatment, this high blood pressure associated with your pregnancy can be life-threatening. You are both Catholic, so alternatives are not a possibility."

"Bloody Hell, no!"

"Ace..."

The father became agitated and spoke over his wife. The toddler squirmed and lightly stroked his father's face. His mother took him, trying to alleviate what she knew was going to be an explosion.

"Crikey Doc, this is 1983. You guys outta be able to handle this. I mean, shit. We are talking about my family here – four lives in the balance. We can pay for the best care and specialists. I run one of the largest cattle stations in the country, for shit's sake. Just give her the best plan, Mate."

"Mr. Sorenson, the first thing is, Jane must be moved here to Melbourne as soon as possible. She cannot receive the prenatal care she needs in the bush. Your business requires you to be away from the station for weeks on end. This is not possible if all four are to come out of this healthy and happy."

He looked at his patient. Her internal struggles with the situation were just below the surface and not helped by the volatility of her husband, whose aggressive, military personality tended to want things his way with a monumental stubbornness.

Ace said aloud. "I have some property near Port Melbourne, a nice house, and near the tram."

"Do you have family here?"

"Naw, just us. Jane is a Yank."

The energetic youngster tossed his teddy across the floor and slipped off his mother's lap to stumble after it. The woman looked defeated in her attempts to keep him under control.

"I have an excellent nurse, I can recommend, Mr. Sorenson. She is an expert in prenatal care. Only thing is, she is black. Is that ..."

"I don't give a shit about that, Doc. Is she good, is all?"

"As I said, she is one of the best in her field. You will be very satisfied, Mr. Sorenson. Here is her telephone. Her name is Kirra Yugambeh. You can also count on her to look after this little guy."

Ace stood and reached for the baby.

"We'll set it up and move this thing along. Let's go."

"Mrs. Sorenson, please see the receptionist for your next appointment."

The woman nodded. The doctor would remember that Jane Sorenson left the office as if in a trance. He also recalled that he forgot to reassure her that all would be well.

Thomas Paul Severino

Chapter One: Inala

Nick Sechi's Journal

"There. It's like the ocean, Mate. As far as the eye can see. My grandfather's little camel ranch has overflowed the Northern Territory as Ace's Inala."

I held on to Kayne as my acrophobic vertigo subsided. The view from Urlatherrke was breathtaking in the morning sun. The colonists had named this place, sacred to the indigenous peoples, Mt. Zeil. It is the highest peak in the Northern Territory and the highest mountain on the Australian mainland west of the Great Dividing Range.

Kayne pointed to the west and swelled with pride as he held my hand. We stood on the summit cairn and took in the view at 1,531 km following a five-hour climb. He was happy and much recovered from our case in Eastern Europe, at the peak of his cognitive powers and physical stamina – all wounds healed.

He tossed his Akubra hat into the air and flipped mine from my head. His long black hair was savagely flying around his handsome face in the updrafts. Grabbing his mane and pulling it back with one hand, he drew me in against him with the other.

"Here, give us a pash, my love."

We did a hot kiss-up to the consternation of a few fellow climbers and the delight of others. One couple actually captured our passion for their social media.

I laughed at the photo bombers and, while still in his arms, pointed to the stunning vista.

"Gays in their natural habitat. Make sure you mention he owns all of that, boys and girls."

We turned back to the view.

"Just about 50% of the Territory land is used as grazing land for livestock, predominantly beef cattle. Unlike in the US, cattle are raised on the open range. You cannot see the Inala Station compound from here as it is closer to Western Australia. Inala hosts cattle and sheep, buffalo, and camels, although the latter is for nostalgic reasons. It is the sixth-largest cattle ranch in the world. Captain Ace Sorenson built a wonder, Mate. Truly."

His eyes were shining as he described his childhood home filled with memories and many family trials.

"I think what makes me most proud of my Da is his relationship with the Aboriginal People. Half of his corporate board is made up of Native folks. His policy of preservation, respect, cooperation, and support has enabled the communities within Inala to thrive. It is a model copied by other ranchers across the country."

Nearby, a group of tourists selected rocks, apparently searching for a souvenir of their experience.

"Here, Mate. This mountain is a significant cultural site for Australia's Aboriginal people."

"You mean the Aborigines?"

"They are Aboriginal and Torres Strait Islander Peoples. It is most proper to refer to them as First Nationers. More correctly, the Traditional Custodians of the Land. They believe that land is family. You might want to consider that before taking a piece of their spiritual being away with you. Just a thought."

Some were convinced. Some were not.

Eying the VHF repeater stations perched on the summit, I said, "Unbelievable, I got a signal. Kayne, what time is it in Sofia?"

"You mean Kris? Rippa, Mate. Great idea. It's 2:30 AM at his school. I say we give it a go."

He punched in the speed dial.

Close to flipping to voice mail, Kayne's nephew picked up the call.

The fifteen-year-old whispered, "Uncle Kayne, I mean Kayne, is everything OK? Is it my Dad?"

"Naw, Kris Mate. Sorry to disturb your sleep, lad. Nick and I just thought we'd show you the homeland, live and in color from the Red Center. Go to FaceTime, my little love."

"OK, hold on."

His picture came up as he closed the door to his bathroom at the Lycée Victor-Hugo de Sofia, where he had just begun the first semester of his tenth year. He was in his PJ bottoms with a blonde 'bed head' and a very sleepy look. Strong Sorenson features even on one so young, high cheekbones, dazzling blue eyes, and the build of a young athlete. A Norse variation mixed with his dad's gene pool reflected his mother's heritage, which added interest to his boyish face.

"Very cool. So, is Nick there with...."

I shouted while looking over Kayne's shoulder, "Good morning, 'Your Hind Ass.' Get that blue blood butt outta the sack, kid. Hit the gym, boy."

Kris grinned, " Don't make me whomp on you, Nicko, when I next see you, as they say in Bronx. I enrolled in MMA classes and am playing soccer, as we discussed."

He did a single gun flex.

"Got a ways to go, kiddo."

I laughed as I thought, *Naw, Kris. No one says "whomp," except perhaps in Texas. And it's "The Bronx" or, better yet, "Da Bronx." But, there would be time for his complete social education as a very cool guy when he came to the US.*

His uncle interrupted, "Make sure you keep up your grades, jock boy."

"Am too smart for my own good, Kayne. The dons are intimidated by my smarts."

"Are you happy, lad?"

"Aww yeah, Kayne. The school is fine. Still the same. My cousins are cool, and all since the summer fuck up and that. Ah, sorry, I cussed. Met some super classmates. Oh yeah, thanks for the Italian stay. Tan's fading a bit."

The sleepy boy prince continued, "Nick, your family is completely dope, man. I got a letter from your Mom wishing me the best at the opening of school and looking forward to getting together when I get to the States. Very cool."

"Kris, did you meet with the recruiter from Notre Dame?"

"That's set up for two weeks from tomorrow, ahhh... today, that is. I forgot the time."

He raked at his hair.

"Yeah, we need to get you back to bed. Remember, lad, the college thingo is not written in stone. You have plenty of time. We can decide together, OK?"

"Sounds good, Kayne."

"And now, lad, have a look."

He turned the phone's camera to the opposite side and moved it over the landscape. He spoke with excitement and great reverence.

"This is Inala."

**

We had flown to Australia from Naples a week ago and made our way to Alice Springs in the Northern Territory. We rented a Prado Gx 4WD, complete with a roof rack and high-performance suspension. We loaded it up with camping and hiking gear and hit the shops for Outback kit, shorts, jackets, boots, shirts, and those classic Aussie Slouch hats. The drive took 3 hours and passed through the wondrous West MacDonnell National Park.

Our campsite was set up near Glen Helen Gorge at the foot of Mt. Zeil. A refreshing swim in the Finke River surrounded by the steep ochre cliffs of the gorge, and we were soon digging into some delicious food and wine from the Glen Helen Homestead Lodge restaurant brought to our campfire.

As the fire died, Kayne remarked, "It's a 9-hour climb, up and down, my love. I suggest we start at dawn. Ouch! Your feet are cold. We could move this into the tent if you'd like. Although, the skies promise to remain clear tonight."

This next comment sounds entirely made up, but it's true, I swear. As Kayne looked up at the sky, I could see stars in his eyes. He jumped up and tossed some wood on the fire before returning to the covers. The firelight played across his body, illuminating a modern savage in the bush. He was spectacular.

I pulled his naked body closer to mine under the blankets and said, "Have you no special tactics, Mr. Aussie Explorer, for keeping your side-kick warm?"

"Ohhh, you are a frisky pup."

He leaned in for some heated make-out and more under Southern Skies.

***

Under a pre-dawn moon, we began our ascent. Orb Weaver Spiders webs blocked most routes, silvered with morning dew drops. We climbed along the western spur of the mountain. Kayne explained the unique wildlife. Halfway to the summit, he pointed down the river.

"The Finke is perhaps the oldest river in the world. Geologists say it is between three hundred fifty and four hundred million years old. Natives call it Larapinta."

He came up behind me and held me tight, knowing my fear of heights and my life-long struggle to control my acrophobia.

I caressed his strong arms.

Kayne lifted a pair of binoculars and remarked.

"My love, I believe we are being followed."

Thomas Paul Severino

Chapter Two: Red Ochre
Nick Sechi's Journal

We traveled from the settlement of Urlatherrke to the southwest. As we came off the mountain, two Native men who had been observing our climb suggested we head toward the town of Areyonga and Watarraka National State Park.

"They speak of you in the village near there, the savage white and the red-haired one. My people call to your spirits."

We took the four-wheel drive along the Red Centre Way via Larapinta Drive through the West MacDonnell Ranges to the Park and set up camp along Kings Canyon. We walked toward the town of Areyonga. A short distance from the Park, we arrived at a village of the Pitjantjatjara Community.

As we arrived, Kayne said, "Follow my example, Nick."

He picked up a pebble and tossed it into the air, saying, "I am Kayne. I am in your country. Please welcome me."

I did the same.

"We acknowledge the traditional custodians of country, the Pitjantjatjara, and recognize their continuing connection to land, waters, and community. We pay our respect to you, your cultures, and to Elders both past and present."

A grey-headed Elder came towards us and said, "You are the ones we have seen in the fire. You are welcome to this land. I am Midnight Johnstone."

Black eyes paired with sparkling sets of white teeth smiled on the faces of giggling, night-colored Pitjantjatjara children with gorgeous, curly hair. They pointed and stuck fingers into their mouths in amazement at the two strangers and our "unnatural" physical features.

"The children are laughing because you are so white, Sir."

Elder Midnight Johnstone smiled at me and shook his head.

"No, no, no, too white, like the sun that burns in summer. Impossible. The Red Center will burn you black as the night sky. You must be careful here."

The Elder motioned to four young men who came forward with small pots of colored earth. The Elder instructed younger men to use our bodies as a canvas for their intended artistry. We removed our shirts.

Kayne sported a raw umber tan acquired on the lidos of southern Italy when I was slathered with SPF 30. Kayne said we resembled a cup of frothy cappuccino when we were naked together.

The women tried unsuccessfully to shoo the children away. Kayne laughed at them with his ice-blue eyes twinkling. One of the children ran up to me and touched my red-gold hair, now plaited with feathers, shells, and strips of hide. I had decided to grow it longer since Europe. Looking into the little girl's eyes, I seemed to see a whole world of wonder, ancient history, and tradition. Her "Auntie" pulled her back with a reprimand.

Kayne also had a few admiring examiners fascinated by his wavy hair, now shoulder-length and loose.

"They think that you two are magic creatures from the Dreaming, sent by the gods," remarked one of the painters. "You will please stand, Sir."

Kayne reached into the pocket of his khaki shorts and pulled out a small, carved gecko medallion. He did the old standard sleight of hand that made the object disappear and then reappear as he gently tugged it from the ear of a little girl. This had the effect of spellbinding the children, who reacted with owl-like eyes, open mouths, and gasps of delight.

The adults and Elders smiled and cautioned the children to be on their best behavior. An Elder woman shooed them away a second time.

Midnight Johnstone gestured to our shorts and said, "If you please, Sirs."

The intention was evident, as was our embarrassment. I reacted with a full-body blush, which created additional interest among the people. A woman handed blankets to two of the artists and spoke in Pitjantjatjara.

The men unfolded the blankets and held them up as screens. Kayne gave me a look that said, *In for a penny, in for a pound, Mate.*

The Elder spoke, "She told them that the whites are crazy shy about their male parts and instructed them to accommodate your concern."

We removed our shorts and briefs under the gaze of appraising males. I was sure we passed muster, as gauged by their approving smiles.

"You must have many happy wives and many children, Sir."

Kayne smiled. "I am one who prefers men, my brother. Especially this white god."

Our Aboriginal friends spoke a few words in their language and nodded their heads. One turned and addressed me.

"Are you a superhero, Sir? We know of these creatures." The speaker was wearing a Captain America t-shirt.

"No, my friend, but he is very close to being one." I nodded to my very fit partner. Kayne harumphed.

"Ahhh, his spirit journeys between earth and shy. Most impressive."

More head nodding accompanied whispers from the folks.

Trying very hard to be respectful, I inspected the loincloths we were given to replace our shorts.

Kayne chuckled and said in a stage whisper, "That tiny garment of kangaroo opossum skin will go over spectacularly back in the boy bars of Wilton Manors, my love. The gay boys will be all up in that."

"Tell me about it. Should I ask for a larger size? Most of my ass is showing."

Kayne laughed, "Simply delicious."

His covering had more stringed shells, emu feathers, and leather strips. I examined the trimmings that descended down the outside of his right thigh. One of the artists, anticipating my question, said, "It is because he is the Elder, and you are his young attendant."

Interesting take on the relationship, but OK... for now, anyway.

The young man pulled Kayne's hair into a savage man bun and dressed it with colorful hangings. Exotic trim hung down his back to the cleft of his ass.

The blankets were folded and put away. The decorating continued, backs, butts, legs, and feet. Painted swirls of color and intricate, totemic animals covered our bodies. The Elder drew closer and pointed to Kayne. His eyes were full of magic and wisdom. His voice possessed a lilt and cadence when he spoke as if he were singing.

"You are a son of this Earth Mother, yes, Sir?

He gently tapped the ground with his walking stick.

"Yes, my Father. I am of this red land. But my people were colonials, deported convicts, to be precise."

The Aboriginal waved away the last comment and said, "The land is your mother; your mother is the land. It is the starting point to where it all began and the ending point as all life circles on the Dreaming."

He looked closely at Kayne's face.

"The Sky-Father has touched you there with a heavenly fire-bolt. He has gifted you with great abilities to think and see as no other man may. Sir, you are intellect."

He touched the "Mark of Cain"-- a scar on the upper right corner of Kayne's forehead.

The gathered folks began to murmur softly, point, and nod.

The Elder spoke again, indicating me, "And he is your life partner, Sir. Your spirits are entwined. True, my son?"

"Yes, my Father."

The Elder gestured and spoke in the traditional tongue to one of the men who brought the basket of red ochre to the leader. He turned and beckoned me closer.

He said to Kayne, "It was not a question, Sir. It is an observation. I hear your songs entwined in the air surrounding you both. Strong bonds, but there is war around and within. It is a very powerful linking and one the gods have blessed."

He took the red earth color in his fingers and drew on Kayne's forehead. He placed a vertical strip on Kayne's lips. He spoke in Pitjantjatjara again. Kayne opened his mouth, and the Elder put the red earth on his tongue.

"This is where you started, and this is where you will go. Take the mother inside your being. She will bless you."

He turned his attention to me.

"Sir, you burn with earth-fire inside. It is part of the Mother and comes from in here. From down and down and up into the sky." He placed a leathery hand on my chest.

"You have strong physical energy and much passion, Sir. You are wild as the wind when it seeks a home. It takes much to tame you, but your nature is to be unfettered and free."

He touched my heart. His gaze was ancient and spiritual. Working the red earth paint with his fingers, he painted a glyph on the left side of my chest. He anointed the inside of each of my wrists and then gave me a similar lip stripe.

"His Mother-Earth is yours, also, young Sir. Taste. She brings you together and will protect you."

I took the offered pigment on my tongue. It tasted raw and ancient, a bitter communion.

"The land is your food, culture, spirit, and identity.

He pulled Kayne closer to me and instructed. "You must always obey this." He touched Kayne's head.

"And you, Sir, must always allow him to lead here. For he flies without boundaries, and that is essential."

He touched my chest again.

Another member of the family presented us with long walking sticks and flagons of water. Women began to dance to the droning of a *yiḏaki,* which colonists called a "didgeridoo." More musicians added the rhythms of clapsticks.

The Elder moved one hand across the dry-hot expanse beyond the village.

"Go, my sons. Go walkabout your Mother. Join together in her arms. She calls to you and will send you spirit guides."

Chapter Three: Bush Tucker

Nick Sechi's Journal

We did not walk far.

The Aboriginal people's village was in the bush just west of Areyonga and not far from our campsite in Watkarra National Park. Kayne pointed out the plants and animals along the way. We saw a few bush quail in the dry sand and rocks, playing tag among the low wildberry scrubs. We gave a snake a wide berth. A mob of red kangaroos, being lazy under the swollen trunk of a Boab tree, watched us with feigned interest.

Further on, our way seemed to be blocked. Kayne said, "The cattle coming our way are obliterating the bore, Nick. I hope we can find the trail. No worries, however. The sun will guide us and the land."

A curious heffer and her calf, both with ear tags, decided to familiarize themselves with the imitation Natives on Walkabout and came close enough for a lick. I remarked with interest at the brand's design, a large letter "I" entwined with the letters M, K, T, and E.

Kayne ran his hand over the steer's flank.

"Kick hates that Ace used his real name initial, 'T' for 'Thomas,' but a lot of good his complaining got him. 'You're my namesake, lad, not some bloody football hero. Fuckin' good name, Thomas.' A few swats from Da, and he left off grumbling."

"Kayne, if we go on more of these near-naked hikes, I'm gonna need more clothes, starting with shoes. These native sandals are not exactly Air Jordans."

He gave me a cuff.

"And all this time, I thought you were warrior-tough."

We found our campsite next to an isolated waterhole, a natural pool surrounded by red ochre canyon walls and the soft, sharp scent of green eucalypts. The water was refreshing in the dry heat, and we watched the formation's steep walls blaze in the afternoon sun. The earth paint washed off, and we got playful in the private, Eden-like setting, as Kayne would say, "a bit of the slap and tickle."

While we were about to come out of the water, a Toyota Landcruiser went up the path. We backed up into the waist-deep water.

A tall Aboriginal woman in a brightly colored sarong and blouse with a matching headscarf pulled back her lustrous black curls. She climbed out of the vehicle and extracted a leather backpack from the space behind the driver's seat. She had a broad smile and was laughing a bit as she called out, "Put your britches on, Mates. We need to talk to you."

She tossed me the satchel and turned to help the other occupant out of the SUV. She was a stately woman of about sixty-five. The Elder ignored the scrambling naked guys in the water and proceeded to the rocks outside the tent that served as our campfire. She bundled up sticks and branches and began to build a fire. The younger woman brought out two bags of groceries from the truck's cargo hold and joined her.

Now in his safari shorts, Kayne shook out his hair and raked it back. He gathered up the loincloths and other trimmings. I brought the backpack and joined him with our visitors. We slipped into a pair of T-shirts.

The younger woman took one of the native wrappings from Kayne's hand and held it up to his hips.

"Are you sure you would not be more comfortable in this, Dr. Sorenson? Although, the two of you are a bit too... what do white fellas say? ... gym-toned to be mistaken for natives."

"I apologize, Ms., but you have us at a disadvantage."

"Apparently, in many ways, Doctor." Her entire face smiled. The Elder rolled her beautiful black eyes.

Before introductions could be made, the older woman drew closer to Kayne. She pressed her hands together and held them against her mouth. Her eyes flooded with tears.

I started to speak, but the younger woman held up a hand for silence.

Shyly, the woman raised a hand to Kayne's face and touched it as one would feel a flower petal. She brought the other hand to his hair and caressed it as it fell to his shoulders in wet waves.

She nodded, pointed to his eyes, and looked to her companion before turning back.

"You did not tell me who we were meeting, little sister."

A tear hit Kayne's lower lid and slipped down his cheek. He addressed the woman.

"I know you, Mother."

The woman nodded.

"Yes, you do."

He gulped and continued, "Nick, this is Kirra Yugambeh. In the Murri language of southern Queensland, her name means 'to live.' She was my mother's nurse during her pregnancy and, for a while, wet nurse and amah to my brothers and me."

They did a tearful hug-up, alternating between holding each other close and stepping back to do a broader assessment. They spoke in words meant only for each other-- a smattering of English and the Murri language.

Ms. Yugambeh said something in her native tongue to the younger woman. Her companion replied, "Yes, they are both handsome men, Auntie. You did well with this one."

The Elder reached out to me and said, "They have powerful songs all around them. I see the beauty. Look at the eyes. Like the heavens above."

She pointed to me and said, "The children back in the village were convinced you were a god, you know. What color is that?"

"It is called 'hazel,' ma'am."

"Ahhh, so beautiful, like the color of the dawn sky after a night of rain. But alas, you are too white." She shook her head.

I blushed, and the two women smiled again.

"Officer Sechi, I am Allira Nangala. I am originally from Alice Springs."

We greeted each other. Kayne also shook hands and said, "Professor Nagala, how is your research in quantum mechanics coming along at Monash University in Melbourne?"

"Hitting some snags, Dr. Sorenson. I am afraid my Ph.D. is on hold until I can overcome some challenges, but I am hopeful... here, hold on. How did you guess? That's amazing. The press on your uncanny deductive abilities is, apparently, very true."

Kayne smiled. "I never guess, professor." He took her right hand and turned it palm up, saying, "When we shook, I noticed a distinct red coloration. As an educator who uses a whiteboard, I, too, have erased the surface with my hands when in a hurry. Conclusion: Teacher and/or researcher."

He went on. "You wear no metal of any kind, no rings or jewelry. Your brand of watch is non-metallic, and its display is digital. The operation of atomic research instrumentation must be in an errant, metal-free environment to produce accurate readings. How many quartz movement analog display watches have you damaged using your lab's MRI? Your taste for non-metallic accessories has carried over into your 'civilian' life."

He next pointed to her Landcruiser, the back of which was pasted with colorful, clever bumper stickers.

Quantum Mechanics: The dreams stuff is made of.

I had to laugh at one with a soggy-eyed feline with a message: *I may or may not brake for Schrodinger's Cat.* Big science nerd joke.

A sticker on a back window featured a crescent wrench and proclaimed: *Quantum Mechanic: Entanglement, Superposition, Uncertainty.*

The SUV's dealership logo advertised a business in Melbourne, and on the front left, a parking barcode announced Monash University.

"So simple when you explain it. Anyway, my research has hit a snag. My Ph.D. is, consequently, on hold."

"I am very interested in hearing more, Professor."

"Right now, Auntie and I would like to share some bush tucker, a traditional dinner with you under the stars. But we must get you into warmer clothing as the evening desert temperatures will be much cooler than anticipated."

**

"Darana Cooper, your father's companion, is a dear friend. She is my 'big sister.' We are of different people. She is Napaltjarri, and I am Arrente. Her folks are from Boojara, Western Australia, and mine from the Northern Territories or, as we call it, Yolngu."

We dined on emu marinated in finger lime and seasoned with native basil, stewed bush tomatoes, and purple yams. For dessert, there were Davidson's plums from Queensland and native raspberries from Victoria.

I pointed to a white and yellow dish.

"I especially like the roasted almonds."

Kirra said, "That is mako, witchetty grubs, best cooked in ash. Very high in protein. I am glad you like it."

I made an "mmm-sound" while my inside voice screamed, *Holy Shit!"*

Kayne raised a glass of spiked fruit drink, "Cheers to the Red Center, the Woop Woop, Nick. And to new and old friends."

"Cheers."

"And so, we will first talk of family. How are your brothers and the Captain, Master Kayne?"

Kayne pressed his lips together, inflated his cheeks, and moved his ice-blue eyes from side to side, looking very much like a boy caught with his hand in the cookie jar.

Kirra smiled and said, "I see. Let me fill in the blanks, and you tell me if I am wrong.

"The Captain is the Captain, still fighting to run the universe and very perplexed because everyone else will not fall in line. Master Mitchell is

29

a wonder of business and a devoted family man. His spirit is rich, powerful, and wondrous – a heavenly being, indeed. Master Thomas is still going at 300 miles an hour. He has the combined totemic energies of the dingo and the Taz Devil. Master Eric is either missing in action, institutionalized, or worse. His spirit is the desert scorpion, earth-bound and filled with hellfire, but I know of another side to him.

"And you, my sleek, phantom cat, a renowned psycho-criminologist who is head over heels in love with your Boswell and gorgeous partner. Both of you are protecting the world from the... what do you call them in your blog, Nick? ... oh yes, the 'Big Bads.' Right?"

I nodded.

Kayne said, "Your analysis is entirely on target, my Mother. We were assisted in our last case by Ace and Darana, a sort of *deus ex machina*. I believe they are returning from Europe at this time. He is still a force of nature, and she tempers his 'crazy' expertly, the soul of patience and intelligence.

"Mitch and Kick were married a few years back and live in Colorado. Mitch is a psychiatrist, and Kick manages their properties and businesses. He is a fantastic athlete, and it takes all Mitch's energy to keep him from blasting into space."

Kirra turned to Allira and explained. "Master Mitch was adopted by Captain Sorenson and Miss Jane when the boy was an infant."

Kayne passed his mobile with pictures of his brothers and said, "And very much, Da's favorite."

Allira pointed to the screen.

"Whose dog? How handsome."

I spoke up, "That is my 'Beautiful Butterfly.' His name is Chouko. He's an Akita."

Kayne smiled and said, "He is a most unique animal, all heart and handsome like his master."

I blushed a bit and added, "Yes. I miss him a lot, to tell the truth. Here he is with our buddy Gints," I pulled my blanket closer as the desert night was getting colder.

Allira said, "Whoa, are all you guys just like a posse of underwear models. Look at that guy, Auntie."

"Hmm. This is a big boy. Also, too white. Will also be cinder-burnt in the desert like this. Black men are more hardy, you see."

"Auntie, you are a tad racist, I fear."

The nurse shrugged off this remark. And continued, "You are leaving out the Black Sheep, Master Kayne."

Kayne looked off for a long moment.

"Eric is somewhere in Europe. He is alive and handling his condition as well as can be expected. I do not believe there will be a happy ending to my brother's story, my Mother."

Kirra patted the hand of her former charge.

All she said was, "There is much of what I read concerning your case in Europe that filled me with deep grief and sorrow. The universe has its reasons, my son."

Thomas Paul Severino

Chapter Four: The Sign of the Five

Nick Sechi's Journal

"Why have you sought us out here in the remoteness of the Outback, Professor? It is at least a 24-hour drive from Melbourne, and given the semester schedule, your visit must have a keen and essential purpose."

Professor Allira Nangala wrung her hands.

"I am here to ask your help, Doctor and Officer Sechi. I fear for the worst at this time for my colleagues and their families.

"At Monash?"

"Yes. I am a part of an independent research group supported by the University. The story begins with my father."

"Please go on."

"Three years ago, my Father, Steven Nangala, was killed mysteriously in his lab. He was stabbed to death. The police had a murder weapon with only my father's prints. The report from the police mentioned that his body was positioned on the floor of his lab such that he must have knelt and driven the blade into his torso, falling on top of the knife as he died. They ruled out foul play and, consequently, did not look for any suspects. The case was determined to be a suicide."

"I am sorry for your loss, but why do you suspect murder?"

"Dr. Sorenson, my father was in excellent mental capacities before he died. He believed he was on the threshold of a breakthrough in his work. There was no suicide note. I have tried everything to convince the police that treachery was involved."

I asked, "Why would anyone want to kill your father?"

"My father was not an easy man and made many enemies. Da was on the bad side of a few international energy conglomerates. Parallax Industries, a worldwide industrial consortium, was the most aggressive. They wanted his research, and he was unwilling to move in their direction."

"Allina, what is your father's research?"

"Cutting edge government research, very classified with implications for advanced weaponry development. My father resisted government control, refusing to limit his research to military use. He made enemies at the highest level, creating some real dangers to his life. Parallax tried to force his cooperation with them with the pressure of government agencies through alleged bribes. My father exposed them, and there were lawsuits."

I said, "I'm sorry, Professor. Do you mean Parallax was trying to steal your father's work?"

"Exactly so. With the help of corrupt government officials who were indebted to them for huge payoffs."

Kayne said, "I remember hearing about this. Please go on."

"Foreign countries and rogue nations would love to get their hands on this work. Dad was not an easy confederate for any government meddlers who wanted to steer his focus into different areas. He was very critical of our government and could not abide those who call for massive military build-ups. 'Damn warmongers,' he would call them."

"I see. Please continue."

"Dr. Stephen A. Nangala was a man of firm convictions. Despite the very overt discrimination of many of his scientific colleagues, he mentored five Aboriginal graduate students in chemistry and atomic physics, three men and two women. Anatjari Bradley, Gurumarra Peris, Colin Gibbs, Renna Goodes, and I were guided in our graduate work by one of the greatest minds in physics, my father.

"However, when approached by activists who sought him out to leverage him as a spokesperson for the rights of Australia's Aboriginal people, he refused. In many ways, my father was blind to the underlying causes of the social problems of our people. He used to say, 'If I can come from the Bush and rise to the heights of my profession, any black can do the same.' He wanted to be left alone with his science and his hand-crafted community of scientists.

"There were significant protests at the University, complete with hanging him in effigy. He was caught in the crossfire between the alt-right and liberal extremists. "

Kayne thought for a bit and then said, "Possible corporate espionage, government collusion, racist agitation, ardent social justice critics, all centered around top-secret research -- a motive for murder?"

"I believe so, Doctor. The animosity continued to be very violent and very public right up to his death. My father once confided in me that he felt that he had a bull's eye on his back. He imagined that his assassination would somehow further either the white or the aboriginal side of the social issue connected to the project.

"There is more to this, gentlemen. 'The Nangala Five' have been unable to duplicate or continue his experiments. Essential pieces are missing. So, not long after his death, the public demonstrations died down. It was assumed that he took the unreproducible secrets of his work with him to the grave.

"Da used to say that he had a buried treasure protecting his work-- a hidden component that was a fail-safe setup to protect the research. At the right time, he would recover the treasure and reveal the pieces that would make the project function properly."

I said, "I don't get it. A treasure?"

"My father had a very active imagination, often very childlike. He loved stories of nonsense, adventure, and mystery. He extracted five sets of essential project equations and hid them somewhere."

Kayne said, "Let's back up just a bit. You mentioned weaponry. Please be more specific."

Allira traced her finger in the sand by the campfire light as she spoke.

"For many years, scientists have been developing particle beam weapons that would be many times more destructive than any laser. Such armaments would be composed of a power source and an accelerating tunnel.

The power source sends subatomic particles through the tunnel at hyper-speeds. It then focuses these particles into a beam that would be fired at a target. The packets of energy shot from the particle beam weapon enter the object and pass energy onto its atoms. This impact would be like tossing a ping pong ball into a room of mousetraps loaded with ping pong balls. Thus, the reaction is self-perpetuating. The target explodes in a matter of seconds after impact."

Using a *Star Wars* reference, I said, "The Death Star."

"You are not too far off, Nick. However, the major obstacle in developing a particle beam weapon has been creating a manageable power source. It must produce millions of electron volts of power and tens of megawatts of beam power. My father was developing the power source for particle beam weapons that was manageable, affordable, and pretty much boundless in its scientific potential. It is the invention of fire for the Third Millennium."

Kirra looked into the night sky and added, "Master Kayne, it has been seven years since Dr. Nangala died. The bad spirit of his death has haunted this child tremendously. A few months back, we asked an Elder of the community to visit her in Melbourne and do what he could to relieve her misalignment with the universe."

"What was the result, please?"

Allira picked up the story, "He visited the lab and place where my father was killed. He told us of the great sadness and destruction that the place held. My father's spirit seemed to cry out for justice. Just before he left, without speaking, he took this book from Da's desk and handed it to me."

She rooted through her backpack and removed a slim volume.

"I suppose the Elder was in touch with the connection this book has for my father and me. For our people, all objects are living, and they share their souls and spirits with us. My father would often read this story to me at bedtime when I was a girl. I cherish this and the memories associated with it."

Allira Nangala handed the book to Kayne. Embossed on the ruby-red cover were a chess piece and a title in gold, Through the Looking-Glass and What Alice Found There by Lewis Carroll.

Chapter Five: The Nangala Gambit
Nick Sechi's Journal

Kayne turned the rich-looking volume over in his hand without opening it. He thoughtfully fingered the embossed chess image and then handed it to me.

"Did the Doctor play chess, Professor?"

"What a curious question. Yes. In his last years, my father had a cyber partner, a Mr. Lockwood. They played on the computer. The game went on for quite a while. I remember Father was white, and Lockwood was red."

"And had you the occasion to meet this Mr. Lockwood?"

No, Doctor. I don't think Father ever met him, either. I mean in the flesh."

Kayne pushed his flopping left-side bang off his forehead. *Boss is thinking big time here, children.*

He asked, "He had an actual chess set?"

"Yes. Father got it when he was in England, Cambridge, as a matter of fact. Rather oversized, but he treasured it. Odd...."

Allira Nangala's voice drifted off.

"Continue, please. You were about to say something."

"He kept it in his office. Just before he died, pieces went missing. I assumed they were the defeated pieces in his game with Mr. Lockwood. You know, removed from the board as each piece is taken. But, now that I think of it, they were both the white and the red chessmen and not placed to the side, just gone."

"Do you happen to know what pieces were missing?"

The academic searched her memory. "I believe they included a White Pawn, Both the Red Queen and the White Queen... hmmm ... O yes, my favorite, the White Knight... and... umm... and the ahhh, ahhh... the Red King."

"You are sure that the Red King was among the missing chess pieces?"

"Yes, why?"

I spoke up, saying what I knew Kayne was thinking.

"In chess, the King never is removed from the board. Defeating him ends the game. And he is tipped over onto the chessboard. It's checkmate."

Chapter Six: The Dreaming
Nick Sechi's Journal

Allira and Kirra left the volume with us and began their journey back to Areyonga. Kayne promised to take good care of <u>Through the Looking Glass</u>. He also committed to getting back to the Professor regarding the case of the hidden scientific treasure and the murder of her father. She left her contact information.

As she left, Kayne took the hand of his former amah, saying, "You must come to visit Inala one day, my Mother. We will arrange a reunion for all of us, yes?"

Kirra wiped away a tear and nodded. She kissed each of us goodbye.

We snuggled up once more under the clear skies. Kayne tipped the book open against his thighs and held a flashlight in one hand."

He arched an eyebrow at me and was about to speak when, anticipating his question, I said, "A few times, actually, mostly as a kid. To be honest, I found it a bit difficult to understand and went back to my comic books. There was a Lewis Carroll festival once at Fordham, but I had some exams and criminology reading to get done."

"We share something quite extraordinary when we can read each other's thoughts, my love."

"Can you tell what I am thinking now, Boss?"

He swatted my exploring hands under the covers and smirked.

"The Alice Stories represent a genre of literature popular in the Victorian Age called nonsense stories, mostly written for children. Carroll's story revolves around a game of chess. The appellation 'through the looking glass' has come into the lexicon as 'on the strange side,' 'in the twilight zone,' 'in a strange parallel world.' It comes from the exotic and mysterious world Alice finds when she steps through a mirror.

"Carroll has included his fanciful poetry in the tale, 'Jabberwocky' and 'The Walrus and the Carpenter.' The book appears to be annotated in the margins by Dr. Nangala. Have a look."

Some pages were notched, worn, and dog-eared. I continued to flip through and said, "The illustrations by Sir John Tenniel are so cool. Classic. Look at this one. What a pair, Tweedledee and Tweedledum -- chubby and sour-faced. You know these guys were trouble from the get-go."

Kayne took back the book. He flipped back and forth through the fourth chapter. Kayne shined the light through several pages from the back. He smelled the paper.

"This chapter seems to have been of special interest to someone, evidenced by the grease and dirt on the pages and... hello! Hold the firelighter behind this spot next to the drawing of the snoring Red King. Have a care, my love, and do not burn the paper."

The black and white drawing glowed against the flame. An image began to form in the lower-left corner, near the feet of the sleeping King.

"Lemon juice. A secret message writing worthy of a child."

"Kayne, it looks like symbols of some kind, letters, but...."

He jumped up and retrieved a shaving mirror from our kit.

"This is so appropriate."

He placed the "looking glass" next to the symbols.

I read, "S... A... N."

"Steven A. Nangala."

I shook my head and said, "Not getting this, I'm afraid."

"As the heroine of these tales, Alice would have said, 'Curiouser and curiouser....'

"It would seem that Nangala identifies himself as the Red King who, at the end of the story, is checkmated by Alice as she wins the game. Alice is undoubtedly Allira, whom he has entranced through these fairy tales as Carroll was with Alice Liddell in the summer of 1862. He believes that Allira will unravel the riddle and locate the lost calculations."

"So, where does this get us?"

Kayne flipped to the end of the chapter.

"The chubby twins tell Alice she is only an element of the King's dream. See?" He read aloud.

> *"He's dreaming now," said Tweedledee: "and what do you think he's dreaming about?'*
>
> *Alice said, "Nobody can guess that."*
>
> *"Why, about YOU!" Tweedledee exclaimed, clapping his hands triumphantly. "And if he left off dreaming about you, where do you suppose you'd be?"*
>
> *"Where I am now, of course," said Alice.*
>
> *"Not you!" Tweedledee retorted contemptuously. "You'd be nowhere. Why, you're only a sort of thing in his dream!"*
>
> *"If that there King was to wake," added Tweedledum, "you'd go out -- bang! -- just like a candle!"*

"Still lost, Boss."

"Dr. Nangala sees his relationship with his daughter at the center of the spirituality of Australia's Indigenous People, the Dreaming. He creates the reality around him."

He flipped through the pages to the end of the book. "See here. These are the final words of the story, the epilogue,

> *In a Wonderland they lie,*
>
> *Dreaming as the days go by,*
>
> *Dreaming as the summers die:*

Ever drifting down the stream --

Lingering in the golden gleam --

Life, what is it but a dream?

"Scholars and philosophers have argued for over a hundred years. Just whose dream in this very arcane story was it? Alice's or the Red King's? And is life, in fact, merely a dream?"

I shook my head slightly and opened my hands next to my head.

"Way crazy, handsome. This boy is so lost here."

"The Aboriginal Community holds as a fundamental component of their tradition the concept of the Dreaming, *Tjukurrpa*. That is reality – not all this." He waved a hand, indicating everything.

"The Dreaming is more than just an explanation of cultural norms and where and how creation began. The Dreaming is a complete guide to life and living and an encyclopedia of the world. It is expressed in stories, art, songs, and dance. It is written into the land itself.

"The Dreaming completely surrounds us and belongs to every Aboriginal person. Every ceremony, every right, every tradition, every bit of knowledge comes from the Dreaming."

"Yes, the Dreamtime."

He caressed my head and neck a bit and said, "No, my love. That is a misnomer. There is no time in the Dreaming. It is for always, designed to be lived in every moment. Past, present, and future are merged. It serves as a guide to day-to-day life, a guide to the spiritual side of life."

Dude makes me nutso-hot when he gets all up in his cognitive powers shit. Then he goes and gives me that loving touch stuff.

My, oh my. Getting frisky here, Bossman.

"Three initials and a chessman, and you're getting all of that. You are like the superhero of intelligence, studly."

He ignored my inference, pointed to Carroll's book, and continued, "So, to summarize: Dr. Nangala crafted the tale of how to find his treasure in layers of meaning connected to the fantastical world of

<u>Through the Looking Glass</u> and the wondrous universe of the Dreaming."

He looked at me for appreciation for his fantastic logic. I reached over and very methodically took the flashlight, turned it off, and set it to the side. Next, I took the book, closed it, and put it away. Finally, I pulled back the covers and climbed on top of him.

"So for your homework, Bossman, I want you to make savage love by firelight, on the raw earth, under the southern moon, and reaching an intense dream-state ecstasy a minimum of no less than three times. Although my lucky number is seven."

The firelight played across our entangled bodies.

Chapter Seven: Night Images

"Is Mitch coming back, Kayne?"

I tried to soothe my brother, "Of course, Kick. He just went on a bit of a search, is all. Seems to me that it's important to know where you come from."

"The Captain is fried to shit, lads. I heard him yelling and such, and you know he never gets angry with his favorite son, St. Mitchell. All about 'this is the thanks I get' and all. I fuckin' love it."

I said, "Eric, you need to stop with that. The last thing we need is your jealousy and troublemaking. It's almost as if you <u>want</u> Da to give you the strap."

"Why don't you make me stop, Kayne the Brain? I haven't kicked your arse in quite a while, you self-righteous bitch."

Kick laughed at his brother. "That's because every time you try, Kayne beats the crap outta you."

Eric looked at Kick and growled, gnashing his teeth. Kick went at him, and I pushed in to break it up. I yelled, "Quit, you guys! Enough problems are going on without us scrapping. Have a care about Da. He feels betrayed that Mitch wants to find his real parents."

"I'm so gonna clobber you, crazy arse. You take your meds?"

"You take yours? And you're the crazy one. Messing with that older guy. Da's gonna find out, and then you'll get it. Ahh yeah, you bugger him, or he buggers you?"

"You just shut up, you little twerp."

Eric made for Kick once more. I pulled him down and got him in a hold. He was getting stronger every day, but so was I.

"Eric, leave off. I bloody mean it."

We three seemed to calm down a bit. Kick said, "Crikey, all the way to Perth. He's gone walkabout."

"Oh, he'll come back, Nutso Boy. He's the Princeling around here. All that big brother swagger... Don't you know? Not gonna trade all this for some lowlifes in the big city who didn't want him in the first place. Pro'ly living in refrigerator boxes under some highway. Plus, the Captain is springing for a full ride to ND for his number one in the fall. So fuckin' pathetic all of this. Makes me puke."

My rebel brother's last words hung in the air as we realized someone had walked into the room. A deep voice came from behind us. It was a voice and a tone that we all recognized.

"Eric, you will report to the tack room immediately and bring the strap. It would seem we have much to discuss regarding what I have just learned concerning your behavior."

Eric mumbled, "Hit me as much as you want. I am not doing what you say." Before Ace could challenge him, the defiant boy stomped defiantly out of the room. Kick's eyes grew big — about to cry. I approached Ace.

"Da, can I say something?"

"Say what you have to say, Son."

"Da, you're upset about Mitch. Please don't take it out on Eric. Whatever he's done, he can fix it. It won't help anything if you...."

"Look here, Kayne Jason. You are about to give your Da advice or orders. Be careful, Master Sorenson. My strap is quite capable of tanning two hides in the same evening. You and your brother, Thomas, get to bed."

"Da, about Mitch..."

"Thomas Michael, you have your orders. There is no discussion needed. Mitch and Eric are not your business right now. Take your medicine and go to bed. You have athletics in the morning."

I got Kick in his bed. He gave me a good night hug and kiss, as was our custom. I stole down to Ace's office in my pajama bottoms. I tiptoed to the closet opposite his big desk. It was a familiar hiding place since I had been an ankle-biter — a kid. I felt the old coziness of watching my Da in secret. He discovered me only a few times.

I settled in the back corner and felt my eyes drooping in sleep. Ace came into the room without my hearing. I came startlingly awake at the sound of his slap on the desk. I watched through the louver doors as he poured himself a large glass of whiskey. He put his head in his hands and cried huge sobs. I felt the wetness of my own tears upon seeing my father crying hopelessly. Ace never cried.

Suddenly, he looked up at the closet, stood up, and walked towards me.

"Kayne?"

***

"Kayne!"

At the top of the mountain was a narrow, twisting canyon covered with Indigenous art -- petroglyphs and fantastic animals. As I came over the ridge, the killers chased a tall man with black hair into the entrance. I pulled myself up, undid my Glock from my holster, and hurried after them.

"Kayne, I'm coming."

The colorful, dreamlike decorations covered the inside surfaces of the labyrinth, and the branching passageways were confusing as I turned back and forth, attempting to find a route.

"Nick, help!"

Around the next bend, a native man droned melodically on an ancient wind instrument. He stopped playing and made a motion with one hand, saying, "Stay to the right, sir, that's the secret. And mind your steps. He pointed to the ground."

"Nick!"

I stopped in my tracks, inches from a trap. The passage's floor was cut open, and I could see the sky below the opening. A steer blocked the way on the other side of the hole. He raised his head and said, "Take the hall to the right."

Where there was no doorway before, there was now one to my right.

Another passageway, another opening, another righthand turn. Now, the painted animals on the walls seemed to go 3-D and reach out for me as I ran past. A crocodile snapped her jaws, a kangaroo lashed his massive tail, and snakes coiled and slithered.

"Nick, I am right here. Where are you?

I came to yet another dead end and turned to reverse my course. The way in was now blocked by a barrier that wasn't there before. I was in a sealed room. A huge dingo snarled from the surface of the wall I now faced, teeth bared from deadly jaws. Covered in blood, Kayne stood inches from the monster. I dashed for him as the floor opened up, and I began to fall.

"Kayne!"

Chapter Eight: First

From the Case Notes of Kayne Sorenson, Ph.D.

"Crikey, Nick, we are quite a pair. Mind reading and now nightmares in sync. It is this mysterious land seeping into us-- a strange night."

We were both sitting up in the bedroll, sweating in the cold night. I pulled him close, burying my face in his chest. He gently stroked my hair. My trembling began to stop.

"I could actually hear you calling me through the dream."

"Damn, boss. I thought I'd lost you for sure this time. Big Bads, monsters, and my fuckin' favorite, dizzying heights. Oh, yeah, and the maze deal from the Budapest case. Funny how things creep into your subconscious and stay there."

"Yes, the human mind is a many-layered puzzle to be solved."

"What did you dream?"

"A reoccurring thingo -- issues with my Da and my brothers. The time Mitch tried to find out who his birth parents were. In these dreams, I end up in a closet in my Da's study, spying on him, and he is just about to discover me when I wake up."

To lighten the mood a bit, I did a puffed-up version of a psychiatrist. "The closet is the classic symbol of the hidden homosexuality of the young and inexperienced Kayne Sorenson, and he struggles with his hunger for man love. He is afraid his father will find out and...."

He smacked me playfully.

"The three of us were out at fourteen, Dr. Freud and Mitch before that. Hard to keep secrets with randy teenagers in the house. A schoolmate decided to make fun of Mitch when he was thirteen. As you youngsters would say, Mitch ate that bully for lunch. No one ever again messed with us. In fact, with Kick, it was the other way round."

"Don't tell me – causing trouble like a pubescent pain in the ass."

"Yeah, loved making passes at jocks. Mitch actually got him out of a fix with a coach. Kick was obsessed with the team captain. Ace would have walloped him a good one."

I grabbed him close to me in a hug-up, both of us sliding down into a sleep position in the down covers.

"Four gay boys in the same family. That has got to be an unbelievable statistic."

"As I've said before, my love, we were a biological wonder. Ace allowed the research – the gay gene theory. We are, after all, identical triplets. Mitch is ever his own man. All of that investigation and analysis stopped after a while when we went to the U.S. for university. Ace told the researchers enough was enough. He wanted his boys to study and work hard. He said, and I quote, 'I don't give a shit about who they bugger, as long as they are good men.' And, when all is said and done, at least we had a lot in common to talk about. But Da faced many very tough times. Keeping us all in check was not easy. Four aggressive boys, all hitting puberty at about the same time—an assignment worthy of only a most dedicated parent or a former Marine. The disasters were immense."

"Eric?"

"Bloody hell, yes. That was a real tragedy. But we all had our struggles, Kick and his hyperactive behaviors, Mitch trying to find his parents. By the way, the end of that story is, when he found the poor blighters, they still wanted nothing to do with him. Fundamental Christians. No tearful reunion for my brother. He came home like the Prodigal Son, and Ace cried."

He shifted next to me – uncomfortable memories.

"Who was your first?"

He stretched out, gazing up at the stars, his arms up behind his head. A small smile crept over his face as he reminisced.

"A bit of a sea change, my love? Well, it was Peter Jamison, a goal man on my high school footie team, two years older than me. We both messed up in a crucial match. Australian Rules Football is sacred here, even at the school level. Coach made us stay after and clean up the locker room and store the gear for a whole week. It only took until the second day. The rest, as they say, was young love history, a very passionate tryst. He was a fantastic lover -- absolutely ruined me forever loving another man."

My turn to smack him. He laughed and brought his arms down and around me.

"Have a care, lad. You'll bruise this fine male animal. Now give us a pash."

"Why? I couldn't possibly measure up to Peter-fuckin'-Jamis... mmm."

He covered my mouth with his and explored his lips and tongue. Slipping over on top of me, he straddled my thighs. He came off me and sat up, saying, "And who was your first infatuation, my love?"

"Jacob Birch, three grades ahead of me, a jock pole vaulter, and my chemistry tutor-- sexy and smart. We used to solve some chemical equations and then make some smoking-hot chemistry of our own. Got found out by one of the priests on the faculty. Huge school-wide scandal. My Dad was classic."

"In what way?"

"He let the school know that their outraged reaction stemmed from institutional homophobia. If we were a boy and a girl, the whole incident would have been treated with much more confidentiality and concern for the students. Then he went full throttle on telling me to be who I was and forget everything else. He was a great believer in authenticity. My Mom was a tad more acerbic."

'What was Viola's reaction to your devilish ways?"

"And I quote, 'Nick baby, you don't shit where you eat.' I'm serious."

We both laughed, and he began to move his body against mine.

"My, my, I do believe that things can change." He kissed me again and said, "Definitely, you are my ultimate. My libido seems to have altered its settings. Peter Jamison would be saddened."

I swiveled under him so that I was face down. I said with a fake pout, "Talk is cheap, buster. Go back to sleep."

He pressed his lips to my ear and said, "I will in a bit, my love. It would seem that 'little Kayne' here has something else in mind."

Chapter Nine: Stalker

Nick Sechi's Journal

"I had that feeling again, Mate. We are being observed."

"When?"

"Last night by the fire, before we went for round two."

"Voyeurism in the Outback? Pretty weird. I wonder what's going on."

We had gotten up with the sun and did a run through the park before the desert heat set in. A few jocks were giving a try to a rock-climbing station in the gorge, and we joined in. As long as I was not looking down, I was fine. Challenges like this, I thought, would help me get over my acrophobia.

Face your fears, Nickboy.

All in all, we did very well and chatted with the athletes. Kayne had to translate. A couple of the climbers were French, and four others were Aussies who launched into the slang known as 'Strine when they found out he was also from Oz. I understood some of it after almost a year with my fantastic man and some interactions with his family members.

"You blokes up for some brecky?" a sandy-haired blond asked. "The lodge has a sportsman's meal that is fair dinkum. Have a go?"

I spoke up, perhaps a bit too eagerly, "Sounds great, Mate."

Call me a body fascist, but I love hanging with fit guys. The blonde and his bud, a black dude with a footballer's body, were superb specimens. My friskiness in these situations never went unnoticed by Kayne. He was forever commenting on my troll-like habit of mentally undressing hot men.

The French couple, Thierry and Justine, joined us. The six of us sat out by the water, enjoying a hearty breakfast and delightful convo. We each talked a bit about our backgrounds. Max and Zach, the Aussies, were from Victoria in the southeast of the continent and were starting a spring vacation. They were coming from Tasmania and spoke of its wonders. Eventually, they had also been "up top" and visited The Kimberly in Western Australia.

The French couple were first-time explorers of the Land Down Under and had come to the Outback after touring Queensland, New South Wales, and Victoria in the east. Their favorite was the wine country of the Yarra Valley in Victoria. Max directed them to the Barossa Valley north of Adelaide.

"It's one of the oldest areas in Australia for excellent wines. Look here, Zach and I brought a couple of bottles of a very robust Shiraz with us. What say we get together for dinner and raise a glass?"

Kayne was delighted and said, "I have some homework to do today, but that sounds like a capital way to end the day."

He translated another invitation, "Thierry and Justine are going rowing on the river and invited us all to go along. I need, as I said, to cuddle up with my book for a few hours, but I can join you later for a swim."

Zach said, "Sounds pretty tame for a pair of Marvel's Avengers. Do you blokes really fight crime? You sure got the bodies for it."

I jumped up and did a jab-jab-kick-spin to the delight of our new friends.

"The boyo here is the muscle, and I just tag along for the excitement. No offense, my love. Nick is a police officer in Florida, and I am just a lowly school teacher."

"OK, so, I call BS on that. Such humility, Boss. Kayne is an internationally renowned psycho-criminologist. His cases range across the globe. He also teaches graduate school in Florida. That is where we met. It's all on my website, *The Sorenson Mysteries*."

"Excuse me, folks, but my friend Bridget over there claims you are underwear models here for a shoot. I guess it's because of your abs. Just asking." The waitress at the outdoor café was giggling as she inquired.

After translation, Justine assured her that we were.

A minor upset had broken out a few tables away. The staff was trying to chase away a dog who had decided to look for some scraps.

Being an avid canine lover, I recognized the breed immediately and commented, "Wow, that is an Australian Cattle Dog. She is so beautiful."

Kayne said, "We had a few of them when I was growing up on Inala, our cattle ranch just a few kilometers from here. The Cattle Dog is a breed of herding dog originally developed here in Australia for driving cattle over long distances across rough terrain and...."

He never finished. The interloper headed straight to Kayne, sat before him, and put her head in his lap. We were all astonished, and no one more so than he.

"I am so sorry, Sir. We did not know she was your dog."

"May I have a bowl of water, my dear?"

"Certainly, Sir."

Kayne said almost to himself. "But not my dog. I wonder...."

Thierry said, "*Non, mon ami. Je crois que vous constaterez que les animaux nous choisissent et non l'inverse.*"

Kayne chuckled and said, "Thierry believes that animals choose us and not the other way around."

We took turns petting her grey and bluish fur. In addition to water, the server brought some cooked chopped beef for our new friend.

"Kayne, could she have wandered away from an Inala drive?"

"I'd be surprised, my love. Da's dogs are all collared and marked. Too many poachers. This beauty has neither."

The dog finished her breakfast like she hadn't eaten in a while. As Kayne leaned down to pet her, she stood up on her hind legs and gave him some loving licks, face and hands. She sat back and barked contently.

I joked, "Hey, baby, that's my job."

Max said, "She is definitely a Blue Heeler, a mix with some dingo in there. They are intelligent, active, hardworking, and very protective." He scratched the beauty behind the ears as he spoke."

Kayne said, "I'll check around to see who is missing a dog while you folks are enjoying the...."

He was interrupted again as the pup nuzzled him and insisted they go for a walk.

He stood up to follow her, gave me a kiss, and said in English and French, "I'll catch up with you later. You know, Nick, I think this is our stalker."

He bounded after the dog.

Chapter Ten: Alice

From the Case Notes of Kayne Sorenson, Ph.D.

Fascinating.

The Blue Heeler imprinted on me with delight and enthusiasm. She followed me to our campsite and plopped down next to me for some additional scratching and dog lovin'. She showed her interest and appreciation with a frantic tail wagging, or I should say, she wagged her entire hindquarters. The dog also licked me copiously, slopping plenty of dog slobber.

The town of Areyonga was only a few kilometers away, and I looked online to locate a vet. I grabbed up the keys to our 4WD and started for the vehicle, stopped, reached for the book, and said aloud, "I better take Alice."

The dog's ears went up, and she barked, came close, and sat at my feet, looking at my face.

"Huh? What did I say, girl?"

She wagged.

"Alice."

She jumped up, put her paws on my torso, and barked excitedly.

"Is that your name, Gorgeous? Come over here. Can you sit?" I made proper hand motions learned in my boyhood with the Inala pups. She sat and waited.

"Someone has trained you well, Girl."

I added a single word to our conversation, looking at the attentive dog.

"Alice!"

She barked, ran over, and jumped up on me.

"Very interesting. Your name is Alice."

Alice chased her tail in a circle and barked in affirmation.

"Step one accomplished. Naming the beast."

I stooped to pet her and said, "Now, let's see if you are healthy."

***

"There was an accident on the highway not far from Areyonga about 4 days ago. When the first responders arrived, they found an Australian Cattle Dog trying to pull one of the bodies from the burning wreckage. Most likely, this dog… see the singeing on her fur. She was unsuccessful, and there were no survivors. Pretty stalwart pup."

Dr. Pemulwuy ruffled Alice's fur and continued, "She ran off when approached. Traumatized, it would seem."

"She is about three years old, in excellent health, remarkably intelligent, and has been spayed. I believe her blood work will come back with excellent results. I will text you the report."

He handed me a slip of paper.

"As she has obviously rescued you, Dr. Sorenson, you now have the responsibility to see that she gets her meds. No fleas, ticks, or heartworm for this baby."

I looked at the adorable Alice and thought. *Would it be better for the animal to find her a nice, quiet home? Our lives are fraught with so much danger most of the time.*

Kayne, kiddo, what a year this has been. I found the love of my life. I have a fifteen-year old nephew for whom we are responsible and now a dog. Are the gods hinting that I should settle down instead of fighting wild-arsed crime Big Bads in far-away places? Feet up and smoking a pipe?

As if he read my thoughts, Dr. Pemulwuy said, "Sir, when an animal imprints on a human as this one has on you, it is a tremendous psychic and spiritual phenomenon. This is especially so when trauma has come into play. Alice has told you her name and claimed you. You are her forever home now. To break that bond would injure her in body and spirit."

Alice agreed with a jump up and set of slurpy doggie kisses.

The vet added, "Besides, females across the globe will be eternally jealous, and some men also, I suspect."

I spent the rest of the morning trying to decode the mysteries of Alice's Adventures Through the Looking Glass. Searching for invisible ink in the margins of the pages. I used a mirror to read the reverse messages – *so Leonardo da Vinci!* I was becoming frustrated because the codes were arcane. Still, I was convinced that the missing research materials were divided into five sections and hidden in places across the country. Beyond that, I was stymied.

I turned to the first reference: The White Knight, Alice's savior from the Red King. Near the entry where the eccentric soldier tells Alice of his inventions, the upside-down container, Nangala's secret message was, "A world turned upside down." A "Hamilton" lyric? I was getting nowhere.

Alice, sensing my frustration, decided it was time for us to play. She seemed to say that a good frolic was always called for, refreshing and restorative. She abandoned her new chew-chew toy and began to nuzzle me as I sat before our tent.

She backed off and rolled on her back, alternating her landing position, first on one side and then the other. I looked at her antics– upside down and sideways, then I looked down at my finger placed in the text where the Knight talks of his topsy-turvy contraption. Nangala wanted his decoder to know something about this.

I jumped up so suddenly Alice exploded into a tail chase, a barking barrage, and a circle run around the campsite.

"That's it, Alice, my girl! I got it!"

"Uluru!"

Chapter Eleven: Upsidedown and Sideways

From the Case Notes of Kayne Sorenson, Ph.D.

I watched the canoes come down the river and decided that I needed to join Nick and our new friends.

I stood up, stripped off my Deadpool t-shirt, and jogged down to the water's edge. The five river explorers were stowing the boats and gear. Zach and Max suggested a swim in a nearby swimming hole, but Justine and Thierry declined. Justine had gotten a bit too much sun and needed some skin first aid.

Secluded pools of bright freshwater extended from the main gorge and were surrounded by deep red-ochre canyon walls. Sunlight sparkled on the water and danced up the rock walls.

The four of us jostled each other in a sporty water wrestling tag team event, frolicking like a pack of randy frat boys. Max was a spirited boyo and intent on making off with Nick's and my bathers. In one of our wet wrestling bouts, I felt my shorts yanked to my ankles and ripped entirely off. Nick dove like a dolphin to knock Zach over. His white arse and muscled flanks glistened with sparkling water. He came up with Zack's speedo in his teeth.

The three of us rounded on the mischievous Max. The horny lad who had started it all. Surrounded, he struggled as I raised his hips and reciprocated with a friendly stripping. It seemed naked frolicking was the order of the afternoon and soon developed into quite enthusiastic and very friendly... ah... well...

Suffice it to say that decency forbids me to go any further into the details of our very energetic antics and group play. Still, I will say it was a rippa-- a lot of fun. The sexual chemistry was mind-blowing.

***

"One-hundred thousand six hundred and thirty-two."

"Huh, Boss? What are you talking about?"

"The number of followers you have for your blog, *The Sorenson Mysteries*."

"How did you know I was thinking about...?"

"And we should talk about our return home as you are a bit homesick, I perceive."

"Boss, you are spooking the shit outta me. Come on. How could you possibly know what I was thinking? There is some mysterious energy thing going on out here in the Bush."

I sat down next to Nick and stretched out, laying my wet head on his lap. Max and Zach asked us to dinner, but we had some time before we were expected.

"It's a simple grammar school exercise, love. Why it's..."

"Elementary?"

"Precisely."

"Oh, brother."

"You were petting our Alice and picked up your mobile. You showed her a picture of my number one rival for your love, your 'Beautiful Butterfly,' the noble Akita, Honorable Chouko-san.

"Alice yelped with admiration and put a paw up to your phone. Your serious expression followed. The conclusion is simple. You were feeling homesick."

I looked up into his beautiful hazel eyes and handsome face. I continued, "You then picked up your laptop and began to write – your regular blog entries would be the logical conclusion. Your scrolling indicated you were searching for some information. Your habit is that after you post an entry, you look to see how many followers you have. One hundred thousand six hundred and thirty-two when I looked 20 minutes ago."

"Ha! Six hundred and thirty-four."

I traced my index finger over his lips.

"Fine, make a liar out of me for two new followers."

I asked, "Any regrets or guilt about our carnal pursuits with our new buds? Sexing up with the Aussie hotties?"

"Fuck no, Boss. It's just hot sex and all consensual. Great fun. One thing, though."

I could not decipher his serious expression.

"What is that, my love?"

"I find Australian men very fit, sporty, and eager, but after a few hours, you are only hungry for more. Just sayin'"

He burst into a grin, and I wrestled him for busting my rockos.

"Kayne, what are we doing?"

I was a bit miffed at the question.

"Being playful, my love."

"No, I mean big picture. You know. Are we dating? Just having a good time? Something more?"

He pulled me close to him. Significant conversation time – critical to the relationship.

"I am pretty sure it's love, Nick. I've never felt this way before. It defies my cognitive processes."

I stumbled to put my feelings into words. I always have this problem. I tend to distrust emotions. They are uncharted territory for me. However, cognitive responses to issues of love and romance are a buzzkill. So, I tried my best to let him know what he meant to me. I wrapped my arms around my beautiful and brave man.

"Nick, I am pretty much head over heels, lad. I find you beautiful, smart as a whip, and amazingly strong and brave. There are times when I am not sure where I leave off, and you begin."

"You're my Bossman, Kayne, of my heart and my mind. I am never homesick when I am with you. You are my home.

"And, you fuckin' inspire the shit outta me. When the fears come, I want to climb into your back pocket and stay there. You have my heart, Dude. What I fear most is losing you."

"No chance, my love. No matter how many hot boys we play with. We are a couple."

"A couple of whats?"

"Sluts?"

We both laughed.

***

"Nick, I have concluded that our first stop in our scavenger hunt for Dr. Nangala's missing data is Uluru."

We were waiting for Max and Zach to go to dinner. I showed Nick the text and the secret message. I pulled up a picture of one of the most recognized landmarks in Australia.

"It's less than 150 kilometers from us. That's where we will find the first piece of the puzzle. Most of the rock formation is underground and was formed about 600 million years ago, a time geologists refer to as its mountain building.

"The layers of sandstone that make up the rock are a puzzle. They run vertically, not horizontally. The science is that the rock mass was turned on its side about 400 million years ago, almost upside down."

Alice lay between us and watched. Her eyes went from me to Nick and back again as we spoke. I reached down to scratch behind her ears.

Nick scrolled through his tablet. He said, "The native people who are the traditional custodians of Uluru is the Anangu confederation, made up of the Yankunytjatjara and the Pitjantjatjara people. They believe the mountain was created by the ancestors who left marks in the land and made laws for the people to keep and live by."

He scrolled and said, "Wow, Uluru is listed as a UNESCO World Heritage Site. Climbing is now discouraged. That is very cool, considering the spirituality of the place."

"Yes, the only trouble is, my love, I do not know what it is we are looking for."

Thomas Paul Severino

Chapter Twelve: Uluru

Nick Sechi's Journal

The "island mountain" rising from the desert was astounding. It glowed red in the dawn when we arrived. As the morning progressed, the early light seemed to change the colors of the red sandstone, and we gazed in wonderment.

About 1100 feet high and 6 miles around the base, Uluru seemed to be wrapped in timeless mysteries. The area around the formation is home to an abundance of springs, waterholes, rock caves, and ancient paintings.

"Hey Mate, I think I know you. Inala, right?"

As we entered Uluru-Kata Tjuta National Park, Kayne and I looked at the speaker, a ranger. He was a tall Aboriginal man.

Kayne pointed at the guide, "Campbell Morton. Your Da worked at the ranch."

"Yes, two of my brothers are still working for the Captain. How are you, Kayne? It's been years."

The big ranger turned to me, saying, "This bloke right here was the best ruckman in the state when we were in school. Footy forever, Mate! Crikey, you and your brothers had it bloody sewed up – Inala's Avenging Angels, we called 'em."

"Cam, this is my partner, Nick Sechi. First time in Oz."

"And you are in the Great Australian Fuck All. 'Smatter the big cities like Sydney and Melbourne too dull, Mate? Nice to meet you, Nick."

"My pleasure, bud. Oh... ah... wait...."

I looked at Kayne and turned back to his friend, and continued.

"I acknowledge that your people, the Anangu, are the traditional custodians of this land and asked to be welcomed."

"Very cool, Dude. You are most welcome to Uluru. Just don't call it Ayer's Rock."

We did a fist bump.

"Pretty classy, Kayne. I remember how the sheilas were so frustrated chasing you and your brothers. They thought all this gay stuff was some kinda phase or a curse, you blokes being so fit and all. Four pooftas ... so wild, Mate. And nobody-- and I mean, *nobody*-- messed with the Brothers Sorenson."

Kayne put an affectionate arm around me. "Yeah, and I got me a good one this time, Mate. A keeper."

"Dudes, I am so going to be your guide here, show you the wonders. Kayne, how are your brothers and the Captain?"

"Still crazy as a pack of wet wallabies, Cam."

Campbell looked at me and grinned, saying, "So, as I said, the Angels were unstoppable."

He counted off on his fingers, "You had Kick, who was a manic forward – it's how he got his nickname. Driven as bloody hell. Then, Eric, a fantastic midfielder, intense as fuck, and then Mitch, the anchor. There was no getting by that studly defender. You know he bloody dominated. Owned the backfield! Big, brawny, and powerful."

He led us into the park toward the base of the rock formation. Between the tour talk, he continued to expound on footy matches of their school days.

"Yeah, this bloke was the best follower – the Ruckman of the Angels, more hit-outs than believable. Kayne was a combination tap and mobile striker. Yeah, I can tell from your expression you got no idea, Nick."

I nodded, and Cam continued, "The ruckman is the player who contests at center bounces and stoppages such as boundary throw-ins and ball-ups. Dude is the most important player on the field. They are critical to game strategies and winning center clearances. That gets you the most goal-kicking opportunities."

Note to self: Research -- Google Footie

"You need to get this lad to a footy match, Kayne – best game on the planet. Essendon Bombers vs. the St. Kilda Saints-- bloody awesome, Mate. Get your sporty arses back to Melbourne for the match."

The friendly park ranger spent the next few hours showing us the sites and wonders of the World Heritage Site. For our tour, his knowledge of the climate, geology, plants, animals, and significance of Uluru to Aboriginal culture was very informative.

Cam gestured up and wide at the massive land formation that dominated the Park.

"In the Nineteenth Century, during the expeditionary period made possible by the construction of the Australian Overland Telegraph Line, the colonists named it "Ayers Rock" in honor of the then Chief Secretary of South Australia, Sir Henry Ayers. In 2002, the Australian Government gave prominence to the traditional name. It is a sacred place for the Native People of this country. It belongs to the Dreaming."

I listened carefully to his explanation of that most fascinating concept of a time out of time. As he spoke, Campbell's voice took on an otherworldly feel, kind of a sing-song chant cadence.

"This is a Dreaming battleground. Serpent beings waged many hostilities around Uluru, scarring the rock. After a terrible war, two tribes of ancestral spirits came here to make peace. Still, they were distracted by the beautiful Sleepy Lizard Women. There occurred then much contention and anger. Members of one tribe sang evil into a mud sculpture that came to life as the monstrous dingo. There followed a great battle, which ended in the deaths of the leaders of both tribes. The earth itself rose up in grief at the bloodshed, becoming Uluru."

In the brush, we spotted a small kangaroo.

Kayne said, "Your first wallaby, Nick. Actually, it is a black-flanked rock-wallaby."

"Very cool."

"We are fiercely protective of the plants and animals found here because of our spiritual kinship. According to recent surveys, there are currently twenty-one species of native mammals. Seven species of bats roost in the caves and crevices. The park is rich in reptile and amphibious fauna, with seventy-three species, including four species of frogs. The plant population contains many rare, endangered, and vulnerable life forms. In these months, our animals are breeding, and you can see our plants are flowering. It is our Spring."

We noticed a few hikers attempting to ascend the formation. I said, "Cam, I thought climbing the formation was prohibited."

"Nick, we do not climb Uluru because of its great spiritual significance. We request that visitors do not climb the rock because doing so would violate a sacred traditional Songline or Dreaming track and a sense of responsibility for the safety of visitors. We say the climb is not prohibited, but we prefer that you choose to respect our law and culture by not climbing as a guest on Anangu land. But we can see the caves along the base."

As we drew near the enormous cliffs that rose above the desert floor, we followed a walking trail that brought us to caves and waterholes on the southern side. Stencil art and petroglyphs covered the surfaces and led back into the rock's interior.

Cam continued our tour, explaining that each side of Uluru has a different set of creation stories associated with it. The fantastic rock paintings of the Anangu people surrounded us as we explored the caves.

"These tell the story of the ancestors, the spirit-songs. Certain rock outcroppings represent ancestral spirits. We believe that by simply touching the rocks, they can communicate with the spirits and receive blessings from their ancestors. Here is one such song."

He pointed to a colorful section of a sandstone wall. Around us, other guides escorted groups of tourists through the caves.

"This is Barnumbirr, a creator-being associated with the planet Venus, who came from the island of Baralku in the East, guiding the first humans to Australia. He then flew across the land from East to West, naming and creating the animals, plants, and natural features of the land. You can see his trail along the wall, across the ceiling, and down."

Cam led us further into the mountain, using his "torch," a flashlight, as our illumination. A spring bubbled up, pouring clear, sweet water into a shallow pool. On the arched ceiling and walls, another set of petroglyphs seemed to come alive with a fantastic bestiary, a mammoth snake dominating the art.

"This is the Rainbow Serpent and Dreaming Spirit Walujapi. She is shown as the black-headed python. Walujapi is said to have carved a snakelike track along a cliff face and deposited an impression of her buttocks when she sat establishing camp. She followed a path across Northern Australia, creating rivers and mountains as she went and stopping at especially sacred places. A song attributed to her is still sung by Aboriginal Australians and describes her journey and the features along the way."

"Kayne, have a look, Boss."

In a niche near the spring was a stylized drawing of a horse, its head lowered as if to drink. The water in the pool was deeper in this corner of the cave.

"Interesting. This art is not very old. Aboriginal People still come to these caves for ceremonies and to create new dreaming paintings. As you know, Kayne, the horse is not indigenous. It was brought here by the colonists."

"My convict ancestors and their associates, yes. Very curious. Is this a Bumbry?"

"I would say so. The Northern Territory has the most mobs of these free-roaming horses. While environmentalists regard them as a pest and a threat to the native ecosystems, we value them as part of Australia's heritage. The National Parks work to prevent inhumane treatment or extermination."

Kayne examined the painting as closely as he could without touching it.

"Nick, what does this look like to you?"

"It's a bit weird, but it looks like the rider has some trouble staying on."

Kayne stood up and quickly stripped to his briefs.

Cam tried to intervene, saying, "Dr. Sorenson! No, Kayne. It is against the rules to...."

Kayne dove into the pool.

Chapter Thirteen: Lab Work

"Yes, you can be sure of this information. She confided in me as late as two days ago."

The academic looked down at his shoes. He was uncomfortable with the meeting-- had been from the start.

"So, what you're telling me, Professor Peris, is Allira Nangala is searching for some of her father's lost notes. The missing documents will solve the impasse you and your colleagues are up against regarding the power source for the particle laser?"

"It would appear so. The five of us have worked on this project privately for years, even before the death of Dr. Steven Nangala. We have yet to crack the codes in his research. He broke the project into five pieces. Each of us works on one component of the developing power source. At some point, each of us came up to a dead end. There are chunks of each of the five research components that are missing.

"Allira believes her father hid five sets of equations, essential figures, for the project. Considering the implications of this cutting-edge energy research, he was fearful that the project would fall into the wrong hands."

"Sounds like he didn't trust anyone, his students included."

Gurumarra Peris was unable to look the man in the eye. He was aware that he had been bargaining with the devil. He traced his finger along the surface of the lab table. His actions seemed to underline his anxiety.

"Dr. Goodes seems to have made what appears to be the best breakthrough just recently, but there seems to be a developing atmosphere of suspicion among the five of us. I have begged Professor Nangala to move this project into a more public position both for funding reasons and to allow the work of other scientists to augment our project. I believe that can get us further along, past these dead ends, I mean."

"And?"

"She has addressed the morale problem by getting us into some team building– some group physical training. All good. However, she is opposed to opening up the project. Claims her father's intentions were to keep this research secret because of its potential to change how we look at clean, industrial, and weapons-grade energy. Professor Nangala does not want to repeat the difficulties of the past, like government involvement. We have restarted the project with the conviction that knowledge of this research would be kept under wraps.

"Allira claims that new information is forthcoming. Something about Dr. Nangala's diary and a puzzle he created to hide the missing figures."

"Where are you getting the funds for your work?"

"The estate of Dr. Steven Nangala. Running out, I am afraid."

"Tell me about the diary."

Peris grew more nervous as he explained, "The professor kept a series of notebooks and diaries throughout his life, like his literary idol, Lewis Carroll. They contain a variety of entries, from scientific extrapolations to personal reflections. Much is encoded in some real nonsense entries. He had a very complicated way of organizing his thoughts on paper."

The man in charge said nothing. He turned to gaze through the window and across the quad. A few students were returning from the library at the far end to their cars and dorms. The hour was late, and the University was cloaked in darkness and fog.

He signaled with one hand that the researcher should continue.

"Steven Nangala was a very eccentric man. His interests were wide-ranging. In addition to energy system technologies and quantum mechanics, he also had an avid interest in gaming theory. He loved to model complex problems as chess strategies. He taught me the game. We would play for hours, and I came very near to defeating him on a few occasions. He was also an aficionado of English literature, fairy tales, and nonsense stories. The diary is filled with a mash-up of these topics."

"Get me the diary."

"Impossible. The research notes had to be shared among the four of us if we were to contribute to the work, so each of us works with shared files. That's one set of data, but the diary is another. Dr. Nangala's diary is not on Allira's laptop. Occasionally, one of us asks to search the diary for project information. Still, I am not sure I can get access to it."

"It is very odd that the professor had little interest in the culture of the blacks given the relationship with his daughter and the fact that his five young proteges are Aboriginals."

Peris shifted uncomfortably. "Not all of us are connected to our past, Sir, and it is rather, if I may say it, prejudicial on your part to assume so. I do not see where the private life of the Professor has any bearing on the science of...."

"Careful, Peris. You are about to get on your boong high-horse again."

The ethnic slur caused the young man to rise from his chair in anger. His visitor fixed a murderous stare on the irate Aboriginal, and the professor was numbed to silence. The man loved to irritate.

He continued, "I understand that the girl was raised by her mother in one of your native communities, but the government insisted that she be educated in the white schools. When the government stepped in, Nangala brought the girl to Melbourne."

Peris responded rather non-committedly, "Yes, they were devoted to each other up until his death, that is. So strange the way Dr. Nangala died."

"Suicide."

"Yes, but he showed none of the classic symptoms."

"Suicide." The word was spoken as a warning to say no more.

The man took a thick envelope from his jacket pocket and placed it on the lab table. He did not remove his hand. He repeated, "Get me the diary."

"Look, you got me by the balls, Mate. You know I need that. You never paid me for any of this and promised...."

The interruption was firm and sinister. The man in charge leaned forward and said, "Do *not* remind me of what you perceive are my obligations to you. Your attitude is about to cross a line, so shut your bloody mouth and do as you are told." The speaker's eyes were as cold as a cobra's. Despite the chill in the room, Peris began to sweat.

"Rheumatic heart disease is an insidious affliction. How are your mother and your sister, Professor?"

"Suffering. You know they are badly in need of treatment. Valve replacements. Please do not toy with me."

He reached for the envelope only to have it retracted.

"Our government healthcare funding does need private subsidy, especially for long-term care. And this disease is so common with your people. Such a shame."

The insincerity of the last comment was evident.

A tough-looking man entered the lab and spoke privately to Professor Peris' guest. He caught the last part of the exchange.

" ... now, Sir."

The visitor stood up. His hand was still on the envelope.

"I will expect delivery in three days."

The academic slowly nodded.

"Our relationship will continue to be an ongoing one, Professor. Make no mistake about that."

His words hung in the air.

The man shoved the payment to the young man, stood, and, with his companion, left the laboratory. The professor sat in silence and stared for what seemed to be a long time before reaching for the envelope.

Chapter Fourteen: Detained
Nick Sechi's Journal

"Dr. Sorenson, my superiors have decided not to press charges, although they and I are much puzzled by your behavior in the caves. Do you take stimulants, Sir?"

Kayne, his hair still wet from his plunge, said, "I do apologize, officer. Perhaps it was a reaction to being in such a confining space and all those colors. I seem to have gone a bit off my head."

Superb acting, Boss.

"There is no alcohol allowed in the park, gentlemen."

The captain was eyeing our rucksack. Alice barked from a seated position next to Kayne. I hushed her and added nothing to the narrative. I figured the less said, the better.

Cam was also silent, rather astounded by his respectful friend's flagrant violation of park rules. We were being held at the Park Ranger Station near the Uluru Kata Tjuta Cultural Center. I pulled our backpack from under my chair, anticipating our release.

"You are free to go. Remember the curse, gentlemen."

I said, "I don't get it."

Cam explained, motioning to our gear, "The Captain is referring to the legend that those who steal pieces of Uluru will encounter the most terrible consequences."

"Not doing it, Mate. See?"

I unzipped the pack for an inspection that never came.

"No need, Officer. Please take your friend and leave the park."

Kayne apologized again. I hefted our backpack and called for Alice to lead us out when the door to the interrogation room opened.

"Prison sex is scorching hot, but really, Darlings."

Thomas Paul Severino

Chapter Fifteen: Caravan

From the Case Notes of Kayne Sorenson, Ph.D.

We tucked into the local fare at the Desert Gardens Hotel in Yulara, a small town north of the park and close to the airport. I worked swiftly on my mobile -- an email of thanks, another apology to Campbell Morton, and a flight reservation and accommodations in Melbourne.

Nick had returned the car and secured a carrier for Alice. Having doffed her Outback bush hat, Rebecca poured the delicious white wine and gave us a run-up on her attempted rescue of her best friends.

Nick said, "Girl, the Safari kit is fabulous, right down to the desert boots. But the riding crop is a bit much."

She smacked him on the arse and said, "For the snakes and trolls."

She added, "Anne Klein. Rather pedestrian in a wilderness sort of way, Darling, but I love it."

I asked, "And where is your fine Welshman?"

"Mark is on assignment. Human rights issues in Vanuatu. It seems the country is struggling to address violations of women's and LGBTQ+ rights. I decided to drop in and see what's up down under.

"I have the new phone app, Find Kayne," she joked.

"There is no possible way you could have pinpointed our location, my girl. Are we using tracking devices these days?"

Rebecca rested her chin on her folded hands and raised her eyebrows with a sly glance in my direction.

"Um ... well ... that would be me, Kayne."

Nick flipped open his laptop.

"The bloody blog!"

"It's cool, Boss. I am doing a travelogue thing at this point, so there has been no compromising of the case. I posted our arrival at Uluru last night."

"I knew you were in the Northern Territory since a week ago. Mark and I were on a layover in Darwin yesterday. Thought I'd surprise you, Darlings."

Nick said, "Your *modus operandi* is usually arriving just when we are... how can I say it?"

"Sexing up like pagans, Darling?"

"Something like that."

"Well, it's usually that, or you dudes are up shit's creek without a paddle again. Skinny dipping in a national park?"

"I was in my Aussie Bums, dear girl."

Rebecca smiled and switched gears, "Kayne, how is Ace?"

"He and Darana are on their way back from Europe. They will land in Darwin in a couple of weeks. I hope we can see them before we leave AU."

"Nick, it was so cool meeting and working with your mother and your sister. I am so grateful for their help in the case."

"Yeah, we all did pretty well, didn't we, considering?"

I continued, "Mom and Portia are safely back in NYC. School started, so Mom is teaching. Europe is not the place for the Sechis right now."

Rebecca turned back to Kayne, saying, "And that adorable prince, Darling? He sent Mark and me an email when we were in Provence."

She sipped her wine and sighed, "Another adorable Sorenson male. I told him I have connections in the fitness model industries."

"Rebecca, my love, mind your creepiness. Kris is fifteen, and he is safely ensconced in private school away from trolls and much older women who...."

She smacked him lightly and said, settling into a mocking reverie.

"I am kidding, love. You have seen my hunky Mark and, in the altogether, if I remember rightly. Dashing and so scrumptious. Why those abs and that man ass...."

"Yes, yes, yes, seethingly hot. We get it."

"Well, as long as your brother, Kick, *doesn't* get it. He is quite mad for my Mark."

"Kick has the libido of a musk ox in mating season."

"And speaking of adorable males...."

Rebecca nodded to an interracial couple who were crossing the restaurant and heading our way.

Max took her hand, saying, "Ms. Quinto. So nice to see you again."

"Mr. Caliban. I believe it was Chicago, was it not? I was at the Art Institute planning an exhibit for the Museum in Fort Lauderdale, and you were doing some energy work, I believe."

"Yes, yes. One cannot forget you, Ms. Quinto. This is my friend Zachary Ariel."

"Very nice to meet you, Darling."

Turning to Nick and me, the three of them said the exact same thing at the same time, "You know these guys?" and laughed.

I said, "We met these fine young men at King's Gorge. Excellent blokes."

Nick put away his laptop and gave each of the men a hug-up. Alice contributed some dog licks to the new arrivals.

Rebecca's glance was unmistakable and unavoidable. *I see.*

Max asked, "How are you, big guy?" He gave me a pash, as did Zach.

"Heading out, it would seem. We have caused enough trouble in the Northern Territory. Please join us."

Nick said, "Hey, you're Maxim Caliban, the alternative energy source guy. Kayne, why didn't we recognize him when we ... I mean, before?"

I snapped my fingers and said, "The Elon Musk of Australia... where has my brain been?"

As I finished the sentence, I could read Nick's thoughts, *Thinking with the little head and not the big one, Boss?"*

Zach said, "We prefer to say that Mr. Musk is the Max Caliban of the US. My man has taken the energy industry in Australia to some pretty impressive heights-- major initiatives in private space launch technology as well as solutions rethinking mass transit options for major cities across the globe."

Nick interjected, "But Dude, your industrial rockstar status sucks. You need some media buzz– talking social and broadcast. Get legendary, bud."

The handsome CEO did a breathtaking smile but said nothing. He absently fondled the hair cascading down my neck before he caught himself.

Zach reached over and took the offending hand, saying, "Right. Just as elusive as can be. Max's privacy is legendary. The industry does not favor the public eye, he believes. So much of our research is cutting edge, and the science behind it has vast implications."

Max signaled for the server and ordered another bottle of wine for the table.

He seemed to become more alert and said, "We need to get back to Victoria. It is bloody frightful to cut our vacation short like this, but fortune favors the bold. Business developments call us back. Some scuttlebutt brewing."

Max had a tattoo band around his left bicep that translated his favorite motto into Latin, which he was fond of quoting, "*Audaces Fortuna Iuvat*. Fortune Favors the Bold."

Zach said, "Clean, renewal energy capable of creating vast sources of power is becoming more and more of a political hotbed. Australia needs to lead the way. The weapons side of it all is lucrative, to say the least."

"I believe Caliban Ariel Industries has been talking to my father about solar farms on Inala lands."

Max said, "Crikey, you're *that* Sorenson! Guess I wasn't putting two and two together."

So, Max was that type, it seems. I was getting some intensely longing vibes from the hot Aussie. It appears that the recent casual sex play sessions among the four of us went a little deeper for the lad – a bit awkward.

"Well, well, well... a lot of non-intellectual activity going on when the four of you met, humm Darlings? And Nick, you don't have to tell me what was going on in your mind."

I attempted to toss a breadstick at her, but Nick beat me to it.

I jumped in, saying to the lads, "Perhaps we will see you then in Melbourne."

Max was making a call but answered, "Have to, Mate. The three of you and Lady Alice here must be our guests at Heathcliff, my – I mean our ranch in the Yarra Valley not too far from Melbourne. My company's headquarters is in Geelong, just across Port Philip Bay. Can't say no, Mates."

Zach was pleased with the decision and clapped Nick on the shoulder.

Rebecca bubbled over with, "How very nice of you, Max Darling. We will try hard not to overstay our welcome."

"Kayne, holy crap! Excuse me, folks." Nick's face became filled with excitement like a youngster on Christmas morning – eyes all aglow and mouth wide open. Some new occurrence just beyond our veranda had him mesmerized.

Nick and Alice dashed from the restaurant to the adjacent road to greet a caravan of passing camels. He had snatched Rebecca's riding crop and was whirling it in the afternoon light. The four of us stood to watch, and Rebecca took my hand.

Nick jumped into the air and whooped as the beasts and their passengers, all in a line, glided past with their characteristic side-to-side motion of the ships of the desert. Camels and drivers ignored both boy and dog with sardonic expressions on their mugs.

Thomas Paul Severino

Boyish and full of natural joy, Nick was magnificent to watch, and I was astonished at the depths of my feelings for him.

He mounted up at the invitation of a cameleer, his heart and spirit soaring. Alice raced around the group, sharing the enthusiasm of her buddy and their combined excitement for these splendid beasts.

Chapter Sixteen: Heathcliff

Nick Sechi's Journal

The ranch was set in the rolling hills of the Yarra Valley, near the river that wound its way to the south. Magnificent horses turned and raised their heads to watch our approach from beautiful paddocks and stable yards. During dinner on the manor house's spacious stone patio, we viewed the sunset change the colors of the distant Warburton Ranges.

Throughout the bucolically scented dusk, it seemed as if a sky deity was drawing a dark blue and sparkling cloak across the sky from east to west, tucking it someplace beyond the western hills. Soon, the night sky over Victoria deepened with midnight hues of black shot through with diamond-like stars. The calls of night creatures sounded softly in the surrounding countryside.

Alice was still frolicking with her new friends, our hosts' three border collies, Snipp, Snapp, and Snurr. Despite the late hour, they were filled with energy and the excitement of a world full of new smells.

We were relaxing in very comfortable acacia wood Adirondack chairs on the back lawn of the estate's manor house. Off in the dark distance, vineyards made their approach to the main living quarters. Max was sound asleep, and Zach had arranged some pillows to support his dozing, leanly muscled frame with long legs crossed at the ankles.

The remaining four of us were stargazing and quaffing Heathcliff Vineyard's signature reserve, a 2017 Pinot Noir marketed under the label *Wuthering Heights.* Their other featured vintage was a luscious, green-gold Chardonnay, our dinner pairing. The dark wine caught pinpoints of light contrasting with the flickering of the low-burning fire pit and the carpet of stars overhead.

Zach was waxing eloquently, saying, "Ahh... the Greeks and their preponderance and dominance of western civilization, it's all so much...."

"*Hubris*, Darling?"

"Exactly."

Zach waved a hand toward the heavens, "Contemporary civilization rarely acknowledges that other cultures have had myths and legends that explain creation, the universe, and the starry firmament."

"They did do a good job inventing unconventional sexin', Darling."

I raised my glass and said, "Cheers, Mates. To Greek style."

We toasted and laughed. Now, Alice and her three boyfriends had fallen into some serious lounging, imitating their humans.

Heathcliff's majordomo approached with yet another bottle. Zach acknowledged, "Thank you, Earnshaw. I was just going to launch into my astronomy lesson, and more wine is a pre-requisite." His beautiful midnight-black coloration blended into the night. It caught glimmers of firelight on his face, arms, and animated hands.

Tall and stocky like a rugby player, the staffer courteously extended a blanket, saying, "I thought that Ms. Quinto would like this. Nights can be cool out here, and the star lesson will be extensive."

"Why, thank you, Darling."

The manservant added some wood to the fire. Kayne said, "Dinner was magnificent, Mate. Rippa of a nosh." He shot his pesky forelock, a signature move.

He was a bit "on his face," as he would say, with the pre-dinner cocktails, dinner wine, and now this Pinot. I always knew because his Australian slang, or 'Strine, would kick in, and his normally ice-blue eyes would turn a sexy cobalt.

Earnshaw bowed in appreciation for the compliment and said, "I hope you will find the accommodations here at Heathcliff to your satisfaction."

He turned back to Zach and said in a low and officious voice, "If there is nothing else, Sir, I will take my leave."

Zach reached behind him, grabbed a throw pillow, and sent it sailing at the head of the stoic servant.

"Oh, bollocks you! He so loves the Mrs.-Danvers-in-'Rebecca' routine. Say it, ya mug."

David Earnshaw assumed an even more stern expression, hands clasped at his waist. He stepped back into the shadows. Now we heard him speak the dialogue from the hypnotic scene where Mrs. Danvers tempts the second Mrs. de Winter to throw herself into the sea.

"Look down there... it's easy, isn't it?... Why don't you?... Why don't you? Go on. Go on. Don't be afraid... Don't be afraid ...."

The sinister voice in the dark continued in the character of the devotedly evil housekeeper. "What's the use of your staying here at Manderley? You're not happy. Mr. de Winter doesn't love you. There's not much for you to live for, is there? Why don't you jump now and have done with it? Then you won't be unhappy anymore."

I felt my skin crawl and, to lighten the moment, jumped up and did my best Judith Anderson, saying, "I came here when the first Mrs. de Winter was a bride."

Not to be outdone, Kayne rose and said, mixing innocence and boldness. "I am Mrs. de Winter now!"

Zach spoke again, a Sir Laurence Olivier cloaked in darkness.

"You thought I loved Rebecca? You thought I killed her, loving her? I hated her, I tell you."

We all laughed at the group's aping of a classic. We were tipsy enough to be dramatically overboard.

Rebecca put a hand up that said, "I got nothing."

She toasted, saying, "Queens doing Hitchcock. Does it get any better? Mr. Earnshaw was the best."

He stepped back into view, remained straight-faced, bowed, and said to Zach. "Will it be proper to take this, Sir?"

Our host smirked, "Yes, I believe we're finished with all of that." He waved his hand as if shooing a fly.

Earnshaw approached his sleeping master and took Max into his arms, lifting him from the chair. He bent and scooped the tall jock's legs up so that he was cradling him as one would carry a child, Max's head against the man's powerful chest. Straightening his back, he walked back to the house. Max never woke up. One got the feeling that this was a familiar routine.

Reading Zach's face in the semi-darkness was impossible. As he spoke, his tone became a bit other-worldly.

"So, different Australian Aboriginal groups have different astronomical traditions, but there are some broad similarities. These are very unlike the astronomy that is familiar to the West. Our native star-gazing songs describe many constellations that cannot be seen in northern skies. Even star groups that can be seen from Europe appear differently in the sky in the southern hemisphere. Let me tell you some stories, my friends."

He pointed to the Southern Cross.

"There is Bunya, the opossum. The tip of the four-star cluster is his nose, and his tail hangs down to the left. Bunya ran away from Tchingal, the Emu, and hid in a tree for so long that he turned into an opossum.

"Tchingal is the evil emu that terrorized people. He battled with Weetkurrk – that star there. Their war created the landscape of western Victoria. You can see he is made up of stars and dark nebulae next to Bunya. You cannot see him from the city because of light pollution, but here in the dark skies of the country, he is arrayed in his evil glory."

He pointed to a familiar array of stars and asked, "What do you call that constellation?"

Rebecca volunteered, "That's Orion the Hunter, Darling."

"For us, that group is Kulkunbulla, the two young dancing men. Kulkunbulla is the belt and the sword of your Orion. Both Max and I were born when Kulkunbulla shone brightly in the night sky, and so we sing and we dance. Therefore, our story is remembered and passed on, which is very important in Aboriginal culture."

Zach continued in his lullaby voice, "If you look in that direction, you will see just coming over the horizon Yurree and Wanjel, the two hunters who pursue Purra, the kangaroo."

***

I was floating in the night sky, lifted up way beyond the earth. I looked for Kayne. He was nowhere to be seen. The celestial bodies were moving and growing denser and more colorful against the black curtain of space.

A swath of stars revealed my dog, Chouko. He wagged and yipped at me, turned, and hopped over cascading stars, inviting a game of tag. Alice shot by me, taking up the challenge. The two of them dashed through clouds of nebulae, disappearing into a dark, empty circle.

A regal woman in a chair waved at me and called me "Darling" before tumbling and floating away. She seemed to be in pursuit of a shy hunter who turned into two dancing men gyrating to the music of the spheres.

Two other naked men, made of darkness and stars, came up near me and reached for each other. The third man in a rugby shirt sailed up and took one of the men into his arms, carrying him away. His partner stared at me before vanishing. His tears were falling celestial gems.

Now, the stars were forming more recognizable patterns. Stripes, whorls, waves, and dots of light formed birds, kangaroos, koalas, and snakes, moving across what I knew were the skies of the never-ending age of creation. An emu, made mostly of darkness, came from far away and was intent on battle. She squawked and trumpeted.

Suddenly, two blue stars came at me from the other side. They were dark blue but morphed into the sharper blue of an icy tundra. The being gathered me up and away from the murderous emu, who screeched in frustration. I pulled the sky god closer to me and handed him a white horse.

***

"Ohh, fuck. I am never drinking again."

Kayne handed me water and ibuprofen. All in all, I was not that bad. Additionally, I accepted a cup of coffee and sat up in bed.

"Say, did that big bruiser, Earnshaw...."

I tried to look innocent, pulling the sheet up to my neck.

He gestured to my naked body lying under our sheets and said, "No, Frisky. No one takes my sleeping man into his arms but me."

He hit a "gunz up" he-man pose, and added, "I would have ravished you last night and left a 20-cent piece on your nose, but making love to the unconscious was never my style." He parodied a biceps kiss.

Kayne switched to a triceps shot, side presentation, opposite leg bent, grasping his wrist behind his back and pulling his shoulder back. His waist was impossibly narrow from this angle— so lean-power-lifter hot and such a cocky showboater.

I howled and chucked a pillow at him but missed.

Holding my hand up to the bright morning light, I quoted Auntie Mame, "Ouch! How do you see in all that light?"

The room was sumptuous, and the view was of dazzling hills loaded with grapevines and the lush green lawns of the estate. Rebecca sailed in from her bedroom. Kayne dashed for a towel, and I covered my privates with my hands first and then a pillow.

"Nice ass, Darling."

Kayne said, oozing sarcasm, "In a long, uninterrupted tradition of not knocking...."

Rebecca waved at him, "Oh please, with the modesty, Darling. We all have been in a hot tub together, for heaven's sake. I am practically one of your gay male buds... Oh, wait a minute, that's not right, is it?"

"No, my dear. You are a raving heterosexual female, and Mark will verify."

Never really one to be shy about my body, and since my morning ardor had subsided, I jumped up.

"Who's for a swim?"

I made for the doors to the patio and the glistening waters of the aquamarine pool. Kayne intercepted me with an arm around my waist.

"Hold on, naked boy. He held out a green Speedo.

"I do not believe that skinny dipping is approved by house rules, my love. It is permissible in the wilds of the Northern Territory, but we are in Victoria and must act properly. Think you can fit your arse and manly equipment into these budgie smugglers?"

I did my best trying not to look like a porn star, but it was seriously small.

I raised my arms and turned. "Cool?"

Rebecca said, "Splendid, actually. Darling, bring me up to speed on the case. We three have hardly had a moment alone to discuss."

"Go, Nick."

With some effort, Kayne slipped into the red version of my Speedo, did a package adjust, and shot his forelock. He sat down on the bed with his back to Rebecca. He handed her a leather strip, and she began to pull and tie his long black hair into a savage coif. Turning his face to hers, she pulled on the left side of his bangs, dropping a wave halfway down his forehead.

I explained the case to the point that we had been detained by the park police at Uluru. I went to the backpack and extracted the treasure that Kayne had brought up from the bottom of the cave pool.

"Wait, wait, I need to get a mental image. Arrested, handcuffed, wet, and in your tighty-whities. All for that? Gimme a minute, Darling."

Kayne tapped her head.

"Not quite. Wow, do you need a man?"

"You're not kidding, Darling. Whatever you do, do not destroy my fantasy that Earnshaw-studly is straight."

She looked to see Kayne and me shaking our heads in unison.

"Damn. OK, continue, Nicky. It looks like a pepper mill or...."

"A chess piece? It's the Knight."

I unscrewed the white horse head and took out the flash drive.

"How did you get this through airport security, Nicky Darling?"

"I'd removed the flash drive and stowed it with my laptop. They must have thought the figure was a souvenir."

"Have you reviewed it, Nick?"

"Yes, Boss. A bunch of scientific equations and notes. It looks like the real deal."

"We should get this to Dr. Nangala, but I propose we get all of the pieces and turn it over as one package."

Rebecca was leafing through the Lewis Carroll book. She asked, "How exactly did you know this was under that cave glyph. There must have been thousands through that cavern."

"It was Nick, my dear. He suggested that the painting not only showed a Bumbry horse but the semblance of a rider who had fallen off."

He pointed to the Tenniel illustration. "The Knight had trouble staying on his mount. QED: The clue referred to this particular glyph. Child's play, really."

She rolled her eyes.

"And I am confident that I know the whereabouts of the second piece of the puzzle. We need to head up to New South Wales. I will explain subsequently. First, let's get some bangers and rashers and a swim."

"One more thing, Darling."

We stopped. Rebecca did a one-hand-on-hip, head-tilted inquiring pose and, wagging an index finger, said, "All righty, then. So what's with the two of you and the two of them?

"And this one...." She indicated me. " ... and that Earnshaw *papi*? Nicky, a couple of times, I thought I would trip over your tongue last night. Hot boys with daddy issues. My, my, my.

"And does Max ever have a crush on you, Professor Beefcake. Whatever happened to subtlety, I ask? Have we been behaving like sluts 'down under' again, my Darlings?"

I felt myself blush with embarrassment. Kayne put one hand on her shoulder and the other on his chest and said, "Please, my girl. Your self-righteousness is positively comedic. As to the sexual tensions you suggest, modesty forbids."

Thomas Paul Severino

Chapter Seventeen: The Red Queen's Race

"How?"

"I got into the storage closet that contains his personal effects. Allira keeps the contents of his office on the off chance that there is something we are missing, either regarding the project or anything having to do with his death. I waited until she was super busy. I swiped her keys."

"She will soon know it is missing."

"I replaced it with an empty journal I purchased online. Look at the brand – fairly easy to come by."

He opened the book and examined the writing. "But this is gibberish, utterly useless!"

"Hold it up to a mirror. Nangala wrote like DaVinci, backward."

The scientist placed a hand mirror on the table and quoted.

> *My meeting with the Red Queen: She is ruthless about winning the game. I must act to remove her from the playing board by keeping her and her court continually running but remaining in the same place.... I will create the ultimate safeguard. They will need the chess game, the pieces, the moves. That is the key. Then the Dreamer King will awaken, and the game will be won.*

The man continued, "I am puzzled by what appears to be references to a child's story, chess pieces that come alive."

The nervous scientist said, "The Red Queen's Race has a significant meaning here, I think. Colloquially, it means attempting to move forward with no progress, running in place. Dr. Nangala loved the world of contradiction. His gaming has shut down the project by extracting and hiding the most important parts. He believes this will keep the Red Queen and all who desire to steal the project in suspended animation – getting nowhere."

"And the missing equations are hidden in a chess game? This is most interesting. It is work for a detective."

"Here is more about the Red Queen.

> There are traitors among us. The Red Queen flies across the chessboard! Her pawns surround her. The corporates are beginning to make overtures about moving this work from the academic sphere into the high-stakes world of defense. We desperately need the funds for the transition to the prototype phase. Still, I am suspicious of their interests and must be careful about the lure of funding. I have set the game in motion. Look to the text -- Queen Allira/Alice, to win the game.

"Nangala, at this point, is surrounded by those who would co-opt his project. He senses defeat and struggles to protect his work. More..."

> I have become increasingly aware of the danger represented by the energy protocols we are developing. Looking Glass science is annihilation unless we are careful. If this project were to fall into the wrong hands, it could have disastrous consequences for humankind, in fact, for the whole planet.

Kindly give me some answers here, Professor. It is more nonsense, and it taxes my patience."

"Yes. Clearly, the doctor uses Lewis Carroll's writings as a roadmap for his hiding game. In the Looking Glass story, Carroll has a multitude of reflections and parings – Tweedledee and Tweedledum. In fact, the chess pieces themselves have mirror opposites except for the King and Queen."

"Again, this is a game for children. This is useless nonsense."

"Not quite, Sir. The Nangala project's energy source comes from the physics of the symmetrical opposites of matter and antimatter. Research on this type of Quantum Mechanics began during the Cold War but was found to have too many challenges. A significant obstacle is the difficulty of producing antimatter in sufficient quantities. Stay with me on this."

The man stared at the scientist without expression.

"Creating anti-matter in the lab – suspended by magnetic forces and then combining it with matter results in the total conversion into energy. It's not like nuclear fusion or fission, where only a small amount of mass is converted. With this, there is much dangerous material left over. Have you any idea what this means?"

"So, tell me."

"The road to ultimate nuclear power lies on the other side of the looking glass, the reversal of the structure of matter. Dr. Nangala has found a way to make and contain anti-matter in sufficient amounts to produce fuel cells. He has gone through the looking glass of science."

"Professor Peris, I did not bring you here to discuss the intricacies of the project. I need those equations."

Gurumarra Peris snapped his fingers. "Follow the nonsense. The clues are in the text. The Lewis classic is about a chess game. Consider Professor Nangal's game set … I saw it when I went for the diary. Someone made off with a few of the pieces. Find them, and you will find the figures."

"For a scientist, boy, you are master of the fuckin' obvious."

The man with the diary tapped the pages and stared just over the head of the jumpy academic. He was considering what had transpired with this scientist and the stolen book. Suddenly, what his next moves would be seemed clear. He said, "Hmmm, child's play."

The academic scrambled for a conclusion to this alarming conversation. "Look, I am going to need more of the money you promised, you understand? I risked a lot to be here tonight, and things are getting a bit out of hand at home and…."

The man said nothing. It was as if he did not hear the statement from the sweating researcher.

Peris wrung his hands and said, "Sir? I do not want to be an encumbrance, but I think I must insist…."

The word got the attention of his companion. He looked up, holding the gaze of the distraught scientist.

A woman and a man walked into the darkened room as he spoke. The woman stood behind the man in charge, and the muscle stood behind Gurumarra Peris.

"Go with my staffer here, and you will be given your thirty pieces of silver, as it were."

His dripping sarcasm was accompanied by a disgusted expression.

As the pair left, the dark-haired beauty looked down at the puzzling diary entries.

"As usual, you have nothing. You disgust me. Instead of paying Peris, you should have your man force the boy to tell you more, *n'est-ce pas?*"

"On the contrary, Your Highness, I know exactly who hunts for the Nangala figures, and that is where we need to apply extreme pressure."

The man looked up at her and said one word as if it were a curse.

"Sorenson."

Chapter Eighteen: Blue

From the Case Notes of Kayne Sorenson, Ph.D.

Max and Zach were poolside being waited on by David Earnshaw, who brought food and drinks to a table for the three of us. Max was in a polo shirt, khakis, and the requisite hipster brown leather shoes.

When we arrived, the young executive was attempting to control a very disturbing exchange with his corporate and life partner. Max's temper was boiling over. Both were gesticulating with frustration. As we approached with hesitation, I caught a bit of the argument.

Max was pointing at Zach, saying, "You will ruin us. Is that what you want? Have you seen our financial reports? The energy projects are totally off the charts. Red ink, Mate, and a bloody lot of it."

"Max, there is no way around this, I can pressure the board members, but I need you to...."

The enraged CEO stepped forward as if to strike his lover. "You bloody back off, Zach. I mean it. Lives and fortunes are at stake. You don't, and we're through."

His mobile went off, and he punched it to take the call.

Our intrusion was impossible to disguise, but Zach did what he could to recover some propriety in the situation. Max turned away and walked to the opposite side of the pool area listening and speaking to his caller.

Zach looked at our bathers and joked, "Yeah, I should have gone with a larger size, but mmm mmm, eh Rebecca?"

"No complaints, Darling. Man candy extraordinaire. How's the water?"

"Excellent, refreshing. It would seem we chose well for you also. You look divine, my dear."

"Thank you, Darling."

We swam and ate. Max's conversation was getting loud, angry, and frustrating. After a few sharp remarks, he ended the first call and then contacted his office. He raked his hair as he spoke to one of his senior staff. He paced the edge of the patio and argued, "Look, you are my Executive Vice President or not? Last time I checked, you were.

"Yeah, yeah, yeah, I do not want excuses. I want results. We have numerous resources at our disposal to get what we want. You all know that. Are you listening to me? Find the funds to make us the top player in this. I want to see a plan when I get to the office this morning. End of story."

As he listened to the response, he grew louder and more agitated, clenching and unclenching his fists.

"No, Mr. Ariel is with me on this 100 percent. Cecily, why can't I have what I want? You understand that there is no plan B, right?"

Zach tried to cover.

"Sightseeing today? Vineyard tours? The Stephenson Estate backs up to ours along that ridge. He's Parallax Energy. I have a meeting in Geelong late morning; otherwise, I would give you the grand go-round."

Nick said, "Actually, we are going to hit the Blue Mountains up north."

"Long trip, Mate. Earnshaw will set you up with one of the Rovers, please? Can do it in a day, but it's a ballbuster. Better yet, take the Piper. The hangar is north of the estate. Up and back in a day unless you want to overnight it in Sydney. You are a pilot, yes, Kayne?"

Max was listening and nodding. He waved his assent as he finished his call to the beleaguered Cecily.

"Very generous of you, Mate. We may just stay over."

"Take all the time you need."

"Aren't you all afraid that we may be big-time shysters, and you will never see your plane again, Darling?"

Zach mouthed the word 'shysters' with a quizzical look on his face."

Kayne translated, "Criminals."

"Bloody hell, no, my girl. He's a copper, and this bloke is Kayne Sorenson, Ph.D. And you, gorgeous woman, are the Executive Director and Head Curator of the Fritcher Museum of Art, Fort Lauderdale. And from what I understand, FBI trained. No worries."

***

Nick did his best. We Xanax-ed him up, and he rode behind me, Rebecca, in the seat next to him. As we approached the small corporate airport near Katoomba, NSW, he was actually talking and enjoying the flight as we circled the park. The mountains were exploding in soft clouds of blue haze.

"It's caused by the oil from the forests of eucalyptus trees."

Rebecca wanted to talk sex. Big surprise.

"At the risk of being somewhat indelicate, Darlings.... "

Nick groaned, "Oh shit. Here it comes."

I concurred, throwing a "Since when, my girl?" into the back seats.

"It's just that you guys are so... how shall I put it ?"

"Frisky?"

"How about 'lusty,' Darling? I mean, sex is a heck of a lot of fun, but...."

I teased, "And no one knows that better than you."

Rebecca reached over and gently swatted me.

Nick protested, "Please, hands off the pilot. Not until we land."

I reassured him. "All good, my love, almost there."

Nick took on the question at hand, saying, "Kayne's 35, and I am 26. Don't let all that intelligence fool you with your best buddy, the Kaynester, gurl. He and I are very physically and highly charged in the sexin' department. On top of that, I am Italian by heritage, and we know that my people do two things better than any other ethnic group, girl."

She looked at me with a blank expression. I added, "Cooking and making *amore*. And my man loves him some spicy Italian."

We laughed.

Nick reached over and caressed my shoulder. Rebecca said, "But you two are like satyrs. I mean solving international cases of murder and intrigue while sexing up twenty-four-seven. Not physically possible. Dancing on the edge of the volcano…."

Nick said, "It's simple, girl. We don't sleep."

***

As we came upon our destination, I explained the marvels of the Blue Mountains National Park. We hiked down into the ancient rainforest valley between cliffs hung with lush vegetation and filled with animals of all kinds. The steps throughout the descent brought us through dramatic gorges, waterfalls, and aboriginal rock paintings.

"Dr. Nangala's clues have sent us to yet another sacred place. The park is the land of the Gundungurra and Darug People, the traditional custodians of this declared Aboriginal land.

"This park is another UNESCO World Heritage Site. I believe it is about 665,000 acres of wilderness and encompasses a huge plateau – part of Australia's Great Dividing Range. We are descending to a part of a network of 140 kilometers of hiking trails. We will eventually come up over that way further along in the Jamison Valley, but, for right now, we are headed to the most famous attraction in the park, The Three Sisters."

We stopped to admire the astonishing surroundings. The experience left us speechless for a bit. The Blue Mountains seemed to have a mystical effect on our fellow visitors and on us.

Nick took my hand, saying, "Incredible boss. The Dreaming, yes?"

I could only utter one word, "Yes."

Rebecca was a bit spellbound also.

"This is so beautiful and soul-enriching, Darlings. Primal and so powerful."

"So, I hate to do the business thingy here, Boss, but...."

"Got it, Nick, OK, so, in Chapter Nine, Alice is crowned queen and finds herself in the company of the White Queen and the Red Queen -- three royal Sisters."

I turned to Nangala's secret annotations.

"Meehni, Wimlah, and Gunnedoo."

Nick fell silent for a moment and then said, "Totally lost now, handsome."

"Meet our three queens. Those are the names of that."

I walked us to Echo Point lookout just beyond the forest, offering stunning views of the Jamison Valley and pointed. Three sandstone rock towers rose up on the northern escarpment. The viewing deck floated at almost tree-top level, with the land descending rapidly off its eastern side.

I continued, "According to legend, three sisters, Meehni, Wimlah, and Gunnedoo, lived in the Jamison Valley as members of the Katoomba tribe. They fell in love with three brothers from another community, but their marriage was forbidden. The brothers decided to use force to capture the three sisters. A major tribal battle ensued, and the sisters were turned to stone by an elder to protect them. Their protector was killed in the fighting, and no one else could turn them back. So there they wait for the enchantment that will restore them."

Rebecca stared at the enormous formations. She said, "Darling, are you proposing we scour those towers for a chess piece? We could be here for months. Also, I think this little foray into breaking park rules may actually get you into the hoosegow for a long run."

I smiled at my two companions. "Hey, you mugs, this is Kayne Sorenson you're dealing with, remember? Amazing solutions are my specialty. Take a look at this."

I opened a display on my phone.

"I have a mate who works for BIMworks, Inc. He owes me a favor. Yesterday, he and his buds took a helicopter ride over and around the Sisters, doing a laser scan. Here is the file."

I sent it to Nick, and he opened it on his laptop for a larger view.

"Very cool."

"Now, I assumed that Professor Nangala was not adept at rock climbing, so the hiding place needed to be close to the bottom of the towers."

I pointed at the screen.

"There. Enlarge, please, my love."

The niche near the base of the last Sister, Gunnedoo, came into sharper focus.

"Yes, I can see it. There is something there, Darling, but how do you intend to get to it without being arrested by one of those delicious park rangers in their tight, short pants and...?"

"Easy, Circe. So we need a diversion, and that's where you come in, my girl."

Rebecca blanched as Nick chuckled.

She was frosted.

"Oh, hell no. Kayne Sorenson, if you think I am doing the 'help-I-seem-to-have-twisted-my-ankle-damsel-in-distress bullshit,' you are seriously wrong."

"Come, my dear, these park guards are lusty Oz boys and mostly heteros, so undo your bosom a bit and go into a brainless mode."

I pulled at her luxurious dark-brown hair so that the proper adventurous woman look was replaced by that of a subtly provocative sex kitten. She walloped me.

"Watch it, bub. Kayne, the *male* bimbo routine, shirtless and distraught, is a better strategy." She pointed at Nick and continued, "No one's gonna see me, and you scale that sucker with all of that going on."

We both stopped talking, and I slowly turned and caught Nick in an entrapping gaze. He was closing up his laptop and stowing it in the backpack."

Looking a bit surprised, he said, "What? ...what? Ohh, no... forget it, you two. I don't even have bosoms. Anyway, I am the best rock climber of us all."

Rebecca approached Nick like the proverbial serpent in the Garden of Eden. She lifted his shirt and tickled his six-pack.

"But, Nicky, Darling. Who's gonna pay attention to anything else when you do a little strip for the Ranger boys and the tourists? Hot young muscle... all worked up and... Oh, my stars...."

Nick was still protesting as we made our way down to the closest viewing spot for the Sisters.

Thomas Paul Severino

Chapter Nineteen: Defying Gravity

Nick Sechi's Journal

In the end, we decided that one away would attract less attention.

Watching to see if anyone was looking, Kayne went over the edge near the back of the viewing platform, climbing down about 50 feet to the slanting canyon wall. He ducked under the foliage and headed towards the escarpment on a narrow trail, doing his best to remain unseen by the tourists and park rangers.

Rebecca was behaving like the typical American tourist on the viewing deck, loud and obnoxious, drawing attention to us, asking for help with selfies, and making a fuss over me. She explained to anyone within earshot that this was our honeymoon, and we were deliriously happy.

As Kayne carefully made his way along a narrow trail toward the back side of the towers, he became a bit more visible from the viewing deck. I picked my best shot, announcing in a loud and very excited voice, "It's no use, so stop kidding yourself, Betty Sue. I've been sleeping with your brother, and it's never gonna stop. You and I were fools to marry in the first place."

I acted out the very frustrated spouse, wringing my hands, gesturing animatedly, and shouting. Rebecca took up the fight, protesting and shouting to crowd members to verify what she was hearing.

"Oh my God! I thought I could change him, but he has been so cold and distant. What was I thinking?"

Cell phones went up and on "video." We were the highly charged drama of the moment.

We ranted and raved at each other. I actually pushed away a dude who wanted to help me calm down. Two women attempted to comfort my new "wife." The result was loud wailing and preliminary fainting moves.

I looked north and saw Kayne begin to climb the third tower as three rangers came over to see what the disturbance was on the viewing platform, one talking into his mobile. As one of them approached me with the apparent intention of restraining me, I jumped up on the bench against the outer rail, my back to the open valley expanse. I ripped apart my t-shirt and screamed, "I do not want to live!"

I backflipped up and over the rail into the abyss.

**

The park rangers took about an hour to get me out of the tree. Aside from a few scratches, I was entirely uninjured. My fitness training paid off by providing a spectacular suicide simulation. I added the backflip for the fans with the cell phones.

As I was hauled back up to the tourist platform by the brawny rangers, I saw Kayne making his unobserved entrance up and over the back rail not far from the recovery crew. He retrieved my backpack and stepped in beside Rebecca.

He whispered, "I heard the screams."

Rebecca collapsed in his arms, completing an award-winning performance of the distraught wife coming to terms with her husband's marital infidelities on their honeymoon – totally over the top. I caught Kayne's look and gave him the "thumbs up."

Rebecca looked up at the man holding her in an abrupt mood change and said, "You! My sweetie and you! How could you? You total cad, Darling."

The drama was quickly descending into farce. The cell phones were still recording as we accompanied the rangers off the platform. IDs were requested.

"I am not sure what we just witnessed, a real family crisis or some public performance art." The ranger was confused.

"I'll tell you this, one way or another, you folks need to leave the Park. That is if you are OK, Officer Sechi, is it? After your ah... fall."

He turned to his confederate, saying, "The bloke is not suicidal, just mad as a hyena."

Kayne said, "I will vouch for my brother-in-law. He is just a bit over-excited. Thank you for your assistance, gentlemen."

The park rangers looked at each of us and then at each other. They shrugged, returned our IDs, gave me a souvenir Blue Mountains National Park t-shirt, and wished us well.

"Yanks."

Rebecca added a sultry "Thank you, Darlings" as we made our way to the ground station for the Katoomba Scenic Railway. The funicular is the world's steepest. It whisks passengers up to the top of the Jamison Valley through a cliff-side tunnel. As we boarded the slanted car, Kayne took me in his arms and locked lips until we reached the top station. I only saw him and not the precarious land falling away from us as we went up to the top. *Hot save, Boss.*

"Not bad, kiddo. Dangling in a tree hundreds of kilometers above the valley floor and this steep ride up the side of the escarpment. Mastering that acrophobia like a champion."

Trying not to sound like a film noir character, I said, "I'll take a frisky make-out with you over Xanax any day. You get the goods, Boss?"

He pointed to the backpack. Rebecca extracted a chess piece, similar in size to the Knight but bright red. She unscrewed the top of the Red Queen and dumped a flash drive onto the palm of her hand.

"One problem, folks."

Rebecca and I looked at Kayne for an explanation.

"Those guys."

***

As we exited the park, we quickly made for the SUV and hit the highway traveling the road to the airport. I quickly learned how to drive on the left side of the road.

Kayne explained, "When I was on the trail returning from the Sisters, I was aware that I was not alone. I evaded what turned out to be those two blokes we saw at the tram station. The forest is an easy place to hide, and once they passed me, I returned to the viewing platform.

109

During Nick's rescue, these brogans were pressing a bit close but staying back and away from the rangers. I suspect that is them, following us in the red Toyota pickup."

"You know where we're going, Boss? Just give the directions. I can lose them."

The red Toyota was gone by the time we hit the airport and returned the SUV.

Chapter Twenty: A Phone Call from the Vatican

Nick Sechi's Journal

I was almost too jazzed to succumb to the terror of the soaring aircraft's leap into the high altitudes. Ten minutes into the flight, the Xanax kicked in, and I was calm. I examined the newly acquired flash drive on my laptop. It looked like the real deal.

We were headed north to Queensland and the airport outside the city of Bowen, commanding a square peninsula on Hideaway Bay. As we landed, Kayne banked over the area. The Coral Sea lay to the north, east, and south. The Don River spreads her delta to the west to provide the fertile soil that supports rich farmlands.

The text of <u>Through the Looking Glass</u> provided yet another clue for our investigation. Somewhere below us, we'd find the third chess piece.

From his pilot seat, the professor began his lecture by saying, "Carroll's poem, *The Walrus and the Carpenter*, a typical English ballad filled with archaic language, is one of many references to water and the sea in the story. The eponymous characters in the poem cause a bit of havoc when they come upon an offshore bed of oysters."

Kayne continued, "The logic of Nangala's clues for the next piece of the treasure is simple. Environmentalists are bringing back what were some of the richest oyster beds on the Great Barrier Reef, especially in the area from Bowling Green Bay in the north and Hideaway Bay near Bowen. Our chess piece is there."

Rebecca checked Google Maps and commented, "Talk about a needle in a wet haystack, Darling. That's a sizeable chunk of Reef to search for a chess piece, hundreds of square miles."

Kayne said, "I think we have a clue that narrows the search. Nangala has written 'Catalina' and 'Lucky Country' in his coded, invisible ink entries next to the poem's text. There was an air force base at Bowen for PBY Catalina flying boats during World War II. Their mission was to search for Japanese ships and submarines in the Coral Sea. I believe, among the plane wrecks in the waters off Bowen, we will find the hiding place of the next flash drive."

I said with just a bit of sarcasm, "Oysters and eighty-year-old sunken planes. I am so psyched!"

***

"Nicky, are you OK?"

"Mom? Where are you? I'm fine."

"Oh, thank God. I'm in Rome, dear. University business."

"I thought we agreed you were going to stay out of Europe for a while. Is Portia with you?"

"No, no, she's back in New York. Nicky, I want the truth. Are you married? One of those purple marriage things? Nick baby, I thought you were gay. What's going on?"

Then it dawned on me that my attempted "suicide" in the Blue Mountains National Park had gone viral, thanks to the excited tourists. I tried to interrupt my confused mother.

"Mom, Mom, Mom... it was just a stunt. My acrobatics and all that. I landed in a tree. We're on a case in Australia."

Kayne and Rebecca were holding each other up, laughing. We had checked into the Queens Beach Hotel, Bowen. We sampled some delicious Queensland varietals at the hotel wine bar and were on the street looking for a place to have dinner.

"Still gay, mom, and single. It's all good. And it's lavender, not purple."

"Is Kanye there?"

"It's Kayne, Mom. Remember? One's the rapper. I got the one who killed his brother, Abel, only spelled with a 'K.' We've been through this."

Kayne and Rebecca were just about hysterical hearing this. Kayne mimicked the famous rapper's dance moves, holding an invisible mic to his mouth. A graffiti wall served as his stage background. Passers-by thought we were insane.

"Yes, yes, Nicky. All of this has just gotten me a bit nutso as you like to say, baby."

"I really wish you would get back home, Mom. I'm not sure our last case there hasn't... well, just go home, Mom."

"Nicola, when the Pope calls, you go."

"The Pope?"

My comrades struck jaw-dropping expressions and cooled their street antics a bit. I put my hand over the phone and mouthed, "Too much wine, you guys. You both are cut off." This brought an expected response of even more hilarity.

"Well, practically, baby. It's a project with the Pontifical University of St. Thomas Aquinas, a Shakespeare Symposium. Working title: 'The Bard and the Divine: Theological Perspectives of Shakespearian Theater.' We are almost finished with the planning. I leave for New York on Tuesday."

"Good. The sooner, the better."

"I have to go, Nicky. I will tell your sisters and the family that you are alive and well and still gay."

"Gay as a goose, Mom."

"That's nice. Son, go on your social media and let people know...."

"Will do, Mom. Love to the family. Safe journeys. Let the Roman clergy know that this hottie altar boy is still misbehaving. They will love it."

"Nicola, do not blaspheme!"

"I love you, Mom."

"I love you too, baby. Please give my love to Kayne (*She got it right this time.*) and Rebecca. *Caio, Bambino.*"

"*Caio, Caio, Momma.*"

113

I ended the call and went to my Facebook page. I quickly posted a picture of Kayne and me smooching. *Still alive, very gay, and going strong.*

I turned to my companions, who tried to arrange their faces into a semblance of seriousness but kept busting out in laughter.

"You guys, man...."

Kayne said, "How is Viola?"

"Confused by our hijinks in the Blue Mountains."

"Nicky, let the world know you are a hot uber-gay by posting pictures of you *in flagrante delicto*, as we say."

"Pictures of me having gay sex? Are you nuts?"

"Yes, Darling. Snapchat, Tumblr, Insta."

"Right, I am gonna post pictures of me sexing up."

She held up her phone.

"Need some, Darling? I can send 'em to you."

Kayne slid down the wall laughing.

I chased Rebecca up the street.

Chapter Twenty-One: Bull

From the Case Notes of Kayne Sorenson, Ph.D.

I showed Rebecca and Nick the tablet screen. The underwater picture showed the large cluster of a diversity of life forms that made up a portion of the renowned coral reef.

"RAAF Catalina flying boat, *PBY – 5A* code-named *Lewis Carroll.* Shot down on a bombing mission in December 1943. Yep, there is a boat-plane wreck under all of that. The next image shows its outline. There, see? The location is Gould Reef, 80 km northeast of Bowen."

Nick took back his tablet and said, "That's the dive we want, Boss."

He yawned. We had traveled to the Bowen wharves just before dawn and headed out in search of our missing chess piece. I'd arranged for a Back Cove 34 Motor Yacht equipped for a day cruise with diving equipment for two from Captain Henry Parraqué, proprietor of Lucky Country Reef Adventures.

"Best time to dive on the Reef is from June to November, Mates. So you're in for a good experience. Why, only one day? A liveaboard cruise, 3 to 5 days, is a rippa of a diving experience on the best damn coral reef in the world."

I explained, "Our time is limited, Captain Parraqué. We are particularly interested in diving on that."

I showed the owner the image of the sunken *Lewis Carroll*

"Now that is a problem, Mate. Government issue, that. Because it is a crash, bodies and all. Diving is strictly prohibited. But I do know where it is. I took a bloke there a few years back. Wanted something disposed of." The Captain winked, "We got in and out lickety-split. Marine coppers had no notion."

Nick said, "Bingo! He wanted something hidden, right? Did you see what it was and remember the bloke's name?"

"Naw. Tossed my records of that year just recently. If I remember correctly, the dingus was about a foot long and wrapped in a waterproof sack. The bloke didn't dive, so I put it down there for him. He was very particular about its placement."

I asked, "How much would it take to bend the rules a bit, Captain Parraqué. Can we come to a price for you to take us there and help retrieve the object?"

The fleet owner rubbed his chin and moved his other hand's thumb and index finger in a circular motion. He strongly resembled a Dickens character, grizzly and a bit comical.

"I think we can agree on a number, Mate. But this old sod's diving days are over. The COPD's got me, so the dive is up to you. But I can get you to the site, three hours out and three back in calm seas."

We agreed and boarded the *Coral Sea Aggressor*.

***

Nick was slathered with Sun Block 30 and was setting out the dive equipment as we came slowly through the green and blue reefs surrounding our destination. The bright sun in the cloudless sky made his slick body dance with reflected light, a ginger sun god.

Rebecca and Henry Parraqué had a talk up at the yacht controls. She left the wheelhouse and started to the aft anchor and then to the forward one, checking the mooring lines as she went.

As the yacht eased its way into a passage between Wallaby and Gold Reef, Captain Henry eased the *Aggressor* to the south, following the northern curve of the marine formation. The water was crystal clear to the bottom, and coral gardens bloomed below us. He stopped the ship's progress, and we settled into a sleepy roll.

"Ahh kay, Mates. That fine shelia is gonna tie us up to that mooring buoy just ahead, and we are gonna have an important convo."

Parraqué shouted, "Have a go, lass. Good 'un."

Rebecca secured the aft of the slowly rolling boat, lashing the line to the buoy.

"We're gonna need to set the anchors by hand, but you lads need some reef etiquette 'afore we do."

Ancient Blood

Rebecca had secured another line and commented as she sat next to Nick and me on the deck, "Seems I am the boat bitch, Darlings. At least I have the outfit for it. And let me just say, you guys and your one size too small Speedos... not that I'm complaining... you look like a pair of dick dancers from Club Masque back in Wilton Manors."

Parraqué addressed her previous remarks, saying, "And you be a right pretty sailor gal at that, I will say. Not a bitch, by far, my girl. You are my first mate."

She gave our captain a mock salute.

"Ahh Kay, lads, prime directive: Do not touch the reef. I mean the coral itself, the seagrass, the bottom substrate, any of it. Oil from your skin will kill what one of those little coral buggers took fifteen years to make. Remember, the garden below is alive."

I reflected-- *Alice's Garden of Live Flowers.*

"Speaking of, soap and water that shit offin your body, Bluey Lad. That sunblock is lethal to the creatures. We are gonna replace it with something else in a tic. Protection that you will need down there.

"So, as I was tellin', place nothing on the reef, equipment, camera – nothing."

He looked closely at Nick and me.

"You both have dived before, yes?"

I assured him we had and were quite familiar with the equipment and the procedures for a safe dive. Nick nodded his assurance of our skills.

The gruff captain pointed to me and said, "Well, from how you checked out the equipment, I can see you have 'sperience, lad, so you're the volunteer to set the *Aggressor's* anchor."

He pointed to the sand anchor that Rebecca had readied in the rear of the yacht.

"So, blue muscle boy here is gonna go off the back and place the anchor by hand in the sand – no wild things on the sand swatches, ya see? Bluey, make sure there is nothing around it, just sand, hear?"

Both Rebecca and Nick knew that in Oz, "Blue" was a nickname for a ginger or a redhead. Not the first time Nick had heard it, I recalled.

Nick smiled and said, "Aye, Surr. Ya can depend on your Boatswain to keep us from runnin' on the putty." The Aussie tar imitation, complete with navy 'Strine, made Rebecca and me laugh.

The Captain said, "I'll give yas a yank on the chain, and ya then swim under her and to the front of the boat. You are gonna handset the forward anchor also, and then I am going to give us just enough chain on both to hold us still. That plus the forward mooring will keep us tight and doing no damage in this chop."

He pointed to the rear of the boat, telling Nick, "Naw, use that hose and that soap there to get that bloody grease offen yer arse. Stand in that tub there. No runoff into the sea."

As Nick hopped into the makeshift shower, I looked around and saw three diving expeditions off to our starboard, but most likely two km away. At this distance, we had a bit of privacy to do what we had to do.

The Captain watched the lathering Nick, "Now, don't be shy, lad. Nobody's interested in your arse or your privates. Soap 'em and rinse 'em good." Nick complied.

The Captain turned his attention to me. "Now, c'mere, Hollywood, and listen to me ifin you wanta know where is that treasure. The Catalina boat plane wot's down there has waist gunner mountings on each side. You want the port side gun blister. I placed the package behind the seat. The blister is open, and the case is Teflon-coated, so there is no coral. Be careful not to break any pieces of the reef in the extraction, you hear?"

Nick rejoined us, Speedo intact and body clean as a whistle.

"I am a bloody fanatic about this reef, Mates. I totally buy into the native spirituality of the entire mess. This here is sacred ground to our Aboriginal brothers and sisters. It is a big part of their spirituality. We need to have a proper reverence for this magical place.

"The whole shit-and-kaboodle is 1400 miles long. The Great Barrier can be seen from outer space and is the world's biggest single structure made by living things. Humans think they are the alpha dogs on the planet. Hah!"

The Captain of the *Coral Sea Aggressor* wiped his nose with disdain on a colorful kerchief.

"Had me a right lovely Native wife, but she passed. The woman had a tremendous soul. Taught me a lot about this...."

He drifted off for just a moment.

"Aww right. Let's get to it, Mates. Pass me that bucket, Hollywood."

The material in the pail stunk to high heaven. It was a rank and foul odor.

"Arms up, Bluey."

"Now, hold on, Dude. What the fuck?"

Captain Parraqué painted Nick head to toe using a sizeable natural sponge with a thick, offensive mixture.

"What is this? It's fuckin' awful! Shit!"

"It's hagfish slime, boyo. Shark repellant. Gonna save your arse down there. You're next, Hollywood."

***

In full diving gear, Nick went over the rear of the yacht to set the aft anchor with the Captain on deck. Parraqué next moved forward and slowly lowered the second anchor. In a bit, Nick had resurfaced off the forward deck of the *Aggressor,* and I lifted him up to the starboard side.

"Damn, it's beautiful down there. The main reef is off that way a bit, but man, what colors! Did you see the green turtle pass? She was inches away from me."

He was exuberant and glistening with seawater, my sexy Aquaman. Diving mask hanging from his neck, tanks belted to his back, he checked my regulator and tank valves.

"You ready, my love?"

"Born ready, Boss."

We backdropped off the stern and moved together through the turquoise waters, searching for the sunken boat plane. Around us, the Gould Reef swayed and blossomed, growing ever denser beneath and around us as the swaths of colorful sea life moved into lush formations resting on hard Acropora and Porites corals. We discovered pathways through the dense wildlife and dove through a weightless wonderland.

Carefully, we made our way through diverse coral gardens interspersed with colorful bommies, the reef's outcrops resembling columns partially exposed at low tide. A skittish octopus and three parrot fish circled the underwater pinnacles.

Through channels lined with waving seagrass, skates, and rays frolicked with iridescent fish species feeding off the vegetation and coral. A blue starfish hung out near a darkened cavern, housing a very shy leopard moray eel. It was indeed a wonderland of spectacular biodiversity. I could see Nick react with delight to the many creatures that swam with us, toward us, or lazily watched us pass by. Our bubbles trailed up to the surface like lacey veils rising through the crystal blue as a school of cuttlefish and a bumphead parrotfish avoided a sinister manta ray, ignoring our intrusion.

After about ten minutes of swimming on the charted course, the tail fin of the PBY – 5A, aka "The Lewis Carroll," could be seen beneath us. As a small pod of dwarf minke whales passed ahead of us, the boat plane could be seen lying slightly on its side, wholly encrusted with 80 years of living reef. On the lower blade of the fin, one could just make out a Betty Grable-like cheesecake dolly. The image, pock-marked with corals, was of a blonde bombshell, busty and leggy in a blue and white pinafore that barely covered her derrière-- sexy Alice at the bottom of the sea.

The opening in the mass that was the port gunner blister came into view as a dark hole. I clicked on my lantern, gave Nick a thumbs up, and slowly made my way into the cavern that ended in the waist gunner mounting port.

The living reef laid claim to every inch. The machine gun was still recognizable at a rakish angle poking through the open gun blister. The inside was less encrusted. There were no human remains to be seen. Near an inquisitive pair of sea snakes, I found the Teflon bag exactly where Captain Parraqué said it would be. I hung the treasure from my belt.

I turned around in the very cramped space with extreme care and began my exit, careful not to annoy either of the snakes. As I slowly moved out of the narrow cavern, I looked for Nick. He was about 6 meters from the opening.

Suddenly, a gray and white mass moved from behind him and directly toward me. It was a bull shark about three meters in length, and it was intent on feeding. Her attached remora fish seemed to serve as attendants waiting to clean up the remains of a messy meal.

I tried to get out of her range. Still, I knew her species were outstanding swimmers with acute vision and maneuverability. I kicked my legs to flip my body and turn my back to the beast at the last minute. I tried to control my panic as she lashed her massive jaws at my air tanks, straps, and hoses, gripping hard. Her death hold shook me from side to side, and I could hear her teeth grinding against the metal and nylon straps. She was snagged. I frantically fumbled for the tank buckle.

Nick flipped over the head of the shark and was immediately on me from above. He used his diving knife to cut my tanks and regulator free as the shark increased her whipping. The monster was thrashing her head and body with a sawing motion, pulling the three of us into a deadly dance. We were in a cloud of air bubbles between the reef and the surface, turning side to side and up and down.

Nick's sawing arm came much too close to the beast. As I held my breath, I remember thinking, *Just one drop of blood, and we are done.* Nonetheless, Nick was fast and relentless, kicking his feet against the side of her body to gain the leverage that would separate us from the shark.

As her mighty tail wrenched us back and forth, her jaws became more entangled in my diving gear as my tanks were torn asunder, with one going halfway down the throat of the monster. I flailed my arms like a psychotic trying to wriggle out of a straight jacket. As one arm came free of the straps at the shoulder, I was facing the beast. Her dead, blue eyes seemed to focus on her human prey. Rows of her sharp teeth chomping on my diving gear were inches away.

Nick would not back off. He worked the buckle between my back and the jaws of the shark. I expected a plume of blood from one or both of us to shoot into the bubbles and water around us. I awkwardly reached up for his regulator and handed it back after taking a breath.

With the accuracy of a street pickpocket, as the belt came apart, Nick took the treasure package from my side before it dropped out of sight. He brought the heavy piece up over the head of the ripping shark and came down on her snout. The startled creature gagged on my equipment and struggled with the metal and plastic mess of my mangled underwater air system. She descended just below us, fighting to get free of the metal and rubber wreckage. Retching, she coughed up the throat-clogging tank.

I reached for Nick, and we buddied up on his mouthpiece, rising to the surface. Below us, I watched my air tanks drop to the sand strip below, disturbing a family of eagle rays but missing the delicate branches of coral. The bewildered bull shark seemed to lose interest in the tasty humans rising above her and circled below, switching her attention to a pair of giant potato cods who wandered in for a look. The fish rushed away in two different directions.

Rebecca and Captain Parraqué pulled us into the yacht's skiff as we broke the surface. Nick came up last and fast, heavy with the only set of diving tanks left from the battle. The dingy was surrounded by three more inquisitive bull sharks that wanted in on some action. My bathers were torn, and my upper thigh was scratched and bleeding slightly.

Nick and I tried to catch our breath. We said precisely at the same time, "Are you OK?" After assuring each other that we had all of our essential parts, we stared at the herd of cold-eyed, dangerous, but beautiful mammoths surrounding us. Slowly, they began to seek other interests.

Rebecca remarked, "Looks like the sharks just savor your hagfish slime, Captain, Darling. I think we need to thank the Speedo Company for saving one of the world's hottest man arses on the planet."

With that, she reached over to my partially naked butt and extracted from the torn, hanging nylon a sizeable shark's tooth.

Chapter Twenty-Two: Born This Way
Nick Sechi's Journal

Kayne yawned and stretched in the pilot's seat. "Can you take over, my girl? I am quite knackered from our adventures in the Coral Sea. I need about 20 minutes."

As we kept the setting sun off to our right, the late afternoon light flooded the hills and mountains of southern Queensland. We kept the rising full moon over the coast to the east and flew southward to the capital of New South Wales. Kayne had declared a few exciting days of "all things fabulous" in Australia's gayest city, Sydney.

"I got this, Darling," Rebecca said as she pulled her headphones into position. "Have a good nap, Shark Bait. We'll wake you up for cocktails in Darlinghurst."

I examined the third chess piece, another queen, but this one was white. "What I don't understand is why that bull shark passed right by me and made for you, Boss."

"Doesn't care for Italian food, my love." He yawned.

"Balls."

"Your tanks, Nick. They were bright yellow, as were your bathers. Sharks hate bright colors."

I joked, "Children, another reason for fabulous attire at all times. Gays rule the planet!"

Kayne was checking out of the conversation. I reached over and caressed his savagely long black hair and kissed the top of his head. Captain Parraqué had drilled a small hole in the shark's tooth, and it hung by a leather thong at his throat. His breathing became regular as he slipped into a deep sleep.

I realized how close we had come to disaster and how thankful I was that we had made it through with bodies and minds intact. I also realized that I neglected to take my Xanax, and I forgot to be afraid.

***

"Crikey, you landed the bloody thing!"

"What is it about being a woman that implies she cannot land a plane, Darling? Shall I revive my lectures on how not to be a Neanderthal and bring you boys into the twenty-first century?"

"My apologies, love." He kissed her. "Well done, my girl. You good, Nick?"

"No, Boss, I am starving – gimme food, drink, and plenty of monkey love."

"Ah, the testosterone flood... men are such carnal creatures. Absolutely barbarian, Darling."

The grounds crew, with hand-held lights, guided the Phenom into a private hangar with a black Mercedes parked to the side. As we stepped from the plane, the staff moved our luggage to the trunk of the car. A young woman in Caliban Ariel corporate livery handed the key fob to Kayne.

"Your car, Dr. Sorenson. Welcome to Sydney."

I took the key and joked, "Relax, Doctor, as your driver and valet, I will make your stay most comfortable." I asked the woman, "OK for me to drive?"

"Yes, Officer. Both you and Ms. Quinto are on the manifest. GPS set for Oxford Street."

She lowered her eyes and then looked up at me with a shy smile.

"I just love the blog, Sir."

"Hey, thanks."

Kayne took the diplomat's place in the back seat, and Rebecca hopped into the front passenger seat.

"Don't you love the Aussies, Nicky? So damn classy."

"Got one classy Oz boy in mind for some lovin', yeah. Really hot with that shark's tooth choker and his black mane. Loves me all the savage visuals, gurl."

***

Earlier that morning, Rebecca booked the ADGE Apartment Hotel, just steps away from Oxford Street's gay nightlife in the heart of the Darlinghurst district. As night came on, we checked in and collapsed in our two-bedroom suite at this hip boutique aparthotel for a few minutes. The styling seemed to be bold and a reflection of urban Sydney living.

"Lord, I need a drink, Darlings, and I am talking top-shelf." She waved dismissively at the liquor that came with the room. "How fast can you be ready to hit the bars?"

We were actually pretty quick out the door. We started at the Colombian Hotel on Oxford Street. Kayne insisted that the venue was the premier place to begin a night of fun in gay Sydney. The main bar had a panoramic view of the busy street.

"So, what's the plan, boss?"

"Some outrageous diversions, perhaps two days of drugs, sex, and rock and roll before we head back to Victoria. Alcohol is the drug of choice, my lad.

I have a 'rez' for dinner at Pompilio in Little Italy on Stanley Street, a few blocks away. Then some dancing at ARQ and night-capping at Slide. Tiptoe home at dawn."

I raised my hand and said, "I am all in, handsome. Still have a bit of a rush going on from the dive on the Great Barrier. Oh, yeah, and girl, I never did get to say that your acting skills back at the Blue Mountains -- awesome. Gonna land you on stage again, no doubt about it."

We toasted our lovely friend.

"And before I forget. All of this...." I flew one hand over Rebecca's outfit. "Totally Gaga."

We walked up Crown to Stanley Street and enjoyed an excellent meal at Pompilio before heading back to Oxford Street-- fantastic comfort food. The wine was off-the-charts delicious.

As we walked, Rebecca said, "So, let's get this party started, boys. I am so in my element, Darlings. Everyone seems to be of young hipster age here."

She gestured to a passing couple.

"And the men are so fit and delicious."

"Yes, my girl, Darlinghurst is home to the highest percentage of Gen X and Gen Y in Australia. This neighborhood is well-known worldwide as the center of Sydney's gay community. Oxford Street is the yearly parade route of the Sydney Mardi Gras and the spiritual birthplace of the LGBT rights movement here in the Lucky Country. Gay businesses, clubs, and bars abound here."

"That puts our Nicky at the low age range. Such a hot baby. And you and I are in the middle, Kayne. So many men...," Rebecca said wistfully.

She sang, "Oh, I wanna dance with somebody...."

Kayne smirked, and we made our way through the crowd, "Come on, Whitney. Steer all of this into some ABBA, Kylie, and Dannii. We're in Australia, remember? Hey, is that my bud 'Huge' Jackman smooching on Chris Hemsworth in leather? Need to join up on that hot mess."

***

ARQ is one of Australia's largest and most popular gay dance clubs. We arrived at about 11:30 PM. Let it be known worldwide that Rebecca never waits in line. Kayne and I watched as she discussed options she was willing to tolerate with club entrance security. After about three minutes, he waved us through. She gave the "studly" a peck on the cheek.

"And that's how it's done, Darlings. Learn from a pro."

Kayne rolled his eyes, stripped off his t-shirt, tucked it to hang from the center of the back of his jeans, and said, "Let me show you how it's really done. The usual? This Aussie boyo is gonna get 'em for free."

We nodded, and he headed for the bar.

The lasers crisscrossed the vast dance floor space. Together with the extraordinary sound system and the smoke jets blowing across sweating, half-naked, muscled bodies, the club's designers had created a portal into a dimension of music, sex, and dance. I joined the muscle boy crowd, showing off my torso with my top jeans button opened, and pulled my companions into the mix of sound, light, and skin. We danced our asses off to fantastic music for hours.

Guys gyrated around us, often making contact that ranged from flirtatious touching to salacious body grinds. More than one couple freak danced the mesmerizing Rebecca. Admirers handed us more drinks after asking what we were drinking and accepting some kissin'-up as payment.

Kayne pulled me close and dropped to a squat. He began to lick the sweat from my navel upwards. He had company. Two frisky dudes were tasting my back and shoulders and muttering the most exciting things into my ear. A crotch grope sent the signal to my brain that we had reached a turning point, and allowing reason to prevail, I pulled us from the dance floor. Time for a refill and a bit of calmness.

Kayne pulled me close for a bit of a make-out as Rebecca exited the dance floor. A muscled-up couple stopped to hand Kayne a phone number as they headed out. I relieved him of the note, put it in my mouth, and chewed it up before taking it out. This was one wild night, and he was all mine.

"One more here or Slide?"

"Slide, Boss. Otherwise, Rebecca is gonna have some of those pictures she was talking about."

We stumbled out on the sidewalk. And headed up the street.

***

"Holy Mother like no other! Look at you chaps. Bloody hottern fuck. Get your arses in here and up on that stage."

The club MC was styling like a cross between Joel Grey in *Cabaret* and Annie Lenox in her *Little Bird* video– divine decadence with a top hat, a serious cane, and smoking hot makeup. They was someone who always appreciated fit, shirtless men and a dazzlingly beautiful woman.

We conferred with the DJ, and Rebecca took the mic. He pumped out the music track of Lady Gaga's *Born This Way.* With Kayne and me as her backup, she crushed the iconic song. We "Vogued" around her and lifted her as she sang and danced, imitating the sinuous and suggestive moves made famous by the diva. The audience went wild.

We each did an encore. I did a Timberlake mashup of *SexyBack,* that fetched some of the boys on stage to bust a move with me. Someone tossed me a Blake straw fedora, which I totally tricked into my performance. *Bringing Justin T back, you sexy boys.*

Kayne unbuttoned one more button of his jeans and brought the house down with a smoldering version of *Dancing in the Streets.* When he called out, "Here in sexy Sydney," in a modified lyric, the place erupted. The shark's tooth bounced and whirled on his sweaty chest.

Until the predawn hours, our drinks were also on the house in this unique and fabulous club surrounded by the art deco touches of a former bank building. Folks stopped by our table to suggest a wide range of hookups.

It was very close to last call when the MC approached our table and placed an unusual object on the table before Kayne.

"What the hell, boss? A coat hanger?"

Chapter Twenty-Three: The Harbour

From the Case Notes of Kayne Sorenson, Ph.D.

As the first lights of dawn came over the bay, I scrambled over the ladder barricades on the southeast tower. I headed to the top of the Sydney Harbour Bridge, the "Coat Hanger." Nick remained on the ground beneath the structure. He and Rebecca searched frantically for guards or the police, finally stopping a cruiser and pointing to the figure at the top of the span. I made my way up and across the slope of the arch.

As I reached the top of the span and raced forward, it became apparent that the man ahead of me was bound, ankles, knees, and hands behind his back. He was standing too near the edge. I was within two meters when the floor beneath him gave way. He dropped down through the opening and descended to the roadbed.

Diving toward the prisoner, I spread my body flat on the surface like someone attempting a rescue on thin and shattering ice. I caught the prisoner by the clothes between his shoulder blades with one hand. With the other, I grabbed hold of the exposed girder. His weight pulled us both down, and my grip was impossible to maintain. I lost my grasp on his shirt in an effort to keep my hold on the walkway. The captive seemed to fall away from me in slow motion. In seconds, he was gone.

I fell through the hole after him but kept my hold on the bridge. I swung wildly in the night air and grabbed with my now free hand. Luckily, I caught a holdfast and managed to pull myself up into the arch's surface. Below me, I could see the blood from where I lay panting, 70 meters above. It pooled around the dead figure as the sparse traffic screeched to a halt, and a small crowd raced to the site of the crushed man.

***

"Zachary Ariel. Holy shit, no!"

Rebecca, Nick, and I cooperated closely with the Sydney Police crime scene unit, the latents team, the forensic investigators, the M.E., and the photographers. I explained to the officers what had happened topside. The prisoner had been trussed above a trick flooring that, as I approached, collapsed beneath the captive, sending him down. Most of the loose planks had tumbled into the harbor. Security cameras verified my unsuccessful attempt to free the victim.

We were questioned by the police at the New South Wales Roads and Traffic Authority offices in the southwest tower. The agency managed multiple CCTV cameras overlooking the bridge and the roads around that area.

"Dr. Sorenson, you knew the deceased?"

I explained that Zach had been one of our hosts in Victoria and an executive for Caliban Ariel Energies. I added that we planned to return in a day or two to Heathcliff. I provided contact information for Max Caliban.

"And why were you on the bridge at 4:30 am?"

Nick handed him the wooden coat hanger and explained what happened at Club Slide.

"Jimmy, get the club MC in here for questioning and get this tested for fibers and DNA. Why exactly do you think you were being set up?"

"The killer is a psychopath, Captain. He needs a public stage, and terror and fear are his intoxicants. This maniac is only totally fulfilled when his power is widespread and inspires dread. Look for a mature male who is in his prime."

"Captain, I can't get a positive ID on the tag number for the Toyota that followed these folks from the Blue Mountains. I suspect the plates were rigged, phony, but we'll stay on it."

Nick asked, "Officer, can we review the bridge security cams? Surely, they captured the incident."

"Here you go, Office Sechi. Have a look." The police officer directed his technician to run the tapes. The younger officer said, "By the way, Mate, I am a follower and big fan of the blog. Can't believe you guys are here."

The lighting was obscure, but it was easy to see Zach compelled to walk to the center of the span by two men in ski masks. A third male stepped from behind some equipment and directed the setup that would send Zach to his death. He was trussed up quickly, and his three abductors left him on the edge of the uppermost part of the structure. They then traveled to the opposite pylons on the north side of the bridge.

Nick commented, "It looks like work was being done on the bridge's crest. The set-up for his fall was already up there, as were the bindings that held his arms and legs. They knew the cameras were on. This was a quick-in-and-quick-out intrusion. Three guys, each 1.88 meters tall, I say somewhere in the neighborhood of 90 kilograms apiece. The boss guy is a bit bigger, it would appear."

"Captain, we got two bodies in the Harbour Tunnel. Could be our blokes." The newly arrived office pointed to the computer screen.

"Gentlemen and Ms. Quinto, care to see what we got?"

The bodies were indeed those of two of the abductors on the bridge's two pylons. One was being extracted from the ventilation shaft directly above. It had become ensnared on the overhead grating, which hung open. The second had hit the tunnel pavement after a long fall, obliterating most of the skull. Both bodies had been mutilated. The hands had been hacked off.

Traffic had been stopped, and law enforcement vehicles surrounded the corpses laid side by side on the roadbed.

I examined the corpses and presented my initial conclusions.

"Death is by strangulation and the severing of the major blood vessels on either side of the neck to the brain. This man's head was almost completely severed. The dead men were dumped here through the shaft above. The first caught on the grating, and the second fell entirely through.

The mutilation occurred after they were strangled somewhere above. The bodies were disposed of down this shaft, both falling from a great height to land here. You can see the result of the impact on the large bones and skull. This one crashed headfirst into the grill above, dislodging part of it so that the second body fell all the way through."

Rebecca asked, "Captain, where does that go? She pointed to the ceiling shaft above the corpses.

"The bridge pylons here on the north shore contain the venting chimneys for fumes from the Sydney Harbour Tunnel."

"In that case, lead on, Captain." I pointed upward.

***

The equipment room above the tunnel in the north tower was a disarray of equipment and spattered with blood. A wire garrote with taped ends lay amid pools of blood and tissue. Other tools used in the double murder were scattered near the ventilation shaft.

"It was imperative for the killer that the identity of his victims not be known or that there be some delay in ID-ing them. No hands, no fingerprints – even dental will be a challenge considering the damage to the sculls. Psychopathic killers often collect trophies of their work. If not, I suspect the missing body parts are at the bottom of the harbor as we speak.

"Our man is vicious. In a two-against-one situation, he quickly incapacitated one, killed the other, and then, in a turnabout, made short work of the first confederate. Look at the blood spatters to the left of the opening. The killer is incredibly strong.

"He aimed for a head-first landing to further obliterate the identification of his victims. Removing the side access to the shaft, he dumped one and then the other, not bothering to re-cover the opening."

Rebecca had been given a police officer's trench coat to keep her warm as we traipsed above and below the harbor in the chilly, early morning. Pulling it around her, she nodded to a pile of clothes in the corner of the equipment room.

"Costume change, Darlings."

A black jacket and pants lay amid two sets of construction outfits and boots.

The Captain said, "They arrive as construction workers. Do the deed in black and leave in the first set of uniforms, one of them anyway."

132

Nick opened his tablet and said, "Here's the guy."

He tapped up a feed from the security cams, having been given access. It showed a shed at the base of the tower. Workers in grey and yellow overalls were walking toward the traffic management office-- all but one. A well-built man attempted to keep his face out of camera range as he hurried in the opposite direction carrying a toolbox.

He climbed in and drove off in a red Toyota.

Thomas Paul Severino

Chapter Twenty-Four: Max
Nick Sechi's Journal

"I have so many questions."

Max Caliban had come up from Melbourne to claim his partner's body. Members of Zach's family had accompanied him. They performed a ritual purification as ancient as the first people of Australia over the body of their native son. The corpse would be flown back to Heathcliff, and the funeral services would take place in five days.

"Who would want to kill him? And why the connection to you, Kayne? Someone is playing a deadly game with us."

I asked, "Max, why was Zach in Sydney?"

"Caliban Ariel is working on a major project involving a highly controversial new technology that could change the course of the industry for years to come. We are in discussions with the major players in the energy game, many of whom would like our technology for their own. Zach was here for meetings. I was holding up my end back in Victoria."

Kayne said, "It appears that this is, literally, a cut-throat game, my friend. You have our sympathies."

"But it's some kind of macabre joke. The setup on the bridge... the other two deaths... so much blood and gore... high melodrama. What the fuck is going on?"

The distraught young man fell into a seat with his head in his hands.

"You, or to be more precise, *we* are being sent a message. Just what that message is, I am not sure."

"Max, Darling," Rebecca said as she stroked his head. "How did you and Zach come to be partners?"

"It wasn't too far from here, where we met about six years back. We were both in grad school-- a fight coming out of a bar on Oxford Street. Some arse-hole and his mates were going on about the trashy wogs all over Australia. Just about all of us were on our faces. I jumped in, and Zach and I kicked white trash butt clear across Darlinghurst."

He smiled, remembering.

"We hit it off. Spent a few days in that 'the mystery of you' stage of new love. Dated a bit more at university. When we finished our degrees, I offered him a job at Caliban and a place to live in Victoria. Last year, we upped the partnership. Zach's strategic revisions to the company raised it to international status. I am president and CEO. He is … was… the Vice President for Research and Design."

He looked off through the window of our suite.

"We were waiting for Australia to pass same-sex marriage and do it up official and huge next spring."

Silent tears coursed down his face as he looked back to the three of us and said, "Folks, I have a confession to make…."

Kayne anticipated the revelation. "How exactly did you come to the realization that we are working on a case requested by Allira Nangala?"

"Yeah, I knew back in the Northern Territory when we met. Corporate espionage is pretty powerful in my business. So much is to be gained or lost in the race to be the first in cutting-edge technologies. We try to keep it all legal at CA. Just poking around, that sort of thing.

"We have been in a discussion involving Professor Nangala and my senior staff regarding her late father's particle laser research. There is much to be done to move both sides, the academic and the corporate, to a place of agreement.

"We know that Allira Nangala met with you, and we suspect that it has much to do with the missing pieces of her father's research. Kayne, Nick, and Rebecca, please be advised. Many fierce interests are out there that will stop at nothing to get their hands on that technology. It is a murder game."

Rebecca asked, "Could Zach have been close to obtaining the missing figures?"

"That, I do not know. I can give you his appointments here in Sydney to follow up. I suspect any one of a number of our competitors is behind this."

Kayne had kept Max in an intense stare. I couldn't understand what he may have been thinking. Kayne often said he had an excellent sense of people, their authenticity, and truthfulness.

"Please continue to use the Phenom to complete your case. Also, may I ask for your assistance in bringing the murder of my Zach to justice? Only then will his spirit rest."

Thomas Paul Severino

Chapter Twenty-Five: A Three-Pipe Problem

From the Case Notes of Kayne Sorenson, Ph.D.

As exhausted as I was, I could not sleep.

Nick and Rebecca crashed after Max left our Darlinghurst suite. I sat in bed, listening to the rhythmic breathing of my handsome man stretched out next to me. And contemplating the horrifying events of last night and this morning. My logical processes told me there was much to uncover about the tragic murder of Zach Ariel.

Max had all the psycho-physical signs of a prevaricator of the truth. He frequently looked at his left ear when discussing his relationship with Zach and his company's interests in the Nangala research. Additionally, he often fidgeted with his hands and failed to meet my eyes as he spoke.

The lad was lying. But why?

I closed my eyes and began my meditation exercises, my Method of Loci. The house started to appear. It was often varied in shape and details, but many of the architectural elements were familiar.

The mansion was large, imposing, and dark against the night sky. Somewhere in the distance, heat lightning forked across the horizon. In a hypnotic swirling dance, a strong wind bent the trees around the building.

I looked up at the tower with its widow's walk and saw a figure standing upright, bound. Intermittent flashes of light in the background illuminated the captive on his precarious perch. He struggled at his bindings.

I ascended the steep front steps and opened the door to the large entryway. The entire house was empty of furniture and decorations. A stairway wound up from the foyer to the three floors above.

A young man stood in the dark with his back to me. As I approached, he turned and closed the laptop that had colored his face blue-green in the dark.

"Boss."

"Nick, my love. You will be in the front room there. Go now, please."

His form dissolved, and the whisps of his image swirled around and past me into an open door to my right. It was a first-priority room, and I had put him there before.

Seventeen very black men, women, and children descended the steps. They were Aboriginal and Torres Strait Islander People with traditional trappings and accouterments, spears, musical instruments, baskets, and bowls. Their clothes were decorated with dot and hash mark art prints. Turtles, fish, birds, reptiles, and snakes moved across their garments.

Alice appeared at the top of the first landing and barked at the community of Native folks.

"Alice, go stay with Nick. There's a good lass."

The dog dissolved into smoke and circled over the banister, above my shoulder, and into the Nick Room.

An elder from the group on the stairs approached me and spread two lines of ochre across my face, beneath my eyes, and above my cheekbones.

"I will help you, Darling."

Rebecca leaned over the railing on the second floor and spoke in the Arrernte language. The troupe reversed direction and, while singing, followed her path into a room at the front of the mansion's second floor.

"I will help you, Darling. Give me your hand."

My beautiful friend vanished and reconstituted, her ethereal trail flying up to a higher story. She held in her hands two chess pieces, a knight and a queen.

As I gained the first landing, nine rooms opened into the space. The stairway continued upwards. Ace and a brown steer were in the third room to the right, my mother was in the suite at the far end, and Nick's mother and sister were one room closer. Blood pooled in front of three doorways. A burned St. Lawrence, a Native American woman, and a bloody-faced Mother Courage each peered around the open doors of the three sanguineous rooms. Two Native American warriors in traditional Ute battle gear stood guard near the bloody carpet.

At the other end of the open corridor, two different men leaned in a corner, being intimate. One was a tall blonde, and the other a dripping wet brunette. The dark-haired man spoke in German, and the blonde in Hungarian.

"We have missed you, my Kayne. Come join us."

"While our crimes are most disgraceful, our torment of your body and mind is far from finished. No one ever stays dead. We linger in your memory like a fever."

In the dark, at the end of the hallway, my mirror image stood in tight jeans and a torn t-shirt. The glow of his cigarette was almost a commentary on the lusty moves of the men between us. He was barely visible, but he was transformed as the lightning flashed outside the window. His horns and lashing pointed tail were revealed in the surrounding darkness. One of his eyes showed silver, and his mocking smile was indelible.

The devil spoke. "Taking care of my prince, brother dear?"

"Gentlemen, return to your respective rooms, please. You have ceased to have any mental hold on me." I waved my arm in dismissal, and the specters retreated.

From behind me, a strong young male body pulled against me, his arms reaching over and hugging me to his torso. His hot mouth spoke into my ear.

"You are full of doubt, my dark warrior. I will correct that, and you will be mine forever. We are destined to be together always."

Nick.

No. Cognition reboot.

The naked and very excited Max disengaged and pulled me frontwise to explore my mouth with his. As my body responded with intense ardor, I pushed him against the wall. As we came together, the walls of my palace shuddered and began to fade. My cognition was giving way to my lust for this gorgeous man, and my meditation, the ancient Method of Loci, was falling apart, eaten by the acid of intense emotion.

We moved up the disintegrating stairs to the upper floor. My clothes fell away so that I matched his nakedness. I gasped as Max worked his hands, tongue, and mouth over my very responsive but tired body. I scooped him into my arms and mounted the remaining stairs. I heard a snarling laugh from 'Lucifer's room on the floor below between cries of ecstasy in the chamber where I had stowed the sexually charged blond and brunette.

"Thinking with the little head again, brother? How often have you chided Kick in his frisky moments with that line?"

My brothers, Mitch and Kick, were seated on a divan on the third-floor landing. Well, Mitch was, anyway. Kick was sitting on the top of the back of the sofa, ready to launch into his acrobatics like a tightened mechanical spring.

I kissed Max and set him down.

"The bedroom... through there."

He swirled through. Instantly, the solidity of the memory palace came back into focus.

Using hand motions that communicated, "Is he taking his meds?" I received a nod from my older brother that Kick was in compliance.

Mitch said, "The reason you are here is to sort out the complexities of the situation you find yourself in — the murders and the hunt for the missing figures. You are struggling, as usual, between cognition, which is your forte, and raw emotion, your nemesis. Mind control, my brother. Resist your lust."

Ever the instigator, Kick said, "Poor Nick. You need to sex that boyo up like you invented rutting, Bro."

The walls flickered again like a power outage.

A meerschaum pipe appeared in Mitch's hand. He wreathed smoke above and around us. Their clothes changed to Victorian garments. Mitch was in a long midnight blue dressing gown and slippers, while Kick sported a dark, three-piece suit and spats. He balanced a derby on one knee while furiously taking notes – an ersatz Dr. Watson.

A Holmesian Mitch said, "Why would the boy lie, my dear Kayne? You observe that he is attracted to you physically but has a shit load of secrets surrounding the specifics of both the murder and the missing data case."

Kick paused in his scribblings and said, "That boy has daddy issues, Bro."

"Elementary-- greed. Despite his protests of love and devotion for his late partner, Darling, he is not who he seems to be. You know that as well as the rest of us. Admit it, Kayne."

Rebecca had reappeared costumed as Irene Adler, Sherlock Holmes' one and only, complete with an elaborate hat, veil, bustle, and décolletage. She draped herself seductively over Sherlock/Mitch.

Kick pointed to me with his pencil, "It's what you get, Mate, for sleeping with your clients. Again, I say, 'Poor Nick,' bro. You'll invariably lead his pure heart astray."

Mitch, Rebecca, and I looked at my brother, astonished by his rather poetic articulation. We were thinking, "Dude, where did that come from?"

"I do not get the sense that he is the psychopath for which we have evidence. He is not physically powerful enough to have killed with the force we have seen. And he has an alibi. He was at Heathcliff at the time of the murders."

"Fuck, Kayne. Even I am suspicious of that guy. What the hell is blocking this as far as Max is concerned?"

Nick came up behind me and touched my forehead near my scar. I shot my forelock, avoiding his eyes. Guilty of betraying lust.

"Accessory."

"Bingo, Boss! Now, who is Max protecting?"

"I will find out. I will make him open up. Need to check out other energy captains Max referenced. There could be a deadly conspiracy attempting to hijack the project. But...."

Nick turned his back as Max re-entered the sitting area.

"Yes, they are the murderers, not me. I have been completely fooled by those closest to me, but not you-- for your heart is true."

He took my hand and led me toward his chamber. Nick's image vanished. I attempted to direct the others into a nearby room for further mental consideration of the case. They did not move. The mind palace began to shimmer and dissolve for the last time.

Mitch was disappearing like the Cheshire Cat, a piece at a time. He recited Carroll.

> *Twas brillig, and the slithy toves*
>
> *Did gyre and gimble in the wabe;*
>
> *All mimsy were the borogoves,*
>
> *And the mome raths outgrabe.*

I heard Ace join in, "Beware the Jabberwock, my son."

He was just a voice in the dark. Now, melting icicles of color washed out the sounds, figures, and the mansion's structure like rivulets of cleansing rain on a grimy window.

I felt my body heat up as sexual desire replaced cognition. I could only call out one word, "Max."

***

"Max? Who...? Hey boss, is all that for me or...?"

Nick pulled back on the covers, exposing my tumescence. I stood up and walked away from the bed. He looked after me with a bewildered expression.

I made sure the door to our bedroom was thoroughly locked. I came back with two belts and two neckties and proceeded to lash him to the bed frame. My face was a stoic mask, and my body pumped up for one purpose only.

He began to resist, but I pushed him back on the bed with a firm hand to his chest. As I restrained him, Nick grinned and said, "Ohhh yeah, bull. Let's heat up dis shit."

I placed one hand on his mouth to silence him and then replaced it with my jock, stuffing it in. His body arched; he was revved for intense play. I undid my hair and let it fall over my face, neck, and shoulders. My shark's tooth swung out as I bent my head over him. He was totally jazzed by the "Kayne the Naked Barbarian" session about to play out.

I moved around his bound, muscled body with my hungry mouth. I climbed on top of him. We became pure, primal passion for what seemed to be a nightmarish and endless time.

Chapter Twenty-Six: Parallax

Nick Sechi's Journal

Reese Stephenson was the CEO of Parallax Industries. His office was on the top floor of the PI building on George Street in Sydney's CBD – the Central Business District of the capital of New South Wales. He pointed out the sights of the city.

"That there is, of course, Sydney Cove, the point of first European settlement in the state. Due to its pivotal role in Australia's early history, it is one of the oldest established areas in the country.

I understand you were at the Harbour Bridge during the awful carnage last night. How very, very unfortunate."

As he turned away, Kayne reached over to me and popped the collar on my polo shirt, covering a nasty neck bite, evidence of our rough play last night.

The executive continued, "If you continue around, you can see our fabled Opera House. The design is meant to conjure up sails on the harbor. You really should be up here at night – fantastic. Behind it is the Royal Botanic Gardens."

I said, "I read that they are trying to get rid of the bats that roost in the trees to save the foliage."

"Ahhh yes, our grey-headed flying foxes. They are a protected species but are destroying some of the Garden's rare trees. So, scientists are trying to scare them off with recorded noise. The researchers are not quite sure if the plan is working on those little Draculas."

Stephenson continued his aerial tour from his office in one of Sydney's tallest skyscrapers.

"If you haven't seen the treasures of the Art Gallery, it is quite a winner. Also, the Taronga Zoo will well acquaint you with our Australian animal population. It is a short ferry boat trip from the Circular Quay to the zoological park."

"Mr. Stephenson, we do not want to impose on your time. So, if I may, I would like to ask you a few questions regarding Parallax's interest in particle beam energy source technology."

"May I ask why?"

"Seven years ago, Dr. Stephen Nangala met an untimely demise of a violent nature. He was considered the world's foremost expert in this field. Parallax and Dr. Nangala were in some disagreement over a proposed partnership with your company. There seems to be an entanglement of interests, including your rivals at Caliban Ariel, the government, and some prospective international investors. Removing Nangala would have eliminated an important obstacle to your company's interest in the project, provided his research came along in the deal."

"Dr. Sorenson, I am frankly appalled by what you are suggesting. There was no connection between my company and the death of Dr. Nangala. I remember a perfunctory inquiry by the authorities from Victoria, but there was never any basis for accusations. His death was ruled the suicide of a very depressed individual."

"But your company is dead set, to coin a phrase, on getting his project. You must admit."

"I will be honest here. Particle beam theory and the energy sources to make it a reality could revolutionize modern weapons. The development of the power source alone is a game-changer for renewable energy industries and associated medical and industrial applications of this technology. Parallax and its international partners are poised to lead the world in a transformation that will bring civilization into a genuinely space-age universe.

"Beginning with our affiliates in the Pacific Rim and grounded in the abundant mineral resources of this country, particularly in the area of rare-earth metals, the achievements and scientific breakthroughs appear limitless. Let me emphasize it again: We are talking about construction, medicine, communication, transportation, etc."

Rebecca said, "In other words, the company that gains the Nangala research is slated to acquire a mega fortune."

Stephenson said nothing.

I asked, "Regarding your acquisition of Australia's rare-earth metals, Mr. Stephenson, can you respond to the criticism that your company has committed some grave incursions into the traditional lands of the Aboriginal and Torres Strait Islander Peoples? I believe there are lawsuits and a very public movement for Parallax to end its mining operations in the Northern Territory.

"Parallax is not going to respond to in-process litigation, Officer Sechi. And furthermore, it is hard to see any connection to your case involving the deaths you mentioned."

The speaker was a woman in her mid-forties who joined the meeting unannounced.

Stephenson said, "This is our corporate counsel, Rosalie Brenner, of Barkley and Macklin."

The lawyer continued, "Parallax has been a leader in assisting native communities throughout areas of our investment. We are excellent community partners."

Kayne interjected astutely, "On the contrary, according to numerous reports published by watchdog committees like Australia's First Nations Commission, in the Northern Territory, with the highest concentration of your mining facilities in this country, malnutrition among native communities is the highest in Australia.

"In addition to the starvation and extremely high levels of poverty, Parallax, in the '90s, unloaded a considerable amount of building materials on the Aboriginal tribes through a parent company under the pretext of creating affordable housing. A deadly scandal ensued. The structures were built with below-grade supplies and materials containing asbestos, resulting in elevated incidences of mesothelioma in the population.

"Inala Companies have led the way in the Territory to set up and fund asbestos remediation efforts. However, I understand Parallax has refused to admit culpability and has, in fact, dissolved their association with the construction companies in question."

"Dr. Sorenson, I will be honest here," Stephenson said. "Parallax has evolved in its political economics since my grandfather founded the company in 1951. We have changed our mining and energy production programs to more environmentally friendly processes. Parallax is attempting to become a leader in the industry regarding respect and repair of the land, sea, and air we use. But this takes time."

"And money."

"Yes, Ms. Quinto, and money. We have addressed the cost factors and profit margins. We are no longer the energy robber barons we once were. But it really is amazing what corporations can do with emerging technologies. It holds much for the future of Parallax."

Kayne said, "And yet, I will repeat. Your company is notorious for its oppression of Australia's First Nations Peoples not only in the past but continuing into the present day if the media is to be believed."

I scrolled through my phone and called out a variety of sins committed by the parasitic white industries, which exploited the Aboriginal and Torres Straits Islander People for centuries. I added to Kayne's list of accusations, "High levels of poverty... Health care for these communities is a disgrace. There are incredible statistics of Aboriginal people dying of renal disease and world record rates of rheumatic heart disease. Many families in the Northern Territory do not have consistent running water, sanitation, and power. Very little is done by the corporate sector to help these folks."

Kayne spoke up, "And then there is the 'Intervention.' I remember how my father and several of his fellow ranchers protested in Canberra in 2007. He even refused to allow the military on Inala lands."

Ms. Brenner said, "I understand Captain Thomas Sorenson was taken into custody because of his resistance. He actually hid the children, defying the law."

"Many national heroes have spent time in jail for their defense of human rights, ma'am, and the disobedience of an unjust law. Might I remind you of such a personage by the name of Nelson Mandela?"

Ms. Brenner said nothing.

"Bring me up to speed here, Boss."

"About eleven years ago, the government sent the army into Aboriginal communities in the Northern Territory to remove children from their families. The claim was that the Native children were being abused by pedophile gangs.

"Behind this claim, later proved fraudulent, were the whites who viewed Native communalism as abhorrent and in opposition to the corporate structures of those who profit from Aboriginal Australia. It was a huge ideological muck-up by the neoconservatives who ruled Australia and demanded strict assimilation of the First Nationers.

"Captain Sorenson advocated for an end to this atrocity and reached out to some of his mates among the Northern Territory police and members of the Australian Crime Commission as well. They provided critical evidence refuting the government's claims, using an exposé by child psychologists and other medical professionals to show the abuse claims were fiction.

"The damage was done, however. The government's actions did great harm to autonomy policies in the Northern Territory. It has taken years to restore the dignity of self-determination and connection to land and culture. After two centuries of extermination and land theft, the harmful discrimination policies of assimilation continue across the entire country. This is an attempt to make people forget whose land this really is."

Kayne took a breath and continued, "The chair of the board of advisors to the Minister for Aboriginal Affairs in 2007, during the Intervention, was Roland Stephenson, retired CEO of Parallax Industries."

Stephen said, "Ah, the sins of our fathers, yes?"

Kayne said, "Mr. Stephenson, did you meet with Zachary Ariel yesterday?"

Silence.

Rosalie Brenner answered, "Mr. Stephenson was questioned by the police this morning. You will find with them a record of his encounter with the deceased."

"We actually spoke little of the business of our companies. My property in Yarra abuts Heathcliff, and we are at issue regarding planning for next fall's grape harvest."

The somewhat distracted CEO glanced around at the rest of us. He seemed to come to a determination. After a pause, Stephenson said, "I find your insinuations appalling, and I must say that I fail to see a connection with any of this to the murders of Ariel and Nangala."

Rebecca said very slowly and quietly, "But Mr. Stephenson, I thought Dr. Nangala committed suicide."

Chapter Twenty-Seven: Rites of Passage

Nick Sechi's Journal

We returned to Heathcliff to find the estate alive with energy. Alice and her dog pals greeted us with much love and curiosity. Max offered accommodations for Zach's immediate family during the funeral services and burial for his beloved.

"I am happy to see your return to us was safe and sound."

"Thank you, Earnshaw, Darling."

Kayne said, "We would like to offer our condolences regarding the death of your employer, Zach Ariel. We are sorry for your loss."

"Please allow me to provide you with the details of the obsequies. You do have some time before we will leave for the church."

I said, "We understand the funeral will be at St Mary's Parish Church in Geelong and that Max has requested Zach be buried here at Heathcliff."

We were interrupted by the CEO of Caliban Ariel in somber black and slightly 'on his face,' as Kayne would say.

"Earnshaw, we were not finished...." Max did a self-correction as he recognized the three of us. He extended his hand in greeting, swaying slightly. The handshake became a clumsy hug-up. He held a cocktail despite the early hour.

How changed, I thought. In Darlinghurst, he was sad but logically provided us with a somewhat truthful-sounding backstory. Now, he was angry, distraught, and very drunk. *What had he experienced since he returned to Heathcliff to allow the grief to overpower him?*

"Yes, my Zach will be buried up on Sunset Rock. It was a favorite spot of ours. The family has agreed and will provide a traditional burial mixed with good old Catholic stuff. Look, they dug the hole already, nice and neat."

He gestured to a hilltop on the horizon. A dark canopy was etched against the blue-green, misty hills. One could just make out black feather banners marking the site.

"Do you know what that arse hole, my company's board chair said when he got the news? Do you?"

He stumbled over the words and sought an answer in each of our faces.

I laid a hand on his shoulder and said, "Hey, listen bud…. "

He shrugged me off and said, "That prick said, 'Best thing that's happened to us. Now we can begin to revive this company.' Though I didn't hear him, the bloody wanker."

Kayne moved alongside the angry, grieving young man. "Is there anything we can do for you, Max? Surely we can be of some assistance."

He helped the young man into an over-stuffed sofa. Rebecca sat next to him and placed a comforting hand on his back. Earnshaw seemed to disappear as he stepped back to observe from against a richly paneled wall. I went to the coffee bar across the living room and returned with a cup of strong brew. I handed it to Rebecca.

"Max, Darling, Let's switch." She took the whiskey and replaced it with the coffee cup. "We need you sharp and alert for the next few hours, Darling. Church and all that."

"Did you see the coffin was closed for the viewing?" He had no notion that we had only just arrived. None of us commented, allowing him to express his anguish.

"He was squashed and mangled from that fall. They mutilated my beautiful Zach."

Max blubbered as he turned to Kayne. "Find out who did this. I want justice, Kayne."

***

"Lord, Let your mercy be upon us."

"As we place our trust in you."

The voices of the Senior Choir soared across the nave of St. Mary of the Angels Basilica, Geelong. The procession followed the cross-bearer and acolytes up the center aisle to the transept. The coffin was clothed with a white pall, which symbolized the baptismal robes of the deceased Zach Ariel. Clouds of incense smoke wafted over the large assembly. The pomp of religion embedded in a colonial culture reigned majestically, gathering one of its members into the promised paradise and comforting the faithful left behind.

Max had arranged for the family and friends to be flown from his estate to the Avalon Airport on the northern outskirts of Geelong. The body would be flown back for the internment at Sunset Rock. Corporate friends and associates of Caliban Ariel were represented in full force.

The family filled the front pews on the right. Aboriginal family members and Max Caliban, struggling to come off his morning drunk, sat with a few close friends, senior members of his company, and the faithful Earnshaw. Reese Stephenson, CEO of Parallax Industries, members of his board of directors, and Rosalie Brenner sat three pews in front of us near the middle of the beautiful church. Local, state, and federal representatives also paid their respects by attending.

A tap on my shoulder caused us to move in to allow two women to join us. Kirra Yugambeh and Professor Allira Nangala slid in next to us for the funeral service. Kirra whispered, "This is the 'Sorry Business,' and many traditions meet in this place. Kumanjayi is on his way to the afterlife."

The funeral was rich with Catholic traditions, beseeching God to bring the soul of the departed into the joys of the Resurrection of Jesus. Max eulogized his beloved as a faithful and loving friend as well as a respected corporate and community leader. One got the sense that the family and the business had been generous to the Church and the charities in Victoria. The entire service had the trappings of a state funeral.

I stepped out of our seats to take communion and returned to say a silent little prayer for the family. At the end of the service, the cross-bearer led the clergy and the casket to the rear of the church to the soaring strains of the *In Paradisum*.

May the angels lead you into paradise;

May the martyrs come to welcome you on your way

And lead you to the holy city, Jerusalem.

May choirs of angels receive you

And with Lazarus, who once was poor,

May you have everlasting life.

As we neared the vestibule, leaving the historic church, I felt an arm in mine. "Nicky, Darling. Are you a believer?"

"Yes, Rebecca. The Catholics and I go way back. My family is still very devout. Except for my sister, Olivia. Big falling out over the abuses with the kids by the clergy."

"But the homophobia, Darling. Such hypocrisy."

I did a shoulder shrug as Kayne pulled up next to us to listen.

"Yeah. You know I didn't leave the Church. They left me. Anyway, nobody keeps this former altar boy from taking Communion. I still believe."

Outside, on the lawn of the Basilica, we introduced Rebecca to our woman friends. The expanse before the church was filled with First Nationers in subdued colors singing and dancing in small groups. Kayne commented, "Here you see, the whole community gets together and shares their sorrow as a family."

Max and the relatives stood outside, receiving the mourners. Zach's family did not shake hands even when the guest attempted. I noticed that they offered the traditional embrace instead.

After being introduced, Rebecca attempted to ask Karra, "Darling, why did the service and everyone refer to the late Za..." She did not finish. Kirra put her hand up to stop Rebecca from continuing.

"My dear, you must not speak the name of the deceased. It is not permitted. To do so will disturb his spirit. Also, no pictures, as is the custom with the memorial services of the colonists. We use 'Kumanjayi' or 'Kwementyaye' to speak of the deceased. Our brother was of the

Wurundjeri people from their ancestral home in the Birrarung, the Yarra River Valley. Before European settlement, they lived in the Melbourne area for tens of thousands of years."

Allira said, "So you see, Kumanjayi's burial at Heathcliff is really on ancestral land and is most appropriate."

Kayne said, "I was not aware that you were friends of Max and Kumanjayi."

"Oh yes, dear boy. Max was a dear friend of my son, Uriah. You remember him from Inala. It fell to me to tell the family, at Max's request, that his man had died. It is not permitted for a non-Aboriginal to tell the family. Ah, the 'Sorry Business.' My, my...." She shook her head.

I asked, "Professor Nangala, will you and Auntie Kirra be going back to Heathcliff?"

"Yes, Officer. Mr. Caliban has requested our attendance at the burial. Auntie continued to be a confidant of our deceased brother throughout his adult life."

She continued, "I hope we can meet very soon to discuss developments in our little mystery. I surmise that the two of you have made some progress."

"The three of us, Darling. I joined Team Sorenson a bit ago, and I've kept these two boys from going astray — woman power. It seems we have two mysteries to solve while we are in your country." Rebecca's comment brought nods all around.

Kayne said, "Three if we count the death of your father."

We were interrupted by David Earnshaw.

"Gentlemen and ladies, we are ready to return to the estate. Won't you, Professor Nangala and Ms. Yugambeh, proceed to the third limousine? Thank you."

***

As the sun settled over the Warburton Mountains, participants lit torches to surround the gravesite and illuminate the trail that led down

157

the hillside to the sweeping lawns of the estate. Following the burial prayers, we left Sunset Rock to the family and the Wurundjeri. As Max shepherded his guests back to Heathcliff, I noticed that the Aborigines, in traditional dress, began to paint the pine box containing the deceased's remains with red earth.

As we followed the twisting trail by torchlight, behind us, we heard singing along with the droning of the didgeridoos and the rhythm of the bilma clapsticks sounding in the twilight. The dances began as the moon rose in the east. As we reached the mansion, the silhouettes of the First Nation community members stood out against the sky of the coming night.

We settled on the patio in a corner, all to ourselves. Alice, who never left our side since we returned to Heathcliff, plopped down next to Kayne, her head resting on his shoes. Kirra and Allira joined us. A young man in serving livery poured the wine as dark purple as the night. Max pulled in and sat at the feet of his Auntie Kirra. As was his habit, Earnshaw hovered in the background ever attendant on his employer.

Professor Nangala started us off. "I hesitate to bring up the research case, but I suspect, as you surely do, Dr. Sorenson, that the death of Kumanjayi is somehow connected."

"Yes, Professor, there is death here, murder most foul. I believe that the staging of the killing points directly to our efforts to recover the missing data of your father's research. It is a warning to end our hunting."

Kayne explained the coat hanger message that drew us to the Sydney Harbour Bridge. "We were called by the killer to the killing site by the object given to us in the club. It was a warning that the killer is in charge, and we are to take heed. What followed was an orgy of blood and death."

His words hung in the air and brought a pall of silence upon our little group. I asked, "Professor, what is the connection between Caliban Ariel and your father's research?"

"Stephen Nangala received a grant some years ago to develop renewable energy scenarios for Caliban. Unfortunately, he and the company came to a parting of the ways, as it were. The initial work was not well received, protocols were left undeveloped, and the funding was discontinued. Things got pretty ugly on a personal level."

"I was a boy when my father ran Caliban Energy Inc." Max turned to his servant. "That will be all Earnshaw. Please see to the kitchen staff and the guests. I suspect we will retire early once they leave. Thank you."

Allira added, "According to his diary, during this time, my father was preoccupied with developing the energy source for the laser. He writes that he made a significant breakthrough. I suspect this may have distracted him from his contract with Caliban."

Kayne asked, "So, in Max's time as head of the company, Caliban comes back to Dr. Nangala, unable to resist this new technology. Caliban becomes one of the proposed bidders on the particle laser research project." He turned to Max.

Max answered, "Yes, it was of critical interest to our Board. Personally, I made every attempt to patch things up between the company and the University. My partner, I regret to say, had a view regarding this collaboration that opposed the direction that the Board of Caliban Ariel was taking, not in its acquisition but in the purpose for which the energy source would be used. Many called for his resignation."

"Please elaborate, Max."

We were interrupted, however, by guests who were leaving the estate. Among them the Minister for Energy and Mining for South Australia and the chair of the Board of Caliban Ariel. Max introduced them to us and thanked them for attending services. The server refreshed our wine and replaced Max's with a Glenlivet on the rocks.

Max drew his attention back to Kayne's request for more information.

"Dr. Sorenson, Zach resisted the direction the company was going with this project. He opposed our involvement in weapons systems and encouraged a more pacifist approach to our production. In a word, no weapons. Also, he was a huge proponent for the inclusion and advancement of the First Nations Peoples as benefactors of our work."

I interjected, "Makes sense. The Nangala research has been developed by a cadre of Aboriginal scholars. Galactic weapons development would be seen as antithetical to a culture that understands the Universe as an all-embracing consciousness."

"Precisely. So, Zach was unshakable that we create an oversight and regulation board for the particle laser energy systems project that was made up entirely of First Nationers."

Kirra added, "My understanding from many conversations with our dear Kumanjayi is that he went even further with what he called "The Star Project.' He envisioned a not-for-profit that would create opportunities of all kinds for the Aboriginal and Torres Strait Islander People of Australia funded by this major energy breakthrough."

She shook her head, "Unshakeable, you say? I am not surprised. I remember that as a boy, he would dig in when he had an idea about which he was most passionate. Stubborn -- not giving any ground."

Kayne asked, "Max, how strong is the opposition in your company for going in this direction?"

Max fought with a desire to be drunk on his ass and to present even a semblance of his role as CEO of the energy company. He had pretty much abandoned his efforts to serve as host at Heathcliff and left the guests' comfort to Earnshaw and the staff.

Fighting back a grieving despondency, he said, "There are various issues involved here. Um... corporate solvency is the main issue. Competition is fierce in energy development. The Chinese are the bad arses in the game. They are making astounding industry breakthroughs.

"Caliban Ariel has been slow to see the value of renewal energy sources and is in the catch-up mode. When Zach came on, he helped me lead the company in a plan to get back in the race. The Star Project will drown the Chinese in obsolescence.

"So, to be clear, the Nangala energy research is not just for a weapons-based system. It is a revolution in developing, delivering, and using renewable power. This new direction will provide innovations in manufacturing, communication, defense, and transportation. This will significantly lower consumer costs. It is a bloody game-changer."

Rebecca commented, "But your board realized that the big money and the political clout is in munitions."

He raised his glass to her conclusion as if it hung in the air.

"Mr. Caliban, I want to again say how sorry we are for your loss. I just spoke to the Premier, and he would like me to extend his and Mrs. O'Rourke's condolences."

I extended a hand to Max. He pulled himself up to his feet to thank South Australia's Minister for Energy and Mining and introduce him to us. A very distinguished woman, the Honorable Anne Canfield, Chair of Victoria's Aboriginal Lands Parliamentary Standing Committee, joined our group to say goodbye to Max and his guests.

"We will miss Mr. Ariel. He was an important member of our corporate partners initiative, a true visionary, and champion of Aboriginal rights and cultural preservation."

As they left, Max called for another round. Kirra took Rebecca's hand and said to all of us. "Let's return to the hilltop, my friends. I can tell by the music that they are ready to begin the Creation Stories. The Dreaming has come full circle for Kumanjayi. Death gives way to life."

As we left the manor house, I noticed an interesting group near the fireplace. Reese Stephenson, CEO of Parallax, was speaking to his lawyer, Rosalie Brenner, and a rather regal woman in her mid-fifties. As Earnshaw approached, the mysterious visitor clutched her throat with one hand and, with the other, took the wrist of Ms. Brenner.

Thomas Paul Severino

Chapter Twenty-Eight: Creation

Nick Sechi's Journal

We retraced our way up the trail to the gravesite but stopped short of joining the community dancing at the top of the ridge. Fires burned to light up the hilltop. The corroboree, where the Aboriginal community interacts with the Dreamtime through dance, music, and costume, had taken possession of a blazing Sunset Rock.

An elder met us and directed us to blankets just off to the side. Kirra spoke to him in Wurundjeri, thanking him for his hospitality. I stepped forward and prayed the "Welcome to Country," acknowledging the indigenous land caretakers and requesting permission to join them. Not too far from us sat the parents and siblings of Zachary Ariel, surrounded by dancers, singers, musicians, and friends lit by the fire circles.

"That is Kumanjayi's younger brother, Peter. His sister, Miranda, is attending to his mother," Kirra explained. The bright-eyed young man stood, swept an arm to the curtain of stars above, and the full moon presiding over the obsequies. In a deep baritone, he chanted an ancient song. He swayed and danced to the music he made.

"Peter sings of Bunjil, the wedge-tailed eagle, the largest bird of prey in Australia. For the Wurundjeri, Bunjil is a creator. In the tradition, he has friends and companions, Waa the crow, two wives who are the black swans, and a son, Binbeal, the rainbow. Bunji's brother is Palian, the bat."

Auntie Kirra pointed to a group of dancers portraying the characters in the song. She said, "They are the host of shamans who also figure in the creation story. These six, who represent the clans of Bunjil's community, are Djart-djart, the kestrel; Thara, the quail hawk; Yukope, the parakeet; Lar-guk, the parrot; Walert, the brushtail opossum; and Yurran, the gliding opossum."

More dancers circled the story's principal characters as the music took on an intense and soaring sound. Peter continued to sing the Dreaming as smoke and light surrounded the celebrants.

The elder who had welcomed us returned with three other community members. He spoke and gestured in his language. The men pulled Max to his feet and disrobed him completely. They wrapped a brightly colored orange, white, and green cloth around his hips. It covered his privates but left much of his jock boy ass on display. His body was painted with brown-red, white, blue, and green in the traditional dot and cross-hatching style. His forehead, wrists, and biceps were bound with leather strips. The elder plaited his hair with the feathers of a wedge-tailed eagle and placed an elaborate spear in his hand. The men encouraged the intoxicated initiate in the steps of the dance.

The elder shouted to us after loudly proclaiming in Wurundjeri, "He has become Benjil. Behold the hero of my people!"

Max ran up the slope, yelling and waving the spear. He was welcomed by the story dancers, singers, and musicians as he whirled in the sacred circle. His frantic energy seemed to rid him of ghosts and villains that had invaded his soul.

As she continued her narration, Kirra's voice took on a primal chanting sound. "In the time of creation, warring tribes caused the angry sea to flood the entire country. The people entreated Bunjil to stop the rising sea. He agreed, but only if the people stopped fighting and respected each other. After Bunjil stopped the floods, he asked Crow for a strong wind. The force blew the creator and his people upwards into the sky, where they became stars. They shine down on us this night."

She moved up the hill to join the community.

The Elder pointed to the ecstatic dancer that was Max/Bunjil. "He is one of us because of his spirit-love of the boy/man Kumanjayi. The love that is of the Dreaming and crosses over to join the living and the dead."

Max's body glistened with sweat, and his cries came forth with animalistic intensity. He jumped, spun, and leaped in the circle. His arms, legs, and torso propelled him deeper and deeper into the ecstasy. Eyes wide and mouth agape, he completed frenetic moves as if in a whirlwind. I stood up to help him come back to his senses and leave the soul-burning ritual.

Kayne held me back with a single word. "No." He pointed.

A dark figure moved up to the site from the shadows behind us. With the entrance of a non-aboriginal person, the ritual came to a sudden halt. All stopped except the entranced Max.

"Mr. Caliban. It is time to go back to your guests, Sir."

Tears running down his handsome face, Max stopped his gyrations, bewildered by the strange voice. He faced the intruder, blinking and silent for a few minutes, shaking his head in an attempt to come back from the Dreaming. Finally, he spoke.

"Of course, Earnshaw. I will follow."

* * *

The young man clung to his chamberlain as they descended the trail, almost falling a few times. The strong servant clasped the boy by the waist and lifted Max's left arm over his shoulders. Max still held the spear, which he dragged alongside during their descent. Kayne and I carried the "warrior's" clothes. Rebecca and Allira completed the procession back to the world of the whites. Kirra Yugambeh stayed behind to help smooth over any bad feelings caused by the intrusion and "abduction of the god."

Earnshaw headed for the French doors to the main suite off the patio near the pool. We followed to find Max collapsed in a chair and Earnshaw running the shower in the suite's bath.

Stepping from the en suite, the officious and overly protective seneschal took his boss's clothes and said, "Thank you, gentlemen. Your assistance is appreciated, but nothing further is required. Good night."

He nodded to the open doors to the patio.

I could feel Kayne's discomfort with the dismissal, but I took his hand and eased him away from the stoic majordomo.

"The bloke is a bloody nightmare, Nick. I feel it in my guts."

As we reached the patio off the great room where Rebecca and Allira waited for us, we turned back to watch Earnshaw walk across the expanse near the pool to the large fire pit. He tossed Max's costume and accessories into the blaze. He broke the sturdy spear across his knee with furious strength and threw the broken pieces into the fire.

He returned to Max's bedroom suite, carefully closing the doors behind him.

***

The wine steward provided us with new glasses. He began a pour of a rich dark red quaff, explaining, "This is a Wuthering Heights Station Reserve Shiraz. Mr. Calaban's private collection. It is nicknamed "The Tempest." You will find its flavors and aromas controvert its appellation. It is a comforting and smooth varietal after causing some initial aggressiveness."

Allira asked, "May we return to your investigations, Dr. Sorenson? Do you have anything to report on the missing data? Rebecca tells me you have been on quite a hunt. What can you share with me?"

Kayne said, "We have secured three of the pieces from your father's chess set. I deduce that there are two more to complete the set. I would like to hold on to the flash drives they contained and would beg your patience. There is great danger surrounding this project, as the four deaths so far foretell. Until we can alleviate that situation, I want to keep the treasured information close to us."

Rebecca touched the professor's hand. "They are coming for us, Allira. It is evident. The killer and his associate want this information. It is safest with us. It leaves us in a position to leverage the outcome and prevent further violence."

I said, "We win, you mean."

"Yes, Darling."

"You are most likely correct in this. Well, our research has all but halted – we are running in place. To be honest, I am fearful of certain odd behaviors that I have noticed with our research team members. They are becoming uneasy and paranoid as we struggle to move this project forward. Lack of funding is a major issue in the group since no one will pay for incomplete research."

"Allira, I would like your help in re-opening the investigation of the death of your father. Can you contact local members of law enforcement and get us a meeting? I am seeking exhumation, to be honest. To disturb the resting place of the dead is forbidden in your culture, but I assure you, it is most necessary if we are to catch the killer."

The scientist considered the request silently for a long time before speaking. "That will take some time, Dr. Sorenson. If it is to be done, we must keep it secret. Nevertheless, I will see to it immediately."

"Thank you."

Rebecca and I exchanged a look that said, *This was going to be some nasty business.* I noticed she was distracted by some activity in the great room among the few remaining guests.

She said, "Will you excuse me, Darlings? Powder room-- all this wine."

"Dr. Sorenson... the connection with this latest murder...." Allira's eyes reflected a critical question.

"Yes, Professor. Very definitely. Your father's death and Zach's show the same evil hand at work. The criminal element is trying to gain an advantage over the gambit he built in to protect his work. Zach's death was a warning, a public execution. The murderer wants us to understand that we are expected to cooperate, or the most drastic means will bring all opposition in line. That is why the research on the Star Project must be kept on hold for now, and, as Rebecca has articulated, there must be only one access point to the missing files: my team."

He paused to allow his point to be made.

"And, Allira, your conclusions are valid. Stephen Nangala did not commit suicide. He was murdered."

***

"Incredibly creepy is all I can say, Darlings. The downstairs bathroom was occupied, so I wandered upstairs. The facility was between two guest bedrooms. So, unusual sounds are coming from the other bedroom, and your girl just had to investigate."

We had returned to our rooms and were listening intently to Rebecca's account of her eavesdropping.

Kayne said, "Not the first time you have broken in on a bit of sexin,' Nancy Drew."

She swatted her best friend and continued.

"Darlings, I am talking about nailing-to-the-wall *Bumsen*. Screwing."

"Your excitement would indicate there is more to this salacious report."

She held up her phone. I peeked over Kayne's shoulder.

The picture was dim, but the participants were unmistakable. We could see guests from the post-burial reception, Reese Stephenson, Rosalie Brenner, and the dark and mysterious woman-- very wild *Bumsen* indeed.

Chapter Twenty-Nine: A Phone Call from the Tsar

From the Case Notes of Kayne Sorenson, Ph.D.

It was well after midnight.

Nick was talking in a deep sleep after about an hour of our own *Bumsen.* At the sound of the splashing water, I stirred from savage and sweaty thoughts, eased the sleepy head of my lovely boy off my chest, and rose to investigate. *Not much rest this night.*

I stood in the open doors to the patio and watched the naked man swim laps. He powered through the water, getting an intense workout that seemed a bit of a frenzy. He ended by standing in the water and covering his face with his hands, sobbing.

Max regained his composure enough to exit the pool, grabbing the side and pushing himself up and out of the water. He took the towel from his manservant and led the way back into his bedroom. Max was sober, and I could tell that the exchange with Earnshaw was rather heated despite not being able to hear what they were saying.

As I returned to our bed, my mobile chirped on the nightstand. The number was not displayed, but I had a sense of foreboding about the call. A heavily accented voice said. "Dr. Sorenson? Yes, please hold on while I connect you, Sir."

"Professor Sorenson, I urge you to come at once. It seems that Prince Alexander Kristof is missing. I want to apologize. My family and my government are deeply embarrassed. "

I jumped up and said, "Your Royal Highness, are you able to provide me with the facts of the disappearance?"

"I regret that I am not, Professor. I have my Director of Security for the Royal Family with me. He will provide you with the information as we know it. I want you to know I am putting all resources into action to find my adopted grandson. Please come quickly, Professor. We need your superior skills to solve what I fear may be a kidnapping."

Nick roused and looked up with worried concern.

"We will be on the next plane, Your Royal Highness. We will find the Prince. I assure you."

"I await your arrival, my friend. I have been assured by the Abbess of Monastère du Carmel Carmel du Saint-Esprit Boul that all of the good sisters are praying for his safety."

"Then we are in excellent hands."

I punched the phone to Speaker. Nick came closer.

"Professor, I am Prince Konstantin Preslav, head of Security for His Royal Highness the Tsar. Here is what we have been provided with by the Lycée Victor-Hugo de Sofia. His Highness was at a *futbol* match with a neighboring school. After the match, both Prince Alexander Kristoph and his bodyguard were missing. The athletics officials presumed the bodyguard had returned the Prince to his quarters under his own reconnaissance. The school contacted the Palace when the Prince failed to attend the evening meal or chapel before bedtime. We have deployed investigators but have turned up very little, I am afraid."

Nick grabbed his mobile.

"Your Highness, I am sure you know that very little can be done in this matter without my being on the scene."

"Of course, Doctor."

Rebecca stepped into the room, tightening her wrapper around her middle. She said to Nick. "Your text. What's going on?"

Nick showed me his mobile with confirmed reservations for three on Qatar Airways, one-stop in Doha-- 22 hours. I shook my head and held up two fingers. I read the flight information to Prince Konstantin.

"Wait to hear from me, Doctor Sorenson. We can do better than that. I will also arrange for your arrival and transport to the Lyceé and accompany you on the investigation. Thank you."

"We will see you soon."

"One more thing, Dr. Sorenson. It is the Tsar's wish that the disappearance of His Highness, Prince Alexander Kristof, be kept out of the media. It is imperative that not even the slightest whiff of a scandal touch the Royal Family."

"I understand, Sir."

***

"Darling, this is incredibly bad. Who would want to get their hands on Kris?"

Nick and I hurried to throw a few items in a suitcase

"Could be the work of our foes from the European case bent on revenge."

Nick said, "Fuckin' bastards. Kayne, do you think perhaps this is a vendetta against the boy's father. From your telling, his spy games come with some pretty nasty villains."

"On further consideration, possible but improbable. My brother Eric's trademark seems to have been to leave no enemies behind. He has always been rather thorough in that regard.

"This is the hand of a nefarious villain who seeks to thwart us in the present mystery. Our lad is an extremely valuable playing piece. I strongly suspect we are dealing with a foe of titanic proportions. Most assuredly, the folks who killed Nangala and Ariel are behind this. We are in check, my lovelies."

Regarding the next steps, I turned to Rebecca with a request.

"My dear friend, I have a crucial assignment for you. We need you to go to Inala and keep Ace calm. I will call him on the way to the airport. He will insist on going to Sofia, but that cannot happen. You and Darana seem to have an uncanny power to make him act reasonably. If we find... sorry, when we find Kris, one of the options may be to keep him safe at Inala. Ace will muster an army of his ranchers and staff to see that the lad is protected."

"I am going to love this part, Darling. I live for making a strong, stubborn male do my bidding. You can depend on me."

***

"Where are you, Boss?"

"Sorry, my love. Impossible to sleep. I have decided to use the time to mentally review the problem. We still have no viable suspects. Stephenson is a fool. The Chair of the Caliban Ariel Board is not nearly as evil as this. Max is hiding something, but he is not a child abduction case mastermind. I admit I find this case extremely perplexing. Now it has taken some deadly nightmarish tones on the other side of the globe.

"Besides, I have been sending some instructions to Prince Konstantin. I want to hit the ground running, as the Americans say, when we land in Sofia."

About an hour ago, we had been met at the airport by a representative of the Bulgarian consulate. She informed us, "His Majesty's government has arranged for your travel, Dr. Sorenson and Officer Sechi. You will find the accommodations to your liking, I hope. The Amir of Qatar is a dear friend of the Tsar and has insisted that you use his suite."

The Qatar Airways A380 was an exquisite aircraft, and the Royal cabin provided unparalleled comfort and complete privacy. Nick seemed to ease off his aerophobia and was somewhat relaxed in the double bed, laptop open and flying through pages as he typed and searched for background on the principals of the case. A half-empty bottle of *Château d'Yquem 1811* stood on the night table with a personal note from the Amir. Apparently, the prohibitions against alcohol had been modified by the Supreme Ruler to ensure our pleasure on this flight.

"Holy fuck, Boss. That bottle is £78,105.00. I looked it up." He waved the note. "And Amir loves my Kayne Sorenson Mysteries blog. Very cool."

I shook my head, trying to clear my thoughts.

"Nick, I have tried my methods, but I believe my cognitive processes are somewhat blocked. I may have to sort out these mental processes in a meditative state, but...."

My beautiful man took my hand and brought it to his lips.

Nick looked into my eyes and said, "And Nick, I am freaked out worried about my nephew... C'mon, Kayne. Find the words."

He touched my chest.

"Talk to me from here, Boss. That's where you are blocked. Not in your head. You're pushing it all down again, Bud. Your intellect can let the heart take over for just a bit. What does your heart tell you?"

As he closed and removed the laptop, I shifted in the bed next to him. I tried to avoid our conversation's direction with an inane *non-sequitur*.

I opened with just a tad of sarcasm. "I know what your manhood is telling you, Mate. 'A little man sexin' in the Royal Suite would not only be refreshing but also a political statement.' Always my hot and frisky, Boyo."

"Seriously, Boss. We can come back to that, and I assure you we will. I want you to tell me what you are feeling about all this. This shit is extreme, Kayne, and seems to be getting even more deadly."

He seemed to be able to do this more and more, get me out of my total head trip and in touch with that side of me that I suppressed and avoided with expert skill since I was a lad. Nick also struggled to put words to his emotions. Still, his stumbling came more from an unwillingness to appear less than totally masculine. He preferred the physical side of his nature, but his cognition was never to be underestimated.

He pulled me closer, but I pushed away and sat on the edge of the bed with my back to him. *Here it comes. Bloody hell!* I brought my arms up over my face and sobbed silently but with such intensity that I alarmed both him and me.

He did nothing, letting me cry-- anger, fear, frustration, and total embarrassment. I stood and paced the confines of our cabin and finally sat in one of the two lounger seats.

"I cannot believe this is happening to us again. The danger grows each time and now reaches out to those we love with even more savagery. I am the bringer of death and destruction.

"Sometimes, I feel so helpless to protect the innocent lives that become ensnared in deadly violence. I keep thinking of that poor lad in the clutches of villains.

"Nick, this is it. There are too many risks in all of this. We solve this one, and it is back to teaching and being a cop for us. Perhaps we go to a place where no one knows us or become gentlemen ranchers in the Outback."

I sat forward, my head in my hands. A bit of time passed. He was allowing me the space to feel all this.

Nick left the bed and came to sit on the arm of the big chair. He caressed my shoulders and leaned in to speak softly. "Your feelings are legitimate, but I need you to consider something essential. Something that I am surprised you did not think of before."

I looked up at him with a questioning expression. He stood up and sat on the bed opposite me, his hazel eyes filled with sincerity.

"I call BS, Boss. Feelings, fine– all good. But in the thinking behind it all. Kayne, you're full of shit. Plain and simple."

I couldn't believe what I was hearing. Expecting a bit more understanding, I stood up and faced my Nick with some frustration. This 'put your guts on the table' crap was bloody painful.

"I think you had better explain. You are, I had presumed, supposed to be someone who makes me feel better."

Nick put an index finger to my chest and made direct eye contact.

"You want sympathy or the plain, honest truth. 'Cause that's what I am serving up. Kris has lived on the edge of danger since he was born. Putting him in the Lyceé with his own bodyguard was the safest place for him. These guys are good, but we'll get him back and make sure no one can get him. That's number one."

He raised two fingers. "Second..."

He popped me in the head to emphasize his point.

"Kayne, I have said this before, right from the start, Dude, and you just don't seem to get it sometimes. We face the Big Bads together. We

174

overcome our fears by combining our strengths and talents. We protect each other, man. I don't need a daddy. You need a partner, and so do I."

I tried to look away, but he would have none of it, holding my head between his hands.

"And number next, you big lug. Seriously, Kayne? Cows and camels? Schoolteacher and a beat cop? How long before you are bored, and I am just plain nutso? It's been so good not to be reined in by bureaucracy and regulations.

"I'm not a wilderness man, Boss. Born and raised in The City, and I need the stimulation of bright lights and non-stop action."

He spoke with passion and intensity, both of which I had become familiar with during almost twelve months of our shared life. I started to respond, but he stopped me.

"One more thing -- my writing, the blog."

He continued, "The three cases we have worked on have received worldwide attention, going viral from day one. Talking 160,000 followers and climbing. I'd call that superior marketing.

"And I know this is on your mind, Kayne. Boss, except for our whereabouts, I never give away the real names or case specifics and shit. They are serialized, so I wait till we close each case before giving even the veiled details online. The bad guys cannot anticipate our next moves in real time."

He paused.

"Just so you know, Team Sorenson is a pack of heroes, Boss. And fuck, this world needs folks that can be admired for bravery and put everything on the line for justice and inclusion. You know I am doing this blog mainly for the gay kids out there who need role models and folks they can admire.

"The danger -- it's what we do, Kayne, you, me, Rebecca, Gints, Mark, Scott, even Ace and Darana. It's what we signed up for, Coach."

He looked at me with love in his eyes

"Can't lose heart now. We were born this way."

I stood up and wrapped him in my arms. "I am so fortunate that you are in my life, Nick. I realize that I never knew what true bravery is until I met you."

I kissed him with all the love I could muster at that moment, and he responded with his signature passion, genuine and exuberant.

Nick held me off and said, "Now, boss. Let's return to your comment about violating a few moral and cultural principles of our very conservative hosts. I am so ready for all of that."

"Ahh, my always-frisky boy. Your Italian American libido is truly remarkable." I reached out to caress his beautiful body.

He stepped over and picked up my Calvins and his leather belt. He tossed the briefs on the pillow and halved the strap between his hands. He snapped it between his hands so that the crack was like a warning shot, commanding my full attention.

Coming closer, he snagged a strong hand in my hair. He pulled my face close to his, speaking with a sexy snarl. "Remember a bit ago your scorching bondage session wherein you took very rough advantage of the young, nubile, and innocent officer of the law, one Nicola Michael Sechi?"

Even he could not suppress a smile over the word "innocent."

I played along as he tugged me to my knees.

"Sir, yes, Sir."

"Well, boy, what I am about to do to you we're gonna call 'Big Nick's Revenge.' *Capiche*?"

God, I love wild-assed, fantasy sexing.

Chapter Thirty: The Lyceé

Nick Sechi's Journal

The school was super posh. The Lycée Victor-Hugo de Sofia was an educational institution that catered to the scions of the rich and powerful from the international community. Our plane was met by the Tsar's Head of Security, Prince Konstantin, and we were taken directly to the school.

Interviews had been set up with administration members, the athletic department, coaches, the school's soccer team, members of the opposing squad, and the missing Prince's roommates. Apologies abounded, and theories were rife.

The security head ended up quietly interpreting. My French is rudimentary at best and tainted with the nasality of the *Québécois*. Kayne, of course, sailed forth in exquisite French, a master of deductive reasoning and investigative skills. He was a very commanding presence despite very little sleep since Sydney. The interviewees were amazed.

A story came together that Kris had played amazingly during the first period of the championship match. The rival team put a lot of energy into trying to neutralize the hot rookie during the final minutes of the game. Near the final whistle, Kris pulled a groin muscle resulting from a sloppy tackle by a defender from the other team. He was sent to the locker room under the watchful gaze of his escort.

This is where things seem to have gotten a bit confusing. According to the training staff, Kris never got to the medicos. His bodyguard, Lance Captain Jan Yousopov, didn't show either. The presumption was that the army officer made arrangements for Kris to be treated at a local hospital. An ambulance was seen leaving the rear of the sports palace during the excitement of *Victor-Hugo's* win.

The Prince and his team followed up. When traced, the transport was found to have responded to a call from a spectator but, in fact, returned with no patient. No hospital in the area treated Prince Alexander Kristof.

...into thin air.

In addition to the interviews with the Coach and security staff, we were shown Kris' dorm room, which he shared with three other first and second-year students. The Prince's bodyguard shared staff accommodations one floor above. It seemed that more than one royal kid needed protection during their formative years. None of Captain Yousopov's fellow guards could shed any light on his disappearance.

"I would like Officer Sechi to take possession of my nephew's laptop, your Highness. We may find a clue therein."

"Yes, Doctor. We have confiscated it and will turn it over to your adjuvant. It seems His Highness kept his passwords unwisely in this little notebook. A risky practice that favors us in this instance."

"Kayne, check it out."

Next to Kris's bed was his gym bag, which appeared to be his game bag. His training equipment, ankle wraps, socks, undergear, extra gym shorts, and a pair of tennis shoes filled the duffle. A freshly laundered "Robin the Boy Wonder" t-shirt was among the boy's kit.

One of the roommates commented, "That's Kris' fav, Sir. He loves *vos super-héros américains.*

Preslav asked, "Do any of you young gentlemen know how this came here from the stadium?"

No one knew.

Kayne inspected the contents, carefully turning the items with a pencil from Kris' desk. He nosed a few things and focused on a blue and white handkerchief. I made like I did not see the condoms at the bottom of the bag.

"Your Highness, please have the bag investigated for prints." He put the colorful bandana into his pocket and indicated that we wanted to take it with us.

"Time to hit the practice field, my love."

***

"You are doing that incorrectly, Sir. Please allow me to demonstrate."

The trainer glanced over at the Head of Security, who just shrugged.

Kayne placed his jacket, shoes, sox, and his belt on the bench on the sidelines. He nodded to a bevy of coaches and demonstrated to a pair of boys.

"You want to get the defender off balance, yes? Be aggressive. The step-over is done while running at speed. Step back a bit and try to run to me for a tackle."

Prince Konstantin turned to me and raised his eyes at the unusual methods of the noted psycho-criminologist as if to say, "Seriously?" The young half-back came at Kayne, attempting to steal the ball. The jock detective ran at the boy and stepped over the ball in a counter-clockwise motion, alternating feet. He seemed to have sparks under his bare feet.

The studly defender twisted and turned but was unsuccessful in snagging the soccer ball. As soon as he had the defender off balance, Kayne pushed the ball by him.

"Once more, ready?"

Student-athletes began to line up to watch as Kayne's pupil tried the technique.

"Not bad, my lad. You learn fast. Let's go again."

The third time, Kayne pulled a defensive move that kicked the ball out from between the dancing legs of the boy and would have lofted it out of bounds. One of the assistant coaches retrieved the ball and sent a few other players to watch the guest superstar.

"You have it, Your Excellency. I just did not want you to become overconfident. Try it with, I believe that lad is the Josef, the Count of Toledo who is watching so intently, yes?"

He turned to the small group of boys and continued his instruction, "Remember, lads, move at speed. Keep your knees bent and your body low. Yes, that's it, Your Grace. Well done."

The students practiced the step-over move as Kayne walked around and often jumped in to correct or encourage.

"Become a spring as you encircle the ball. No... go at it with a quicker rhythm. Slow step-overs will cause you to lose possession, Your Highness. Nick, please assist the Prince of Savoy. Yes, the blonde in blue with the earing. Thank you."

I did my best and soon had a coterie of spectators of my own. The lad did fine. I counseled him to remove his jewelry when doing sports.

"Cosa direbbe tua madre se ti strappassi l'orecchio a causa della vanità?" (What would your mother say if you ripped your ear because you were vain?) The boy, no more than thirteen, laughed and undid his gold hoop and made me look like a fool with his sharp moves.

Kayne yelled something to the stern-faced Preslav, who dropped his officiousness, removed his uniform jacket, and got barefoot assisting the players. Everyone in Europe plays soccer. I imagined Kayne said something to him like, "Preslav, ya mug. Get in here!"

My fantastic man clapped the Head Coach on the back as a way to thank him for allowing our intrusion and winning the confidence of the little blue-bloods running around the field. He called over the boys and men, "As soon as you have the defender scrambling off-balance, push the ball by him."

He addressed one of the smaller boys, "My greetings to the Duke of Condé. Tell me, Your Highness, are you a defender or not?"

The boy nodded and tried to look tough and disdainful.

"Then get your royal arse in there and steal some balls, ya bantam."

The boy grinned and raced into the mix.

As Kayne walked among the players, one student, a tall Asian youth in a Batman t-shirt with the sleeves cut off, eased his way to the sidelines. He folded his arms across his chest and assumed a wide stance, suggesting a combination of sullen dominance. *I'm not buying any of this bullshit.*

Kayne stepped toward the Asian athlete and mopped his brow with the blue and white wristband. The action seemed to cause the boy a bit of embarrassment, and he turned his gaze aside. Kayne lightly popped a ball against the back of the kid's head.

"You gonna play or what, son?"

The boy bobbled the ball up from the ground and caught it. He slammed it at Kayne with brutal force.

Kayne caught the missile at chest level and dropped it to his feet.

"Show me what you got, *Senshi shōnen*. Bring it." He raced at the lad, dribbling the ball. The kid came at him.

You spin me right round, baby, right round like a record, baby....

Kayne spun the boy outside and inside out as the lad attempted to steal the ball. He turned the rather formidable defender to mush with a fast-paced change of direction. Kayne moved the ball facing one way and then took it with the inside of his foot to go back in the other direction. He kept his body between the Asian boy and the ball at all times.

His stance was low, and his moves were sharp. In a deadly combination of straight and side knees, Kayne confused the boy, who attempted a sliding tackle only to collapse on his butt. Instantly, Kayne got off a shot, and the ball landed in the net.

I wondered how Kayne's slacks kept from splitting. As I watched him shoot his forelock, he again wiped the sweat from his face with the wrist bandana seeming to make a show of its presence on his wrist. He said in English as he turned back to his defender, "I can show you how to stop that move in a tic." But he spoke to empty air.

The young man was hurrying toward the practice field's exit. I intercepted our fleeing Batman as Kayne came up behind. Turning, the young man caught the ice-blue stare of his pursuer.

Kayne bowed slightly and said, "Noritaka-san. Would it be possible to speak to you in private about a matter of grave importance?"

Chapter Thirty-One: The Dark Knight

Nick Sechi's Journal

The senior athlete spoke excellent English.

"How is it that you know my name, Sir?"

Kayne smiled slightly. "You are Kentaro Noritaka, aka Kaito. You are the second son of the recently retired Minister of Foreign Affairs for the Chrysanthemum Throne. Your father is a current member of the Japanese House of Councillors. You are a fourth-year student at the *Lyceé*, an outstanding scholar-athlete. Among your choices for University were Oxford and Cambridge after turning down Harvard and Yale. Unusually, you have decided to attend the University of San Francisco next fall."

Kayne removed the bandana from his wrist and handed it to the young jock.

"This belongs to you. You will please pardon the sweat.

"Finally, Sir. You are in love with or have some fondness for my nephew."

As the boy stared unbelievingly, he sank into a chair in the coach's office, attempting to preserve some of his innate bravado. He said, "You fuckin' well have done your homework." His eyes narrowed a bit but failed to disguise a rising fear. "You sure cut to the chase, don't you. You presume much with your insolence."

The young noble's bravado was teetering on shit—he sought to fight back an inescapable panic.

"I have no time for deception games or evasion tactics, young Sir. My nephew's life may be hanging in the balance."

I dressed and gave Kayne his jacket and shoes. Kaito handled the wet handkerchief wistfully. "Yes, this is mine."

Kayne continued, "It is an insignia, allowing athletes who prefer the company of males to identify each other."

He indicated the boy's t-shirt. "This Batman is in search of his Robin, I conclude."

Kentaro became agitated, jumping up and pacing. He raised his voice.

"I am a man without honor and an unworthy coward, Dr. Sorenson. I am most likely the one who saw Kris last and have refused to come forward because I know that our relationship would be the subject of much scandal and pain for a great many people. Lately, I have, however, become convinced that revealing my sexual identity doesn't matter if Kris is in danger. It's just that...."

The boy clenched his fist and struggled to keep back scalding tears. I placed myself in front of the kid and held up my hand to stop his pacing rant.

"It's all good, bud. So, I could give you the 'You Be You' talk here, but we need to find Kris quickly. Ya got two amazing gay men on the case, and we'll get him back safely. Tell us what you know."

The young Japanese jock tried to catch his breath and regain his stoic composure. He looked at me carefully.

"You're the blogging dude. Yeah, you guys are pretty amazing. Kris showed me some of your cases online. You may call me Kaito, Officer."

He took a deep breath, turned, and addressed Kayne. He said somewhat shyly, "So, we were gonna do some smooching, making out, and all that behind the field house while everyone was paying attention to the match."

He looked at the bandana.

"Some of us... well, yeah, we have these signals that flag intentions and meeting spots and all. Then Kris got injured and had a hell of a time ditching his fuckin' army guard creep. Dude is like a troll if you ask me. Always around.

"Anyway, I was stuck waiting for him where we were going to meet up for a while and then figured he was too hurt or lost interest. Your nephew had a few other admirers besides me, including girls."

He tossed the bandana on the coach's desk. "So I left. I looked for him at dinner. Started texting, nothing."

"Afraid he blew you off?"

"Damn right. Finally, when Kris went missing at the chapel, the schoolmasters went batshit crazy, he being who he is and all."

Kayne asked, "Kaito, is there anything else you remember about that afternoon."

"Damn, man, I got nothing. And P.S., this shit could get me tossed, you know? They'd dress it up like 'fraternizing with first-year students,' but everyone would know."

Kayne put a hand on the anxious young man's shoulder, saying, "You may be assured of our utmost discretion."

Kaito searched Kayne's face before saying, "Thank you."

He retrieved the bandana. "I will leave now."

It was a statement, not a request. The swag of a government official's son was returning.

Kaito turned as he opened the door and snapped his fingers.

"It was an ice truck, Doctor Sorenson. I remember now because the insignia seemed very out of place, parked near the side of the sports palace. An ice truck– the ambulance thing is a fabrication."

We looked up at the boy, who continued to remember.

"Industrial Ice, Port of Varna."

Thomas Paul Severino

Chapter Thirty-Two: Varna

Nick Sechi's Journal

"There is no such company, Dr. Sorensen. We have covered the waterfront on this. The truck is a mystery."

The Head of the Bulgarian National Intelligence Service, General Andrei Ivanov, met with us following a short flight to the Black Sea port of Varna. This third-largest city in Bulgaria is more than 3,000 years old. It is an essential center for business, transportation, education, tourism, entertainment, and healthcare. As the maritime capital of Bulgaria, it serves as the Bulgarian Navy and Merchant Marine headquarters.

"We are searching video feeds from our cameras at major intersections across the city. We believe the conspirators are attempting to spirit the Prince out of the country. INTERPOL is working with us."

The door of the General's office opened. A retinue of security bruisers entered and parted. A distinguished gentleman of 70 years very regally walked into the National Intelligence Service office leaning on a walking cane with a silver wolf's head handle. General Stefanov and Prince Preslav stood and bowed. With a gesture, the visitor dismissed his bodyguard except for a tall blonde man with a military bearing. The elder gentleman extended his hand to Kayne.

Bowing, Kayne greeted the king, "*Vasheto Kralsko Visochestvo, nie sme pochitani ot vasheto prisŭstvie.*"

"*Blagodarya ti,* Dr. Sorenson."

Tsar Stefan II continued in English, "We are grateful to you and to Officer Sechi for assisting us with finding my great-grandson."

The distinguished Bulgarian royal took my hand and continued, "You honor us also, Sir. Like the missing, young *Knyaz*, we, too, are fans of the exploits of... 'Sechi's Avengers'... is it? We are anxious for the next installment of <u>Stage Blood</u> in the Kayne Sorenson Mysteries blog. So much like Conan Doyle, young man."

He pointed at Kayne, "You are his Dr. Watson, no?"

I smiled, nodded, and expressed my thanks.

"Perhaps you know that Sir Arthur based the character of the overly-amorous King in his story "A Scandal in Bohemia on one of my ancestors. But, I digress...."

The Tsar took a seat and waved the four of us into our chairs. He nervously handled his walking stick. His aide remained standing just behind the king.

His Majesty continued, "When last we met, it was to say goodbye to my daughter-in-law. Such a profound tragedy." He turned to Kayne and added, "Your mother was a good and inspiring woman, and she dearly loved my son and young Kristof. How is your father, Dr. Sorenson?"

"Also, very concerned about the return of the boy, Your Royal Highness."

The once titular head of the Bulgarian State gestured to his countrymen, saying, "I want to assure you that you have the full force of the Bulgarian intelligence services at your disposal. Prince Preslav will assist your every request in this matter."

"Thank you, Sir."

"Count Petar Orlov is my chief of staff. We desire to speak with you about a matter that we believe has some bearing on this case."

"Please proceed."

"We believe that the disappearance of your nephew and my son's adopted grandson is connected to a recent attempt to blackmail the royal family. As the father of a very large, extended family, we are often unable to keep the lives of our brood out of trouble, as it were. I will allow the Count to continue."

Count Orlov stepped forward, bowed, and explained. "In January of this year, the palace was contacted concerning emails and other documents related to the Grand Duchess Olga Danilova, granddaughter of His Majesty. They comprise details of her private life going back several years. These were incidents of a very salacious nature. The request by those who possessed this material was for a considerable sum. General?"

"The Tsar was prepared to pay, but suddenly, around March, contact with the blackmailers ceased– no further communication. Our intelligence discovered an organization referred to as *Paukova Mreža*, The Spider's Web. We understand you have halted their nefarious operations in both America and Eastern Europe in recent months."

Kayne responded to the Bulgarians, "Whether we have been successful remains to be seen, Your Excellency. This global organization of death and subversion is very much like the mythic hydra. As one monstrous head of the beast expires, six more arise to replace it. I believe our team has been an annoyance at best."

Count Orlov continued, "Gentlemen, the efforts to destroy the Tsar and his family by this organization will be yet another effort in the anti-monarchy movement in our country. Forces on the political right, both here and throughout Europe, accuse supporters of the Royals of an alignment with the more liberal elements of our nation, a very inclusive party, very social justice conscious.

"Although abolished in 1943, the dynasty goes back to the Seventh Century BCE. The radicals hope to force His Royal Highness into permanent retirement and replace him with the more conservative Grand Duke Michael Alexander. They intend to realign the monarchy with the conservatives and their nationalist agenda."

The Tsar interjected, "My brother is an outspoken proponent of the arch-conservative politics sweeping the continent and in direct conflict with the principles of democracy and human rights. This scandal has the potential of also sweeping him into the office of the Prime Minister."

Count Orlov continued, "We believe the silence of the *Paukova Mreža* is temporary and may be connected to the abduction of the young *Knyaz*, sorry, the Prince."

The Tsar broke in passionately. "Hang the scandalous documents! A child's life is at stake. Find that boy, gentlemen. We will face the fallout of the other matters and survive as we have for nearly 3,000 years. We will accept whatever Olga has brought down on our House. We have done so before."

Kayne said, "Your Royal Highness, I assure you that we will find Kristof and bring him to safety. I must add that I do not see the hand of your blackmailers in this. There are too many inconsistencies. The boy is a titular member of the Royal family with very little cachet. He is a titled noble with no right of succession.

"No, this apparent act of anarchy is, in fact, an act of ransom not directed at your family but at mine. Nick and I possess essential information related to another case of corporate espionage that malicious elements would like to own. Unfortunately, the Tsar and his family are caught in the middle, and for that, we do apologize."

General Ivanov, holding his cell phone, interrupted, "Your Royal Highness, we have located the ice truck used in the abduction of the Prince. Our Fraport Twin Star Airport Management colleagues at the Varna Airport have sent surveillance camera videos of a suspicious SUV arriving at the corporate airfield. One of the passengers seemed to be incapacitated. The description fits Prince Kristof. The plane took off 53 minutes ago and headed east. It is too late for us to intercept the flight. We will try to track their course."

The old soldier continued, "Now, I am getting a report that the abandoned ice truck was found on route E722 near Shumen. The body of Lance Captain Jan Yousopov was found inside. It appears that he was strangled. We are looking for prints and other evidence. I will forward all of this to you, Officer."

Kayne removed a picture of the bodyguard. He mused, "Overpowered and strangled. This was a big and very fit man. We are looking for at least three kidnappers. Nick, the M.O.– same as Zach's killer."

I spoke up, trying to contain my edginess. "Thank you, General. Dr. Sorenson and I have decided to return to Australia as we suspect that is where the kidnappers are headed with Kris, considering the conclusions just stated."

"Then we shall not waste your time in the pursuit of these villains, Doctor and Officer. We will send you on your way with my blessing. I am satisfied and impressed with your efforts on our behalf." Tsar Stefan II stood, as did the rest of us. "I look forward to our next exchange of information, hopefully about the rescue and safety of my great-grandson."

The Tsar looked at his aide-de-camp. "Petar?"

After handshakes all around, Count Orlov led the Tsar out of the office.

Prince Preslav said, "Let us agree then to collaborate on this. As mentioned, the Tsar is most interested in media silence on this. Regarding your case in Australia, we will respect it with the utmost confidentiality. Do you concur, General?"

"Absolutely, Your Highness. Please share with us anything you can without compromising your case, Dr. Sorenson. My agency will assist you in every way."

The Prince asked for an escort to take us to the limousine that would bring us to the airport.

"I will join you presently, gentlemen."

As we left the members of the Bulgarian National Intelligence Services, Kayne took a moment to say, "Nick, why did you break that off so abruptly?"

"Boss, I smell a rat. Something is not right here."

Chapter Thirty-Three: Ace

From the Case Notes of Kayne Sorenson

"Bloody hell. Son, how many times do I have to rescue your fool arses? In my life, I have been up against corrupt politicos, homosexuality, burning buildings, international incidents, crazy-arsed brain problems, divorce, suicide, and vendetta. Now, my only grandson's life is in danger. Shit boy, the old man's done for with all of this.

"Oh yeah, and to top it all off, these women who think they can boss me around like a fool. Bloody Job's Comforters is all I can say to that. Kid belongs at Inala, Kayne lad. I will make a man outta that little pouf. Got a pair o' balls on him, doesn't he? Thems Sorenson nuts, lad."

"Easy, Da. Nick and I will find him. I want him at Inala, also. That is until we get the Nangala case solved. I will set up some security and a tutor, no worries."

"Yeah, Kayne. Let me tell you something straight, lad. Truth be told, that Nick boy is a rippa. Best you marry that ballsey brogan and adopt the boy prince. Make your old man finally happy, yeah."

What he was not saying was that he was not about to raise one more boy.

"Da, Da. Ease off, Mate. You are, as usual, way ahead of the game. Please put Rebecca back on the line."

My father added a gruff goodbye and did the requested handoff.

"Darling, everything is under control. The Master of Inala is going to be fine. I also made those contacts you asked for. Your brothers agreed and are bringing Gints and Scott. Mitch said he and Kick need a vacation before the snow flies in the Aerie Valley. That seems to have taken the edge off the Captain. He and Darana are excited in anticipation of their arrival. Bring me up to speed on Kris, Darling."

"Not good, my girl. The Tsar's security and the school officials have been most helpful, but no real leads. Nick and I believe he has been taken out of Bulgaria. Kris' bodyguard was discovered in the getaway vehicle, unfortunately quite dead... I will spare you the details, but this raises the body count to five. Is this conversation in danger of being overheard?"

"Hold on. I am going outside. I may lose you. This location is really *anus mundi,* Darling. How do places like Inala exist without good cellphone towers?"

I ignored the comment and said, "Rebecca, the best we can tell, with help from INTERPOL and the Bulgarian authorities, is that Kris was put on a private flight to Perth. We know little about the plane or the individuals involved. We are leaving in a few minutes to get there and regain the boy. INTERPOL has arranged to get us back to Perth as quickly as possible. Western Australian authorities have been alerted. "

I could hear Alice barking in the background. She must have been having a rippa of a good time with the Inala dogs.

"There is no reason to discuss this with Ace, my girl. Our line is that everything is being done to rescue the lad and the details will be known and shared soon, hopefully."

"Got it. What's the status of our chess game?"

"Two last pieces, and I know one is in the Melbourne area. I will admit that the deciphering of this next clue was a real challenge. I am working on the fifth."

"Hold on, Darling. It would seem we have visitors. Looks like a helicopter."

Dogs in the background... again barking like crazy.

"Rebecca, go back into the house and have Ace muster the ranchers."

I put the phone on speaker and motioned for Nick to come closer. From the back seat of the Mercedes, we could see that our plane was in the last stages of readiness -- Varna to Perth.

Nick said, "I don't like the sound of that, Boss. Shit, Kayne. Do you suppose it's the Big Bads at Inala?"

"I should have anticipated that, my love. I am hoping that Ace has the muscle to take these guys out."

We waited. I heard excited voices in the background. Rebecca was shouting, "Get those guns up, Mates. This is one of the good blokes."

She came back on the line.

"Mark! Oh Kayne, Darling, it's Mark. Only you could have maneuvered this surprise. Thank you so much!"

"Not my doing, dear girl, but I am relieved he is there. Ace thinks he is grand, which is good, considering. More stability on the homefront. Please bring him up to speed, and I will call him soon."

He looked at me and said, "False alarm, my love."

A Bulgarian officer approached, and Kayne rang off.

"Thank you for your patience, Dr. Sorenson and Officer Sechi. We are ready for you. Gentlemen, welcome aboard."

Chapter Thirty-Four: Nap of the Earth
Nick Sechi's Journal

"How do you lose a bloody plane?"

"We are looking into it, Dr. Sorenson. It was there one minute and then gone. There are parts of the world's modern radar system with some blank spots due to the earth's curvature. Tracking signals beam out in straight lines. Looks like we lost him over the rugged terrain of the mountains of Myanmar. Deliberate evasion. It's called 'terrain masking.' We are contacting that government for help."

The Perth Airport official in Western Australia continued, "He's flying in daylight, so I'd say he's going NOE, Nap of the Earth."

I asked, "Help us out here, Officer."

"Pilot is definitely military. NOE flying is very low altitude and is used by the military to avoid detection by enemy defense systems. He's ground-hugging and will be sea-skimming once he gets over water. Last we had, he was headed southeast, in our direction. But it is anyone's guess right now."

Kayne said, "From what you say, he's going low, fast, and will, therefore, need plenty of fuel. Please give me a minute. Thank you, gentlemen."

Kayne motioned for me to follow him into a private airport security office. He punched a speed dial number on his phone. And placed it on speaker.

"Hey, Dr. Kayne. Everything OK?"

"Hello, my friend. How are you and Gints doing? And my brothers?"

"Mr. Kick is driving everyone crazy as usual, but Mr. Mitch has him under control. The Gints-Dude is just fine. He is out at the Horse Palace, getting some things done for Mr. Mitch. Looks like early snow. What's up?"

"So, Scott. I have a case of kidnapping with which I need your help. The victim is His Highness Prince Alexander Kristof Sorenson, fifteen years old, last seen at the Lycée Victor-Hugo in Sofia, Bulgaria. He's blonde, 5'11", and 155 pounds, most likely in soccer togs.

"I need you to trace the plane that was part of the abduction. Look for a Pilatus PC-24 400 out of Varna, Bulgaria, registered to Oydessos Energies. That's all I have for an ID, unfortunately. The flight is recorded to have traveled east. Radar lost them somewhere over Myanmar.

"Scott, I believe the traffickers will eventually try for somewhere in Australia. This is high security and urgent."

"Count on me, Dr. Kayne, and I will ask for a verbal confirmation on the legality of my operations on this, please. You know I can get in, but how legal do you want me to be?"

"Do what you have to do to get the information and fast, lad."

"I'm on it, Doc. Love to your Nick."

"And to Gints and the brothers as well."

I said, "Scott will hook'em, Boss. His tech skills can get through any firewall."

"Yes, I think we have a chance here, Nick. If they are transporting the boy, it must be for ransom, either for money from the Bulgarian Royal Family or for something from the Sorensons. I tend to think it is the latter. Kris is a titular prince, and more would be gained in kidnapping a *prince du sang*, a prince of the blood."

We were interrupted by a group of three. One was Officer Martin Smith of airport security. Kayne's jaw dropped with astonished recognition.

"I don't believe it." He folded into the arms of the silver-haired, heavy-set visitor accompanied by a young woman. He turned to me.

"Nick, this is Special Agent Robert Francis Wilben of the Australian Federal Police. How are you, Bobby, ya ole dag? How many years has it been, Mate?

"Crikey, lad. Gone by about 15, 17 years now. You were still an ankle-biter in school when the business of your Da's Marine buddy came down. Then there was the help you gave us in Hobart with the mass murderer."

"The Giant Devil of Tasmania. I remember the case back in '07. The entire Bureau was stumped, Nick."

Kayne turned back to the Special Agent, saying, " I told you blokes, it was the vicar of Macquarie Island. The evidence was plain once you viewed it a certain way."

I made a mental note to get the facts of the case for the blog.

"Bobby, this is my dear love, Officer Nicola Sechi of the…."

" … Fort Lauderdale Police Force. You're Nick! Hey Joan, this is the bloke who writes the Kayne Sorensen Mysteries, and this is himself in the flesh. Ow ya goin', Mate?"

The big guy pumped my hand with gusto.

"This is my right-hand gal and soon to take over, as I am months from retirement, Special Agent for Western Australia, Joan Ross-Munroe."

"Very pleased to meet you, gentlemen. I understand we have a kidnapping in progress."

Kayne filled the federal law enforcement officers in on the disappearance of Kris Sorenson, starting with the events at the Lyceé. He briefly summarized our adventures in Eastern Europe, which led to Kayne's introduction to his nephew. He explained the Young Prince's lineage.

"Now that's a barbecue stopper. The ole bludger, Captain Ace, has a grandson. The bounder said it would never happen."

Ms. Ross-Munroe said, "Yes, Dr. Sorenson. We have been in contact with Bulgarian authorities. Prince Preslav and a representative from Bulgarian Intelligence, General Andrei Ivanov, are on their way to Perth."

"Regarding our collaboration, I need to go all honest on this, folks. I have some private investigators working on the disappearance of the plane. I will share that intel when I get it. And, Agent Munroe, I have a special request regarding the present investigation, one that is critical to bringing these criminals to justice. I need you to help me get access to a dead body."

"I will assist you in any way I can. Sounds like we agree, then. You both have the resources of the Federal Department of Home Affairs."

The young woman said. "Let's get that lad back home, eh gents."

Chapter Thirty-Five: Robin

"Get your fuckin' hands off of me, you crap asses. I *will* hurt you."

The boy was distraught but fought to be brave in the face of the nightmare that surrounded him. After all, he had been schooled to be a prince. Kristof was released from his bonds as the sedative effects wore off. The two linebacker-like guards took seats that faced him. He was still in his soccer uniform but in stocking feet.

"I gotta piss, you fucking pig. You boys are so in trouble. Wouldn't wanna be you." He shot a two-handed pistol point from the hip at the two thugs and headed to the restroom in the rear of the plane. Returning, he put his hands on his hips and said, "I need a jacket and some food. *Now.*"

The bigger of the two captors stood and pushed the fifteen-year-old back into his seat. He locked eyes with the young Prince in a deadly stare. The thug closed a menacing hand over the boy's mouth and brought his face to within inches of the young man's. He snarled, "You are in no position to give any orders here, lad. If you want to arrive safely, without injury, my advice to you is to shut the fuck up. You do not want to end up like your late bodyguard."

Kris pushed the imprisoning grip off his mouth and spit into the face of his attacker. The man leaned back and wiped the spittle from his face with a black and yellow handkerchief of a familiar design. He looked at the cloth and again at the boy.

"Recognize this? Too bad your Batman is not here to rescue you, you little faggot." He backhanded the defiant boy.

Kris propelled himself off the seat and reached out to strangle the abductor. He sunk his teeth into the side of the man's face.

In the end, it was required that the young prince would be bound and gagged. Blood covered his mouth beneath the face restraint.

***

"He's a bloody son of the devil. Look at what he did to my face, the little bastard." The thug clamped a cloth over his bleeding cheek and jawbone.

"The Boss says he's an important bargaining chip. Dunno with who, though."

The pilot checked his instruments.

"Last set of mountains coming up. Hate flying so close to land. No radio. Good thing this country has so many wide-open spaces. Sun's coming up, and it's perfect timing. We'll slip 'er in for a landing and be done."

"Where are we stashing the brat?"

"The Boss wants him secured at the hangar, the bomb shelter to the south of the complex. You, Gabriel, and I can head out. Simpson will take over."

"I'm getting to a doctor. Stitches – bloody hell."

"Get back to your charge and secure for landing."

Chapter Thirty-Six: Mr. Lockwood

Nick Sechi's Journal

"He's on the ground, Dr. Kayne. Somewhere east of Melbourne. We traced the trajectory of the flight. There were sporadic shots of him on the radar. Hacked into some corporate and national airports. Needs fuel if he's going further, but those choices are either Tasmania, New Zealand, or back up to Micronesia. And fuck that last one... oh, sorry, I cussed... but he's not zigzagged at all during this flight. I'm wagering his business is in southeast Victoria."

Kayne wrote something on the hotel notepad, one word...

Heathcliff

I pulled up flight information for Perth to Melbourne. The next flight is in four hours.

"Scott, I have to ring off. There is another call coming in. I will get back to you, and thanks."

Kayne put his phone on speaker and held it between us.

"Dr. Sorenson. How about a game of chess?" The voice was digitized.

"Mr. Lockwood, I have been expecting your call. I want the boy."

"And I want a game of chess or rather the chess pieces. Five, I believe. Seems an easy switch."

"Provide me with the location, and I will give you what I have."

"I detect from what you have said that you do not have all of the chessmen. I will only barter for the complete set of five, Dr. Sorenson. Are we clear on this?"

"I expect to have the complete set soon."

"Excellent. I will contact you very shortly. Finish your scavenger hunt quickly. His Highness will be well cared for until then."

Kayne pulled at the front of his hair. "Do not hurt the boy."

"Bishop to King's Rook 4, Dr. Sorenson. Check."

***

I took Kayne's phone and punched *57. Nothing.

"Let me try some other ways. Hold on." I tried tracking with the GPS, again, bupkiss.

"It's gotta be a non-fixed VoIP call, Boss."

"Got no idea, Nick."

"A VoIP call transforms your voice into digital bits, then segments them into separate packets of data that are routed through the Internet and reassembled upon arrival at the other end. Non-Fixed VoIP is a disposable, internet-created phone number that can be associated with any address."

"No matter. I have suspected that things are not what they seem in this case. Especially among the major players. The boy is at Heathcliff."

"I'll book the flight, Kayne. I'll arrange for a car."

"To the airport, yes, my love. But we'll have an aircraft of our own."

***

"I asked him for it as soon as we got to Western Australia. I got a text that the 'Firehawk' had arrived. Got the Xanax?"

"Good old Ace." I mounted into the Beechcraft Premier 1.

"I am not sure the old man is going to play our *Deus Ex Machina* for very much longer, my love. Resolving thorny crises is not something he enjoys."

"So what's the plan, Kayne? We get to Heathcliff, and then what? "

"We find out who has the boy. Max definitely knows something. I have sensed this all along. He exhibits the body language of an equivocator of the truth when discussing his company's connection to the Star Project.

"But Nick, I do not think they will do significant harm to Kris as his captors desperately want the figures. Should Lockwood get his hands

204

on our flash drives, he still needs the bulk of the research. Therefore, they have to have an inside man. Someone who they have coerced to hand over the entire Star Project files."

"Allira?"

"Not necessarily. We need to find out more about the research team."

"Kayne, we only have three chess pieces."

"Four, my love. In the next 24 hours. Trust me."

He banked the plane into the night. The lights of Melbourne glistened below.

Thomas Paul Severino

Chapter Thirty-Seven: The Garden of Live Flowers

From the Case Notes of Kayne Sorenson, Ph.D.

Allira Nangala met us at the airport and drove us to the East Melbourne Police Headquarters.

"I am not quite sure how this came about, Dr. Sorenson. My request for the autopsy came up with a month-long wait. Got a call only a few hours ago saying we are cleared to meet with the police. So fast. Oh, a couple of breakfast sandwiches there and some hot coffee. Fuel up."

"I was able to pull some strings, Professor. Thank you for agreeing to this."

When we reached our destination, we were met by the Executive Director of the Victoria Forensics Services Department, Captain Rachel Jackson. I was happy to be back among the uniforms of a metropolitan police force.

"Doctor, Officer, and Professor, I am happy to assist as I can. Your reputation precedes you, Doctor. Following the autopsy, I have detectives standing by to answer any questions you may have regarding the evidence files on Professor Nangala. Right this way."

Allira passed on viewing the cadaver of her father and completed the additional paperwork required for the investigation. Nick and I donned the requisite masks, surgical robes, and gloves. The body had shown minor decay. Decomposition had been slowed by the sturdy coffin and the cool temperatures of the in-ground burial.

The Anatomical Pathology Technician and the Pathologist stood ready to assist in the external examination and the more detailed internal inspection of the late Stephen Nangala.

I signaled to Nick to proceed. I held his mobile as he examined the body.

"Despite the lack of embalming, prohibited by the ethnic traditions of the deceased, the body shows limited putrification despite the age of the corpse.

"The deceased is an Aboriginal male, aged fifty-eight at the time of death. There are no signs of struggle, hesitation marks, or minor wounds on the viscera. There is a fatal entry wound between the fourth and fifth ribs on the left side of the chest cavity. It is five cm from the left of the sternum. The blade entered the body at a 30 - 45-degree angle relative to the midline of the torso. The insertion wound shows that the knife was swept to the left. Death as the result of this wound would have occurred in no more than four minutes due to exsanguination of the heart chambers, severed blood vessels, and the immediate drop of blood pressure."

Nick examined the dorsal surface of the body and found one contusion across the back of the head just below the *foramen magnum* – the opening where the spinal cord enters the skull. Hands, nails, and feet came up with no significant clues.

I spoke to the attending pathologist. "Doctor, we wish to respect the prohibitions of the deceased's community. There will be no internal examination."

We left.

***

"Dr. Stephen Nangala was murdered in the early morning hours of September twenty-third, three years ago, on the Mornington Peninsula, south of Melbourne. His body was moved to his lab at the University and staged to appear as a suicide. Your investigation and determination of suicide rather than homicide are, if I may be frank, astonishing, considering it ignored a majority of the evidence."

The detectives began to protest, but I continued, "Let's begin with what the body shows."

Nick pulled up a composite of his photos of the cadaver and a biodigital human from my own forensics apps. I slid a transcript of Nick's autopsy notes to the members of the VC Police Department and to Professor Nangala.

"Notice the position of the fatal wound on the left side of the chest. A self-inflicted stab to the heart is a very complicated way to commit suicide. It must be precisely aimed and 'swept' or twisted in the wound to do immediate harm."

Nick brought up a picture of a broad-bladed stone knife.

"From your evidence files, this is the weapon of death, a twenty-centimeter leilira blade. This is an archeological term referring to handcrafted stone blades used as tools and for spears by Indigenous people. The original report suggests ritual suicide."

I picked up the blade from the evidence carton holding it up and turning it.

"It is quartzite, twenty-three centimeters in length, from the Ngillipidji stone quarry on Elcho Island, "Up Top" in the Northern Territory. Why is it in Southern Victoria? Stone and finished blades were traded over long distances.

"It is triangular in cross-section and was made by 'flaking' - removing a small piece of rock from a large piece by striking it with a hammerstone. The core is usually held in hand or rested in the person's lap or on the ground. I understand this blade was never analyzed for DNA."

I looked at the detectives with a mixture of wonder and amazement.

"A large knife such as this would have to be turned sideways so that the width of the edge is horizontal to slip between the ribs. Owing to the construction of the human hand and wrist, this reduced the range of angle of attack and the maximum force imparted. That is if we assume the mortal wound was self-inflicted."

I placed the blade against the left side of my chest and demonstrated. I handed the weapon to one of the detectives. "Try it.

"Furthermore, the blade profile suggests it would have gotten stuck and remained in the chest if the movement was simply to stab or puncture the heart. The weapon was found in the hand of the deceased, not in the chest.

"Professor Nangala was left-handed. The accuracy of the wound by a left-handed person would have been next to impossible. Now, let's look at the blood spatter report. Nick."

I paused as I let him take over.

Nick referenced the digital corpse and said, "Blood doesn't lie, gentlemen. Please note the position of the heart and the ribs. This would have been the entry point, here between the left-side *costae* bones three and four with a twist and drag to the left, like so. The wounds on the left side of the corpse show precisely that – stab, twist, and rake across.

"As Dr. Sorenson has indicated, considering the accuracy needed to inflict the wound, it is implausible that 'the deceased fell on his sword.' That would have produced only a puncture wound. Unless the blade is swept, the heart, a powerful muscle, closes over the penetration point and, in most cases, continues to beat; blood loss is minimal. The victim can live for as much as fifteen minutes following the wound.

"Are we, therefore, to conclude that the victim slammed the blade into his chest by falling, sat up, raked the edge to the left, and then removed the knife before dropping it back down on the lab floor and tossing it to the side?"

I tried hard to suppress a smug expression as Nick continued to destroy the medical examiner's testimony, saying, "So, the evidence eliminates the primary conclusion of your department's report. Please proceed, Nick."

"Just to add a bit more fodder to the argument, if Dr. Nangala, on his knees in the lab, used his hands to stab and rake the blade, it would take a few tries to produce a fatal stab as Dr. Sorenson has demonstrated. You will see there are no hesitation wounds on the chest. Option one was eliminated. He did not do this to himself."

Nick illustrated using the model. "Now, let's consider what the blood says. Your pathologist agrees that when the left ventricle is pierced and raked open like this, with the line of the wound parallel to the ground, the cut, being too large to seal upon contraction, instead widens with each contraction. Blood will be forced violently out of the wound channel under high pressure immediately following the withdrawing blade – remember the knife was on the floor, outside the body.

"What you get is classic horror movie gore-- blood jetting out to splatter the walls and everything else. Blood pressure drops immediately-- instantaneous blackout, death in four minutes max."

He continued. "That is, in fact, what happened but not where the body was found. Observe."

Nick brought up pictures of the lab floor, the body, and the surrounding walls and furniture. He stated, "No copious spatter, only the puddle seeping under the body and a relatively small amount at that, seen here."

I looked carefully at the officers and said, "So, we have a problem with the evidence, do we not? The wound indicates a stab and rip by a right-handed killer, yanking the knife to the victim's left chest. But, no accompanying blood spew that would match the heart's convulsive outpour. Instead, what we have is little blood on the lab floor, obviously a *post-mortem* leakage."

Allira said, "I said this at the inquest. Father would never have had, let alone used, a knife like that. Leilira blades were used by Aboriginal cultures to hunt, for scarification, and for male circumcision. They are mostly ceremonial now. My father had no Indigenous cultural objects, nor did he have any interest in the Aboriginal culture as a whole. My interest comes from my mother's side of the family and her tutelage. My father was a passionate assimilationist. "

She paused as emotion seemed to prevent her from continuing. In any case, after a bit, she managed to say, "There was no note, and Dr. Nangala was not being treated for depression. For that matter, his diary entry of two days previous showed elation at a breakthrough in his research. He was pleased with the safeguards he put on the project, 'The Red Queen's Race.'"

I summarized. "Not suicide but homicide. In an attempt to steal his research, Stephen Nangala was stunned by a blow to the back of the head, momentarily held from behind, and stabbed in the chest from the front by a right-handed man."

As I concluded, I demonstrated the murder on a standing detective. "And he was killed at the Main Ridge Conservation Reserve near Mornington, sixty minutes from the University. The dead body was brought to his lab and staged to appear to be a suicide. "

I spoke my indictment, "Gentlemen, your failure to accurately process the evidence has allowed a killer to go free and a family to be plagued with doubt."

The Medical Examiner said with a bit of derision, "How can you be so sure of the precise location of the murder?"

I retrieved a plastic container from the evidence carton. "These bits of plant material found on the clothing and skin of the victim were explained as coming from Dr. Nangala's plants on the window ledge of his laboratory. His empty watering can was upset onto the floor near the body. It was suggested he was caring for his plants and then committed suicide. In a word, preposterous!"

Examining the very dried plant material with my jeweler's loup, I said, "Very distinctly *Orchidaceae*." I looked up, saying, "Please note, the Professor did not possess any orchids."

Pausing dramatically, I went for the match point. Nick brought up a photo of a few small, creamy-yellow flowers with dark red glandular tips on the sepals.

"My friends, meet *Caladenia robinsonii*, the Frankston Spider Orchid, one of Australia's most endangered species. Its habitat is confined to one small area of the Mornington Peninsula, south of Melbourne. The urban sprawl of this capital of Victoria has reduced the habitat even further. Thus, the gardens of the Nature Preserve are where Professor Nangala's blood flowed."

The effect was palpable. I tossed the container back into the evidence but pointed to it as it landed.

"In grabbing at the foliage as he fell, he left us a message. The flowers speak plainly."

Chapter Thirty-Eight: Nobbies
Nick Sechi's Journal

"Brilliantly done, Boss, but what are you not saying?"

"Took two of us, my love, but thank you. What I am *not* saying is those bonzers were paid to look the other way. I am sure of it."

"I hope Captain Jackson follows up with what could be a case of corruption."

"We shall see, my love."

Kayne was in the passenger's seat. I drove us south from Melbourne, around Western Port Bay, on the B420. We had just crossed the San Remo Bridge to Philip Island. He spoke into his cell phone.

"Bobby, Mate. Yeah, so it's just like in the movies, Boyo... You got it. Contact was made last night, about seven hours ago. Yes, the kidnapper... No doubt about it... Yes, instructed to tell no one... warned that involvement of the coppers will get the lad killed."

Kayne was getting slightly agitated.

"No, listen, Bobby. This is Kayne talking, Mate... I gotta do this my way. Yes... no, Bobby... I *have* law enforcement. His name is Officer Nick Sechi. A bloody good cop. Trust my life and the life of my loved ones to...."

He caressed my thigh and then pointed to the turn-off. Kayne had added a serious pair of Poindexter glasses to his look– one hot geek, in my estimation, for this part of the case. He had an Aussie bush hat and binoculars to complete the look of a field biologist. It was about mid-afternoon.

Kayne continued, "Bobby, I can't do anything until I hear from the Big Bads again, so we're cooling our heels, as the Yanks would say. Yes... in this case, I trust the research that tells me that kidnappers will keep the victim alive as the deal progresses.

"I will handle Prince Preslav. Please let the feds know of the situation, and please keep 'em back. There's a good lad. Stand by for more info as it develops."

***

As he signed off, I interjected while pointing to the landscape, "Not getting the connection. Why are we here? Need more information, big guy."

We turned off to the entrance to the Nature Park on the far west side of the island, following signs for the Nobbies Center.

Kayne turned to me. His ice-blue eyes had gone cobalt with the stress of finding his nephew, and he pulled at his pesky forelock. I sensed his agitation was high.

"OK, so why are we not moving heaven and earth with an all-out militia to storm the enemy and save Kris?"

His voice had a minor edge of emotion, which was rare, as he continued, "First, we actually do not know where in this area he is. Heathcliff is a guess, but we must be sure. The estate has too high a profile to harbor a kidnapped lad. The staff for the estate and its vineyards is quite large. Someone would catch on to strange goings-on.

"In dealing with kidnappers, often one has to play their game, or at least provide a semblance of cooperation with their demands, and then strike for the advantage. Negotiations allow you to get close and keep the victim alive and the criminals a bit off balance. In that regard, we do not have all the pieces of the treasure. It could be a game-changer. But, there is a fourth piece nearby, Nick."

He gazed out at the passing countryside of the island and presented his reasoning. "In the mind of the kidnapper, we find motivation for his deed and a suggestion of how it will play out. Kidnappers of minors are concerned with financial gain, political extremism, or emotional disturbance. Ours is a straightforward ransom situation, and hostage-for-ransom victims tend to survive their ordeal. We are not dealing with a killer who wants to create a sensation or realign a relationship. Those are the most maniacal, as we have seen in previous cases.

"This is cold-hearted, deal-making, Nick. Lockwood needs Kris alive to get the Nangala files. We must keep sight of the logic in the criminal's mind and wager that he will act in ways that the research supports. He will hand over Kris for the figures."

He looked across the front of the car, addressing his next conclusion directly to my face, indicating that this was major.

"And it's Caliban Ariel, Nick. I have no doubt. Max indicated they were on the verge of insolvency, and Scott confirmed this with the balance sheets of the private company. They are in the soup financially. Parallax has huge lawsuits, but C/A is critically strapped for cash. Zach Ariel's new direction, as it were, has brought them close to bankruptcy. They are in a death spiral. Desperate times call for desperate measures—espionage, murder, and kidnapping."

He gazed back out the window again and said rather gravely, "When next we make contact, we ask for proof of Kris's welfare."

"Kayne, so Lockwood gets the research, and what does he do? Publically announce that he has developed this new power source and fight off lawsuits or eliminate his rivals? Going public will expose him as a thief and murderer."

"Not if he creeps back into the shadows after squeezing Allira Nangala's team. They are blackmailing one or all of them. Suddenly, a major agreement is made regarding the Star Project, and the murders go unsolved."

He paused and then added, "Nick, I detect another hand in this. One with a ferocity and menace far beyond Lockwood."

I said nothing.

***

At the western tip of Philip Island, Point Grant looks out across the Bass Strait, where the Southern Sea meets Western Port Bay. The Nobbies sports an information center and a boardwalk journey along the beautiful coastlines of the island's Nature Parks. The afternoon summer sun glistened over the grassy bluffs, hugging rocky promontories descending into the blue water bay. We began to walk the series of switchbacks downhill to cobblestone shores containing numerous tidal pools. Large domes of basalt were alive with seabirds and fur seals. Many of the birds darted to and from holes in the side of the hill.

We stepped along a deep-sea cave carved into the basalt cliffs below us. The pounding sea waves received return fire as a horizontal spew of air and water erupted to the delight of onlookers.

"This place is incredible, man. Friggin' beautiful, but you still have not answered my question, Kayne.

"Let's get back to Alice, Mate."

"OK, the town, the dog, or the Lewis Carroll character?"

He pushed me against the railing and brought his face near to mine in a hug-up that I could not distinguish between frustration or ardor. Fellow visitors along the trail attempted to be nonchalant about male-on-male contact of an aggressive nature as if to reflect the power of the blowhole.

Kayne's mind was racing, the overstimulation thing, and I was attempting to understand his methods in as controlled a manner as possible.

He said, "Carroll called his work a fairy tale. He did not want Alice Liddell to grow up and become 'a melancholy maiden,' sentiments that Nangala most likely felt about Allira. The poem that serves as Looking Glass's epigraph says the story functions as a fairy tale that will not allow Alice to grow old."

With me still in his arms, he looked out over the mighty sea. "To be precise, Carroll calls Through the Looking Glass the love gift of a fairy tale, Nick. 'In thy young life's hereafter, enough that now thou wilt not fail to listen to my fairy-tale.' Nangala underlined it in his secret annotations-- fairy."

I was bewildered, but I smiled at a little girl who was getting too close, investigating these interesting men. "So where are the fairies– and we're not talking fellow gays, right... in Australia? Here?"

He buttoned the top button of his polo shirt. Put on his geek glasses and affected a slouch, disguising his graceful, athletic gait.

Ancient Blood

"Less than a kilometer from where we are standing, my love, tons of little poofers."

Chapter Thirty-Nine: Fairies

Nick Sechi's Journal

The sun settled off to the west. As the dusk came on, we stared intently at the beach and the surf. Special low-level lights allowed us to just make out the white line of the waves across the wet beach. The sand trails wound up from the beach to the low, grassy bluffs riddled with burrows around the viewing stands and up near the Penguin Parade Center.

Humans, not permitted to touch the wildlife, had to stay on the decks, and no photography was allowed. Suddenly, the frothy surf line, caressing the wet sand, came alive. It turned into a string of squat "fairies."

A tiny army of creatures stood up in a line, heads up and flippers dropping on each side. Their backs were a mixture of indigo-blue and slate-grey. Their bellies are white. So, when they reach the beach, you can see them begin their parade due to their white abdomens. These cuties waddled up the sand dunes to the burrows where they were born and raised. Seventeen inches tall and about two pounds, hundreds of them came, wave after wave. Their species had been making this journey to this exact spot for thousands of years.

As they shuffled by their human spectators, I wondered which species was watching which.

***

Kayne spoke to a group of biologists at the zoological center. Convincing them of his scientific interest. We were allowed into the inner sanctum of the burrow viewing labs. The walls of the space were covered with monitors displaying the in-burrow activities of many of the little penguins.

"Why yes, Doctor. We do have some anomalies. But I am not sure what you are looking for in your research."

"Behavioral issues, my dear. The conservation issues are so important. While *Eudyptula minor*, the Fairy Penguin, is not endangered, I suspect that they soon may be. My research with

Professor Nangala of Monash – surely you have heard of her, may result in grant funding that is needed to protect these babies."

The guide accepted the interest, the name-dropping, and the hint of funding hook, line, and sinker. A field biologist, she launched into some detailed descriptions of the few unusual behaviors exhibited by the fairy penguins.

"Occasionally, solitary birds show what we call loneliness behaviors. This sometimes occurs in the young ones who can survive independently but long for a lost mate or parent. They tend to get despondent."

She ran some tapes of some birds in their burrows acting rather despondently. Next, we saw the same birds snuggling up to dolls fashioned in the image of their species.

"We find that they often bring in a seashell, a branch, or a plastic bottle to keep them company. So, we came up with the dolls. They actually thrive until they find a new mate, and then we remove the fake penguin from the burrow."

She pointed to a shelf that ran above the wall of the computer. A row of stuffed fairy penguins stared down at us.

Kayne reached up and removed a slender, wooden object with a large, round base.

"Please tell me about this."

The guide took down the object and said, "Kind of a talisman if you want to know the truth. Seems this kinda appeared in one of the burrows about four years ago. Strange."

Kayne examined the anomaly. "Yes?"

"Too heavy to have been dragged into the burrow by its occupant, who was less than a year old. Alice, we called her. That's her there. Her third set of chicks."

The scientist pointed to a burrow and its occupants on one of the monitors. "Dunno where it came from, but when she was little, she loved that thing. Now, she is one of our most fecund females, to be sure."

"May I."

"Sure, Professor. Anything to help these babies."

We left with the coveted White Pawn.

Thomas Paul Severino

Chapter Forty: Impasse

Nick Sechi's Journal

"Nick, are you jealous? Yeah, because I think you are."

"Kayne, have you totally lost your mind? Jealous? What made you think that?"

"I am preoccupied with finding a fifteen-year-old boy who is missing and happens to be my nephew. It appears that Kris is someone of whom I am very fond. You seem to be trying to distract me from the task at hand."

WTF?

"You know what? Fuck you."

I folded my arms across my chest and stared down at him. He was not getting out of this one.

Kayne stood up and went to the balcony of our hotel room. We opted not to go to Heathcliff. Not just yet. In addition to lacking the fifth missing piece, Kayne needed to speak to Team Nangala.

"Hell of a time to press me on this, Kid."

"I am not a kid, and I deserve better than that."

He turned and threw me a glance that was a quote straight from a parent's lexicon: *Then stop acting like one.*

I felt my temper rising to match his, and my blushing, starting to highlight my anger. I took a deep breath and said, "I simply asked where all of this is going?"

"This?"

"Us."

"You want an answer? Fine. I don't know, I don't know. I don't know. OK?"

I held my temper as best I could, but I was so ready to stomp out. I said with a measured tone, "Under a lot of pressure, are you? Got it, Boss. Total balancing act? Yep, plain to see. Let's count 'em. Huh? Rebecca, Ace, Mark, Kris, the Aborigines, the Bulgarian Royals, a dog named Alice... and the entire National Parks Division of the Australian Government. That's got 'em all. Oh yeah, I forgot Max Caliban."

I walked closer.

"I get it, Kayne. This thing is coming to a head very fast in a monumental shitstorm, and we don't know who the Big Bads are and where the fuck they are.

"Oh, and news flash: I am dealing with all of that and one more little thing you are not struggling with."

He muttered, "And what would that be?"

"You, you shithead. Keeping you safe, sound, and...."

"And?"

I caught him eye-to-eye.

"Loved."

He stopped, looked down, and seemed to grow smaller.

"I will not ask for forgiveness, Kayne, for wanting a little relationship affirmation."

"I do apologize, my love. I need to right myself, I guess."

"Huh?"

"My cognition is in overdrive, Nick. Sunken fighter planes, missing airplanes, bull sharks, murdered lovers, particle beam lasers, a community of noble people who sometimes make me feel like I am from Mars, for shit's sake-- complete overstimulation. So much so that I cannot sleep, and my bloody head hurts. I need to go into my method of loci and set things in order. It's my cocaine."

He noticed my querulous look.

"Bad analogy. Sherlock Holmes took a seven-percent solution to zone out. I use the mind palace referencing my cognitive data to spatial maps. So much clogging up... it relieves the pressure."

I touched him for the first time today and drew him close to me. His eyes had switched back to the ice-blue from the cobalt that usually accompanied his anger. "But I don't, Nick. Honestly, I don't know where this is going. I love you more than life itself. 'Bout all I can do or say right now, lad."

He pulled me close, placing the side of his head against mine. His powerful hug-up felt like the grip of a drowning man.

I said softly, "Well, that's good, Boss. Cause I've just been fired."

***

"Not quite sure, but Captain Mays back in Wilton Manors has been transferred, and the new guy put in for my dismissal."

"On what grounds?"

"The email says misconduct."

"On what basis?"

"It seems there has been some communication from some politicos and government officials back in Europe. My hearing date has been set back in Florida. Two years on the force and two investigations into my behavior. Some fuck up."

"Nick, this is a conspiracy. We'll show that in the EU, you were behaving courageously, saving lives and putting away the villains. We have time to mount a defense. I'll talk to some people."

I checked myself in his eyes and said, "All I ever wanted to be was a cop, Boss. Some career. I'm just glad my dad isn't around to see me go down in disgrace."

He pulled me in as if he could sop up the sadness with a hug.

"Whatever we face, we face it together, lad. We'll get through this. We have two months to mount a case and respond to the charges."

Funny, I should have been feeling sorry for myself, but I felt so good in his embrace. If I had to choose between my badge and Kayne Sorenson, it would be him every time.

He held me in outstretched arms and said, "I know your cocaine, my love. Get your jock on, Superboy. We're going for a run. The body craves."

I pulled my shirt off over my head and said, "I know what this body craves." He took in my shirtlessness and teasing crotch grab with libidinous interest. A promise of some post-training fun hung in the hot night air.

***

We left the Clarkson Court Hotel on the fringe of the campus of Monash University. We circled the many educational venues, alternating jogging and sprinting. Despite being just a few miles from Port Phillip Bay, The air was humid. We ended up outside Monash University's John Donehue Center for Jiu-Jitsu and MMA. Kayne was psyched.

"This is just what we need, my love."

We pulled on our tank tops and entered the air-conditioned building. Night classes were in full swing. The facility seemed brand new with a community atmosphere. Kayne sweet-talked the desk staff, which allowed us to observe in the main gym. I say, 'observe,' but I know my man and his love of martial arts.

As I expected, we were soon discussing form with participants and trainers. An Asian dude in a white *gi* with a black belt came up to us and spoke, "Sensei Sorenson, you honor us with your presence. Officer Sechi, we are pleased that you are here also. We have followed your exploits on the web. I am Daniel Suino, an instructor here at the Donehue. Please, gentlemen, come this way as we intend to take advantage of your visits with our students."

Ten minutes later, Kayne had exchanged his running gear for a black belted white cotton *gi*. I was given fighting gloves, but I asked that my bout occur after Kayne's demonstration. He walked to the center of the mat and bowed to Daniel. He began with twenty straight throws, a jumping scissors kick, and a hook kick combination.

The Sensei defended with counters to various blocks and throws. He brought Kayne down with a leg wheel from behind. Soon, the teacher stopped the match to explain the moves and strategies they had just seen. Kayne also put on his educational persona and heightened the pedagogical experience, taking questions and challenging students to copy his moves. He was in his glory.

He addressed the spectators, "The best striking technique combination for your Mixed Martial Arts bouts comes from the Muay Thai tradition, thousands of years in the making. Start with the elbow strike known as the *Sok Tad*."

He asked a trainer to join them with striking pads. Kayne demonstrated four shots in succession, starting slowly and then adding speed. The impact with the pads blared in the gym.

"It's pretty straightforward but does require good balance and timing. A fighter will aim to throw an elbow to connect with his opponent's chin or temple, keeping the elbow parallel to the canvas. Bring up your pads, Mate."

He then made the same moves on the instructor, who complied with the demonstration but then ramped up the defense and went on the offense. They provided a breathtaking display. Kayne went down more than once but prevailed overall.

Panting and sweating, he bowed to the Sensei and addressed his group. "Regarding the *Sok Tad*, if you time this strike to perfection, folks, the impact can be nothing short of annihilation. It may be a reasonably direct strike to master, and landing it can be difficult on an opponent with good defense and guard, like your instructor."

***

I adjusted my gloves and turned to the crowd gathered around the ring. A shirtless, very fit, young dude covered with tattoos and his trainer came up to me and went nose-to-nose with a mock challenge, shouting, "Hey bud, I'm Joao Galvao, and I am gonna drop you on your pretty boy arse."

I burst into laughter, knowing it was all for effect. Students cheered as we stepped into the ring. Kayne and his entourage of students and trainers came over to my side of the gym space.

The bout was an exhibition. Joao was excellent. I held my own and dazzled a bit. Taking a cue from Kayne and Daniel, Joao's trainer, we invited student comments. We did some in slo-mo, stressing form and accuracy.

Finally, we ratcheted it up and went at each other for a good fifteen minutes with a wide variety of styles, kicks, punches, and clinches. The fury and pace changed as we hooked up in a powerful clinch, grabbing hold of each other, arms wrapped around heads and necks. My opponent anticipated a knee or a kick while widening the distance between our lower bodies and using his own legs to block. I took advantage of him being slightly off-balance to pull him closer and sweep-kicked him to the floor, jumping on top and pummeling him with half force, for which he feigned submission.

Sam, the trainer, broke us up. Joao and I collapsed into each other's arms, congratulating each other with some butt slaps. The fans applauded.

As I lifted the ropes and stepped down, Kayne grabbed me tight. He told me how well I had done and kissed the hell outta me – a big man-on-man lip lock. The onlookers applauded again.

We sat on a bench, and Kayne helped me remove my gloves and wraps.

"No helmet, studly. Dangerous but so butch."

I laughed, still catching my breath.

"You two are amazing."

"Allira."

"So, Dr. Sorenson, Office Sechi, may I introduce Anatjari Bradley, Gurumarra Peris, Colin Gibbs, and Renna Goodes, my colleagues."

We exchanged greetings and chatted about our respective exhibitions. Kayne said, "I was aware that your research facility was near the University, but I am so surprised to see you all here."

The professor said, "We were working late and thought we'd grab a coffee at the Center. They have the best flat whites, long blacks, and ristrettos in the city."

I said, "You all teach here in addition to your research, right?"

Renna said, "And take classes." She looked at Allira and said, "Some of us are working on our doctorates."

Colin said, "And some of us will be."

Anatjari said, "Are you blokes hungry at all?"

Kayne said, "Thanks for the invitation, Mate, but I think we are gonna head back to the hotel. It has been a hell of a day."

Allira smiled. "We will check in with you soon, then. So delightful to see you both."

***

As they left, Kayne whispered, "It's Peris."

"How could you know that, Boss?"

"Never made eye contact once. Nervous as a bride on her wedding night. Of the five of them, he is the most unkempt. His clothes border on the threadbare. He needs cash and is desperate. Nick, he is the Judas."

"Confrontation?"

"First thing in the morning. I just texted Allira to set it up."

***

We exited to the locker rooms so Kayne could get back into his runner kit. Daniel and a few instructors continued the thanks. When things calmed down a bit, Joao came over to our bench in a towel.

"Well done, Mates."

He pointed to me. "Your descriptions on the web of the way you blokes fight is no exaggeration. If you ever are recruiting for Sechi's Avengers, I am your man."

He threw a double biceps shot and stuck out his tongue haka-style. "Let's kick some villain arse."

I smiled, and one arm hugged him a bit. "Your Kiwi is showing, tough guy with the Haka moves. I'll let you know when the recruitment notices are out."

His next remark was as characteristic of his brash personality as it was unexpected. Joao traced a finger down my sweaty torso and placed it in his mouth. I blushed like a teenager caught wanking. Kayne raised his eyebrows and tossed me my shirt.

"You sexy boyos doing anything tonight?"

"Um, yeah, Dude. But thanks." I looked at Kayne and back at the animated fighter. "Gotta take a raincheck, Sexy."

Joao aped the look of a disappointed kid and said, "Wow, ego beat-down. Usually not turned down. At least let me give you my number. The summer nights are hot. Shagging time. And you just may change your minds."

***

"Aussies are so sexual, Boss. Where did that come from?"

"You want the anatomical answer, a psychological explanation, or a combination of both?"

I chuckled and took his hand as we walked back to the hotel. "Was rhetorical, Dude. Since I was a freshman at St. Raymond's, I have understood the energetic male anatomy, man-libido, and how it all works. Especially right now." I placed his hand against my crotch as we walked, doing my best pimp roll.

"Yes, Officer, you are demonstrating the details of tonight's topic with precision and, if I might say so, perfect mastery."

I swatted his ass and raced him back to our hotel.

Chapter Forty-One: Silence
Blog Double Entry

Kayne

I am not aware that we said one word to each other when we returned to our hotel. It was all motion of the most primal. A total escape from, and shutdown, of the cognitive.

I reached to check my phone for a text from Scott, Rebecca, or Lockwood but found nothing. Nick closed the door behind us and went for me, forcefully pushing me against the wall. From behind, he pulled my tank top off and knelt to untie my running shoes, removing them with my socks. He lowered my running shorts, and I stepped away from them, wearing only my jock.

In our love play, we both preferred the intensity of our sexual passion rather than the soft and romantic. Still, tonight would be full of surprises, I intuited. My body and mind responded with the heat of his hands, hard muscular body, and wet, warm mouth. One of the signals of our play was the last person to undress controlled the game, as it were. This is not to say that role reversal and switch-up could not happen throughout the love-making.

We did what came naturally.

As he stood, his face a mask of concentrated lust, he pulled my hair loose and off the left side of my neck. He pressed his mouth against my trapezius and neck muscles, soft at first, wet and hot, then a bit rougher, pulling my head to the opposite side. His hand entangled in my hair, and I felt the force of his mouth with the strength of a biting vampire. I brought my arms up and around him, gasping from the energy of his body against mine. I attempted to push him off, but I urgently wanted his rough play.

He smelled of combat, an opponent's sweat, and his own masculinity. His hands worked my chest from the front and my butt from behind. Nick's mouth invaded mine, owning it. He planted his legs wide, proclaiming his mastery of the play. Sometime during these preliminaries, my jock ended up in the pile of my clothes.

He pushed me to my knees before him. He mocked me with a slow peeling off of his own clothes before grabbing my head and allowing me to taste and mouth-explore his magnificent body. Nick bent, pulled me to my feet, and locked his beautiful eyes on mine.

Since we met, I have been entranced with his body, well-muscled but with the grace of a dancer or an acrobat. Jacked and ripped but not of the roid-boy nature. I liked laying in bed and playing with the ridges of his six-pack or the delicious cleft of his arse. My hands would run up the v-shape of his back, which tapered to his impossibly narrow waist. His blushes turned his entire viscera a red that complemented the dirty blond of his athlete's cut.

But his eyes... as Shakespeare said, the windows to one's soul... deep and tantalizing. Nick's were large and entrancing, ringed with long ginger lashes and full of color and expression. When we made love, depending on the extent of our lustful activity, his eyes would change color, green to gold to soft brown-- exquisite and alluring. I am such a fool for this young man.

We coupled on the bed and responded to each other with powerful energy, extending the sexual athletics, at once reaching a high point and then sliding back to prolong the pleasure. No speaking, only the primal sounds of lust, love, and abandonment. I was literally losing my mind, becoming a being of muscle, blood, and lustful passion in his embrace. Our bodies and spirits came together in a prolonged, raging wave that tenderly abated as breathing returned and sensations softened.

Three rounds, and then we slept entangled.

***

Nick

I don't think we spoke until the following morning. It was awesome. I wanted to nail him so badly, so totally. You know, when you love a guy with a monumental intensity, and you go with it, crossing into pure passion— talking rafters-shaking sexin'— bam, bam, bam.

After our bouts in the gym, I felt the savage energies rise. Even in the locker room afterward, my mind and body went with carnal fires that would not be staunched. I didn't think I could wait until we got into our hotel room.

Once we began, it was like we let our bodies do the talking, start to finish– an energetic dance beyond words and reason. When it was over, there was no mistaking what we meant to each other. Fuckin' amazing.

You see, this is what my man needs. He gets so in his head, the Sherlock thing, with all the cognition tensifying his entire personality, clogging up the emotions. He needs a good round of the nasty to clear all of that out. The best of which is a raging crazy-ass series of ruts with yours truly. Yeah, definitely talking bringing-the-house-down action here– full-on with the energy of champions.

So, I let the Boss know that as soon as we were in the room, "Big Nick" would be the Boss for a while. He dropped the Alpha role and submitted to young muscle and a sexual urgency that would not be disobeyed. In the beginning, I pulled him into complete naked subservience, at least for the time being. He was my plaything– his only pleasure was to be found in pleasing me.

At one point, I found myself getting lost in his handsome face and those fuckingly beautiful Kayne Sorenson ice-blues. When we played rough, he gasped and moaned passionately. His eye color darkened under his drag queen, black eyelashes, lost behind the fierce mass of hair flailing back and forth across his handsome face, neck, and shoulders. I fought the stasis of being in the presence of breathtaking beauty and continued to work his desire to match mine like a total whore master. I would deny him the object of his craving again and again and again until he went mad with lust.

Dudes, EXPLOSIVE! Know what I am talking about? He tensed his entire body and raised his hips, arching up in a full-body clench. I followed with my own award-winning climax.

Reloading did not take long, and he switched up the action with a role reversal. My body's engagement, in response to his dominance, was more defiant than submissive. Wordlessly, I communicated, *C'mon, Boss, that all you got? Fuckin', bring it!* Unsuccessfully pushing him away. And he totally got it. He would not be denied. He loved overpowering a worthy opponent, his sweat-soaked mane falling over his intense face above mine – total savagery.

Yeah, I let him have his hot boy, and he loved reclaiming his "Bosshood," gradually moving from compliant to aggressive and totally dominant.

So you may be thinking, 'What does our Nick need when the shit storm comes thick and fast, for he too is as lust-filled as Hell most of the time? What flushes the crap outta his head?' The answer is this, babies, this.

Unbelievable. After our extended play, it all went a bit mushy and got very romantic. It is a place I enjoy going to, but I have to convince myself that it is real. Like Kayne, I find it scary. He claims I find it unmasculine– so BS, my man.

I am a tough, in-charge guy, as is he. Letting go of all of that and just going to that place that brings two people together is totally mesmerizing -- scary/beautiful. The play of our bodies was exquisite. Did you ever sex up and make love to the extent that you almost can't remember your fuckin' name?

OK, sounding cray-cray, Nick boy.

So, anyway, that was the route our last moments of play went. I didn't know WTF at most points. I got lost and was just filled with him, with Kayne. Kayne. All over like a warm wave that goes deep inside.

Words fail.

Chapter Forty-Two: Stolen

Nick Sechi's Journal

Kayne and I walked into Allira's office the following morning.

Kayne did not wait long before saying, "Professor Peris. I want to know who has my nephew."

The man looked to the floor and said nothing.

Allira took a different plan of attack. "Damn, man. Do I hear that you are an accessory to kidnapping? You have been acting extremely erratically these days. Let's start with where is the diary, Gurumarra?"

The young scientist hung his head and said, "What makes you think I took it, Professor? Or that I know where your nephew is, Sir?"

"The others have been busy with their other interests, but you, it seems, are running in place with the energy project. Obsessed. I am aware of the pressure on you from conditions in your family and the gathering of the vultures around our work. I am not stupid, my friend."

Kayne said, "I do not have time for this, man. You are cooperating with those who would steal this project. I need a description of your contact. A boy's life is at stake."

The young man covered his face with his hands. "These guys play a dangerous game. I am in fear of my life these days. I have foolishly stepped in it and cannot extract myself, it seems. All hope is lost."

The lead researcher stood and began to pace the confines of the small office. Allira said, "Gurumara, did my father ever talk to you about our people and our struggle for social justice?"

"No, I was under the impression that he tried to distance himself from the ways of our people and their community. He was ashamed of being black in Australia."

"Ashamed, no. He was filled with disgust. The history of persecution and extermination of the Aboriginal and Torre Strait Islanders People appalled my Father. He had a wave of righteous anger for those who cooperated with the colonists. He had no patience with advocacy groups who, in his mind, were useless in their attempts to gain rights for our people. Sellouts.

"My father was an ardent assimilationist. He believed that we could only meet the colonials on equal footing if we played their game – threw off the past and advanced as leaders in science, industry, and public service. The key, he believed, depended on preserving and assimilating the forces of nature. He felt that would empower our people beyond the control of those who would destroy us."

She stopped and went eye-to-eye with her colleague. "We are members of the Stolen Generation, Gurumarra, you, me, Anatjari, Colin, and Renna. We were forcefully removed from our families by the Federal Government to be raised and educated white.

"Father collaborated with that dreadful assimilationist program and ensured that we thrived, gaining all the opportunities and advantages of any citizen of this country. He paid a high cost but never questioned his decision."

The quantum mechanics professor continued, "We have lost much in the bargain. However, we cannot allow the events that surround us to use us as pawns in yet another nightmare of death and destruction of the Dreaming. It would be the height of ungratefulness."

She drew closer to her colleague.

"It is time to take control and resolve this, to do the honorable thing."

The distraught man turned away from his colleague and faced Kayne.

"I was contacted a month ago and offered money for our research. I met with a man who sat mainly in the shadows, white, in his fifties, I would guess, an Australian. I can give you the address of the office where we met. It's near St. Kilda.

"Dr. Sorenson, I regret profoundly the part I have played in this terrible crime."

Chapter Forty-Three: *Kopuliram/Bumsen*

"You must be aware of the value of this project. Governments across the globe are willing to go to extreme lengths to get their hands on Nangala's notes. The country which possesses Nangala's engine rises to the top of global dominance."

"We are well informed, my dear Olga, that you have been having some interesting discussions with the pro-Russian party in your country. Tell me, do you think your uncle, the Duke, has the intelligence and the balls to return your country to a position of being a vassal state of the Russian Federation. Shit that would turn back the clock sixty years or more."

Lifting her skirt, he slowly removed her thong. She shuddered with anticipation but stayed in the conversation. She was no man's toy.

"You do not understand me, and that never surprises me, my dear Reese. Bulgaria needs nothing from those Russian fools. Owning and developing this technology will quickly catapult my country to superpower status with the freedom to extend our borders. A strong Bulgaria will answer to no one. Moscow will be quickly drawn into a political regression on the global stage, as will Washington."

She allowed him to unbutton the front of her blouse. His mouth followed the exploration begun by his hands over her neck and breasts. She inclined her head back and arched her upper torso closer to him. His hands caressed with a mounting passion. Her luxurious mane of chestnut brown hair cascaded back, providing an even more alluring view of her well-publicized beauty.

Catching his breath, he said, "You haven't mentioned the Chinese."

She pulled at the back of his head and brought him even closer, devouring his wet mouth. With her right hand, she moved his left between her legs. She liked the fact that he was naked while she was fully clothed. It signaled her dominance in their sex play. She ruled.

"Investors, my nasty boy. You need to bring that Board of yours to understand that working with me is the only sensible way in this. Parallax alone can never control a discovery this big-- or Caliban Ariel either, for that matter." She reached for his genitals but stopped with a slightly teasing touch.

She pushed him back and slapped him hard. He responded with excitement to her forceful humiliation. "And speaking of, just when will I receive that appointment to your Board as we discussed? Do not keep me waiting much longer."

"Hit me again." She complied -- twice. He replaced his hand between her upper thighs, and she stifled a cry. He quickly moved his body into a position to pull her down under him. Still, she slipped out of his grappling and walked to the desk next to the window, leaving him frustrated and lying face-up on the bed.

The Red Duchess moved aside the syringe, the carrying case, and the vial of tawny, brown liquid. She stepped out of her white cotton dress and poured more vodka into her glass. She took a mouthful and sucked air to excite the flavors in her mouth. "Tell me, why can't I get what I want, my pig? You have been given a few assignments in this, and you have failed me. And for this incompetence, you expect to enjoy my favors? To make with the *kopuliram* – the screwing. I despise your arrogance."

She mocked his desire with a laugh.

He looked up at her as she arranged her hair, raking the fingers of one hand through its silky tresses. With the other hand, she raised the glass to her lips again. This time, she moved her tongue across her lips, coating them with the alcohol.

"You men are worthless. Even my cousin, Michael Alexander. He can no more lead a country than you can manage some simple corporate espionage. My uncle, the Tsar, lost the monarchy. He is a figurehead, old, and useless. We need a strong royal leading the country. It takes Olga to make this happen. Strong women succeed where puny men fail. You are all ball-less eunuchs."

She pointed at him like she was scolding a child.

"I set in motion the stealing of that bastard brat. Are you going to get the data from that degenerate fool, Sorenson? I have been given no updates on the recovery of the hidden equations or the plan to make Sorenson and his minions knuckle under and obey.

"Oh, and by the way, I want that girl. She is a wicked minx. Find a way to get her for me. If you are successful, I may allow you to at least watch. More if I decide to be magnanimous."

His excitement continued to rise.

She put down the glass and picked up the leather belt. She turned it in her hand as she said. "Your sincerest apologies for doing nothing to please me in this matter are required, boy. Do not waste my time."

One of the most powerful men on the world energy stage slid naked off the bed. He crushed to his knees in front of his vibrant royal goddess, erotic tease, and soon to be his merciless torturer. The woman reached down and pushed his head to the floor and placed her barefoot on the back of his head, nailing it to the carpet.

"Palms on the floor, my pig."

The Grand Duchess grasped the thick leather strap with each hand and snapped it forcefully. The sound of the crack of the belt cut into the erotic centers of his brain, bringing him closer to the precipice of sexual intensity. The music of the strap on flesh, together with the biting kiss of the beating, would bring them both to complete satisfaction, but it would take hours.

***

Mark held her beneath him, bodies joined in a passionate rhythm. She gripped the sides of his heated torso. Their mouths alternated between kissing, tasting, moaning, gasping, and groaning words and phrases from imaginative and very pornographic scripts. Their brains and viscera blazed with sexual fire and tense desire.

He was good, an expert. Rather than finishing quickly, he coaxed her along to match his ardor, pacing their responses. Her body beneath him, flexing and arching. She reached behind his lower torso with both hands to grasp his gluteals and match his thrusting rhythm by pulling him in deeper. Rebecca's eyes flashed as she tightened her legs around him. Her toes curled with each forward thrust and retraction. They were both building to climax at a parallel pace, one sexy beast.

Their utterances became monosyllabic and a string of sexual gibberish. They called each other by name. They called each other obscene names. They called on God, Jesus, and on the bestial natures in each other, snarling orders and gasping pleadings. A hot summer breeze raced through the curtains of the opened bedroom windows, increasing the sweat of the two glistening lovers and feeding the fires within.

Mouth, lips, and tongues moved over, around, and in each other. They pulled off at the end as one screamed and the other roared in precisely timed and intricately executed ecstasy. It was a magnificently timed sexual tango.

***

"It's all good, Ace. Just having some fun in here."

"Sorry, sorry, Boyo. I heard the scream and, well, sorry, I'm a bit on edge what with Kris and...."

Mark struggled with the towel around his waist and its inability to disguise what he attempted to hide. He moved himself a bit more behind the bedroom door, leaning the upper part of his body out to talk to the man with the rifle.

"Ace, we were fucking. Go to bed, Big Darling, and take that beautiful woman with you. Make the best of this hot summer night."

Rebecca's voice came from the bed behind the Mark-guarded door. Ace smiled at the comment and said, "Well, I imagine you both have more'n one round in ya, so I will leave off."

"Ace, Kayne will get the boy back. I am sure."

Ace nodded and left the doorway. Mark closed the door and leaned against it after doffing his towel cover, his 6' frame in the prime of his maleness. He said, "Such a gracious host but very worried."

A very satisfied Rebecca drifted in after-glow reverie. She took in the visual of the naked man with the wavy brown hair across the room. The very satisfied woman thought Mark was the most magnificent man she had ever seen. Rebecca considered him an incredible beauty with a mind she would explore with wonder and excitement– much like his

240

body. Courageous, brave, rational, and brutally honest, she often bragged of his sexual prowess, intelligence, and perfect manliness. The man looked like an artist's model for the cover of a bodice ripper, even when wet, scruffy, and rumpled.

Responding to his remark, she said, "He's so Kayne, Darling. The apple doesn't fall... and all that, my hot man."

He jumped back on the bed and pulled her into a post-coital snooze position, her head on his chest. A typical couple-- he wanted a post-*Bumsen* sleep while she wanted some pillow talk.

He said a bit sleepily, "What do you mean? They seem to be polar opposites, Ace and Kayne."

"Yeah, but no. So, let's start with the physical."

"Why am I not surprised?"

She bit him.

"Ouch."

"Pay attention. Your problem, Darling, is that you see, but...."

" ... I do not observe. Gonna quote Kayne's aphorisms or get back to the father/son analysis rab-jab?"

She sat up and looked into his gray eyes with her molasses browns. She pushed at his wavy brown-gold hair, pasted to his head with sweat. "In many ways, you are an astonishing gender, and I am just a female who is very appreciative of the physical male."

"That I get." He rubbed his sore groin.

"In other ways, you are a species of Neanderthals, the whole lot of you. Frustrating as hell. But that is not a discussion for a hot Australian night, laced with multiple opportunities for sex."

"Gods be praised." He nuzzled up after pulling her back to him.

"So, they are both fit as can be."

"You saying Ace is another object of your sinful desires?"

She swatted him. "Mark, I cannot reveal all my secrets, Darling."

He laughed.

"You are transparent in oh so many ways, my beauty."

"You know, Darling, you are the only straight man I know who is not intimidated about heated talk about men's bodies, their equipment, or man-on-man sexing. You are very comfortable around my over-sexed gays, even when they hit on you. Wait a *minuto*." She faked horror. "Could poor Rebecca be setting herself up for a heartbreaking surprise, Darling?"

She feigned a look of astonishment. Mark chuckled and said, "Note to self: In the evening's next three rounds, prove to the woman you are a straight man with savage intentions. Exhaust her."

"You are so on, Darling, but only three? Anyway, where was I?"

"You were imagining Kayne and Ace both naked." He yawned.

She swatted him again."Don't you dare fall asleep."

Rebecca continued, "Yes, gorgeous males. Moving on... They have similar personalities, each showing variations on similar themes, like a genetic symphony."

"Your curator skills are coming out, beautiful."

"They are both energetic to the fuckin' max, Mark. Look around, Ace built all of this, amassing a sizeable fortune while preserving the land as best he could and helping the Indigenous communities to thrive. Not bad for a single father of four sons in the asshole of the world."

"Got it. Kayne has primal energy, plus that ADHD thing. What did you tell me? He received his Ph.D. at twenty-four? Ten years later, he's at the top of his game, a world-renowned expert in criminal psychopathology. World speaking tours, university positions, consulting on cases for the well-heeled, and he manages to snag a very hot and uber-classy police officer, one Nick Sechi."

"Exactly. Father and son – each of them is incredibly passionate, sexy, and stubborn, and my last remark would throw Kayne into fits of anger. And speaking of Darling, Ace's temper is like one of the plagues of Egypt. The man takes no prisoners, leaving everyone in the dust.

When Kayne gets angry, it tends to drip like cold nitroglycerin and is just as murderous.

"But both fools for love, Darling. They will plunge their right arm into the fire for a loved one or someone who is disenfranchised...."

"Wait, wait, wait... Gaius Mucius Scaevola."

"Yep, the brave Roman soldier who did just that– the original 'leftie' of myth and legend."

"So in conclusion, 'like father like son' as the adage goes."

"So incendiary! Like I said. You realize that all of this makes Kayne nutso, to use Nick's expression. When I remind him that he is so like his father, Darling – drip, drip, drip...."

Rebecca smiled like an evil step-sister.

"Then why do you?"

'Please, that boy needs his chain yanked from time to time to keep him from believing his own press."

"And who better to yank than you." He kissed her dusky brown shoulder, nibbling just a little as he moved to her neck.

"Ohhhh, Mark... that is so good... but yes, pulling his chain– what I live for, bay-bee."

This time, they both laughed.

Rebecca suddenly got serious.

"Mark, are we doing enough?"

"About what, my dear?" His voice was husky as he lip-walked up her trapezius to her neck and climbed his tongue to just below her ear. As he started to add his hands to the lower parts of her body, she spoke. "Kayne and Nick are half a continent away trying to find that poor boy, Darling. Here you and I are playing a scene from Under Capricorn in West Bum Fuck Australia."

"Those guys know what they're doing, Rebecca... mmmm... ahhh... and the reason for our presence here is not inconsequential."

"I wish I felt that. I'd rather be where the battle lines are drawn, at the front."

He stopped the light preliminaries for the second round. He said, "Rebecca, I have an unofficial source that hears all kinds of things in the cyber universe despite major attempts to keep secrets. My agent is a hacker in the league of Scott and Gints. In fact, they know each other by their aliases and respect each other's work. It is a very secret world, information-wise, covert, and dangerous.

"Anyway, the same interests who kidnapped Kris have their eyes on Inala. Kayne's sixth sense or innate intelligence… whatever… has us here, close to his father and other loved ones. Our job is to see that the web of violence and intrigue does not stretch here and bring harm to Ace, Darana, and the Inala community."

"Damn, so what are you telling me? Instead of making *Bumsen*, we should be sitting on the front porch with rifles ready for the Walking Dead?"

He moved a firm hand and strong arm up her naked thigh. He felt the heat begin to build again. She moved closer into his embrace.

"No, Beautiful. I think Kayne would want us to just take the point on this, you know? I never said anything, but back in Alice, when I was arranging for the helicopter, my contact told me that I was being watched by some militias connected to some very shady operators. Rebecca, Alice Springs is not that far away."

"Mark, why do you have connections with these hackers? It is such a dangerous enterprise, so Girl with the Dragon Tattoo. You know, violence out the ass."

"I cause trouble in my profession as a journalist, you know that. I am the newsboy no one wants at the press conference because I ask the tough questions and press for honest answers, calling BS when I see it. If the pen is truly mightier than the sword, I am the fuckin' vindicator. You see, the military, both friendly and hostile, would rather I reported on some other war when I am an embedded correspondent."

"Yes, but you are brave and resourceful, Darling. Look at those soldiers and civilians you saved in Aleppo."

"Fame is fleeting, beautiful. Anyway, there have been attempts on my life, efforts to imprison me, silence me, and hold me for ransom. I can't have a bodyguard. Too confining and not really cool. So I have Eris. She watches my back in the cyber universe.

"She got me out of Turkey when things got a bit sticky last summer. God, they hated me. This assignment in Micronesia was a way to get lost, but even then, I couldn't keep my big fat mouth shut."

"Darling, I worry, Mark. If anything should ever happen to you…."

"Yeah, I hear that, beautiful. Getting tired of looking over my shoulder."

They held each other in silence for a bit.

Rebecca moved against him and kicked back the covers. She said, "I have an assignment of my own, Darling, for that big fat mouth."

As they came together for another erotic session, the night air was pierced by an extended scream. Rebecca said huskily, "I forgot to say before that both Kayne and Ace are screamers."

Thomas Paul Severino

Chapter Forty-Four: Escape

He was doing calisthenics. He did them a lot in the airless, windowless chamber below ground. When he wasn't exercising, he drew on the wall. Anything, with whatever he could find, although the room had been stripped of almost everything. He sketched buildings, mountains, trees, and faces on the walls and floor. He did math problems.

Kris had heard them talking. The bunker was not suitable anymore, too many observable comings and goings. They were moving him into the city. He saw two men regularly. They gave him a pair of running shoes, brought him food, and took him to the bathroom. There was another voice from someone he never saw, but someone he believed saw him – cameras. He thought the men had Australian accents but did not know if he was in Australia. He tried to figure out the plane ride by hours spent and what places lay that far by plane from Sofia. He drew.

Simpson entered with a roll of duct tape. "Put your shirt on, stink boy. We're leaving."

Kris pulled on his uniform shirt and made two fists. He extended them forward, palms together, knuckles towards his captor, keeping his elbows close to his sides. His abductor wound the duct tape around the boy's wrists.

Wherever he was, it was summer– so, Southern Hemisphere or near the Equator. He blinked his eyes. First time in natural light for a while. The two kidnappers led him to the rear of a sedan and popped the trunk.

"Get in."

Kris bolted but did not get more than a few feet. The bigger of the two men grabbed him around the waist. He immediately went limp, sinking to the ground and dragging the man into a bent-over position. Getting the boy into the trunk was difficult, and he took both of them.

Darkness.

He waited until they were moving at what felt like highway speed before he started to kick out the tail light from the inside. Inevitably, someone will see his leg hanging out.

The car pulled over and stopped.

Kris was on his hands and knees when they opened the trunk, face down with his back to them. He did the limp thing again as they tried to extract him from "The Boot."

"You little shit. I need to teach you a lesson about respect and cooperation."

Once he hit the ground, Kris squirmed and kept his back away from his abductors. He bent over, making sobbing and retching sounds.

"This little pisser is gonna heave. Bloody hell."

His captor made a move to step back. Kris snapped back up, having removed the tire iron from his waistband. With all his might, he brought the metal down on the center of the head of the larger man nailing him to the asphalt. Blood.

The smaller of the two punched Kris hard with a roundhouse to the head, knocking him to the ground. The tire iron clattered on the cement. He saw stars and faked semi-conscious moaning.

One down. One to go.

***

"He's in the back seat. Dude is just about dead, Mate. Head cracked open. This kid is a bloody disaster, Sir. Shoulda put on more men on this."

Kris moaned in the passenger's front seat, whimpering like he was more hurt than he actually was. He pulled his legs up to his chest and rolled so that his back was against the door. He lolled his head as if in a stupor, rocking with the motion of the speeding car.

"Right. I am proceeding to the assigned place. Not coming back. May have a dead guy on our hands when I get there. I'm telling you this kid is...."

Kris exploded. He kicked the driver with all the force he could muster. Double shot. One to the ribcage under the phone-held arm and the other to the man's head. He used the door at his back as leverage for his full-body blast.

The phone fell to the floor between the driver's legs. He fought the pain of the bone-cracking blows and tried to control the swerving car, correcting way too much. The vehicle fishtailed and went up on two wheels, driverside. Kris used the momentum to sit up and grab the keys in the steering column, yanking them out. The steering wheel froze as the car hit four wheels on the ground. The driver tried to grab the struggling boy, but the vehicle began a terrifying spin across the road.

Kris threw himself over the passenger seat and landed on the fatally injured man in the back seat. Blood smeared his face and arm. As the car hit the guardrail and flipped over into the ditch, the boy was attempting to reach over and claw the eyes out of the driver in front of him.

Thomas Paul Severino

Chapter Forty-Five: Darana

A Letter to Nick Sechi

Dear Nick,

You requested I set down the events of November 11 of this year at Inala for your case files. I am happy to oblige in recording one of the most terrifying incidents in my time at Inala. The manor house is quiet now, and I have time to reflect and record. Where to begin?

First, for the sake of your followers, I will relate my connection to the land, the station, the company, the Sorenson Family, and Captain Thomas "Ace" Sorenson.

I am Napaltjarri, but that is a kinship name. It is part of a complex system of our social structure among the Aboriginal societies of Central, Western, and Northern Australia. My community is Ngaanyatjarra, also known as the Nana. We are a desert people who, until the mid-20th century, had little contact with the outside world.

I will not relate the struggles of my people with the federal system over the territory except to say that, in 2005, the land for which we are caretakers was the subject of the largest native title determination in Australian history. I was privileged to have worked on the case. The Federal Court ruled to honor our claim to 187,000 square kilometers in Western Australia. I was a seasoned lawyer by then, thanks to the generosity of Major Mitchell and Mrs. Elizabeth Sorenson, Ace's parents.

My family lived in the Northern Territory when I was a child. Conditions were very tough for a very long time. A spirit of cooperation, mutual respect, and profit-sharing has existed since the founding of the Inala Station and Sorenson Family Enterprises. The relationship between the Sorenson folks and the Aborigines on Inala has been a model of inclusion. The Major insisted that we all thrive together. He was a rabid anti-federalist when it came to Indigenous Affairs and resisted their policies of the assimilation of the traditional custodians of the land, the Aboriginal People. The Major, Ms. Elizabeth, and Ace have all spent time in jail rather than complying with the unjust laws of the federal government.

Ace would say, "One a convict, always a convict. Bloody Feds."

When Ace inherited the business, my brothers and sisters either worked for the family corporation or were in school. Major Mitchell (Kayne's older brother is named after him.) sent my eldest brother and me to Perth for university with the agreement that we would work for the corporation. While I was completing my JD, Ace had finished his military service with the Marines and was raising four sons as a single parent.

After a stint with a private law firm in Broome, I joined the company as chief legal counsel. Soon after, I became Ace's personal lawyer and Chief of Staff for the ranch. In 1991, I represented his interests in the divorce proceedings from his wife, the former Jane Sorenson.

Ours is an intimate relationship of equals – despite his antics so very much akin to a bull in a china shop sometimes. He tends to be a force of nature, all bluster and energy. On the other hand, I draw my strength from the quieter side of existence-- intelligent, calm, and logical. We are the Yin and Yang of Inala these days.

We were delighted to see Rebecca and Mark again after the excitement of Eastern Europe last summer. Ace took them for long rides on some of our best horses to view the land, the people, and our stock. Usually, we would sit under the large Eucalyptus trees west of the main house in the summer twilight and talk while enjoying an after-dinner drink. Mark would speak of his adventures in Micronesia and Asia. Rebecca spoke of the case in which you and Kayne are presently involved.

Their presence with us has helped Ace not to obsess over his grandson's disappearance. And, speaking of that, I must admit that true to form, it sounds like much danger is headed your way. Please have a care, Nick. But there is something about the lad that I have sensed. He will come through this, Nick. The song of his heart is strong and true.

What I have found most interesting is the dynamics among the Captain's family. The Brothers Sorenson are as eccentric as they are loveable. Early in my association with Ace, I was able to be of some help with the "Eric Affair." I have never seen such a broken-hearted father willing himself to keep control of the devastation that came about.

In the weeks following the escape from Trieste (as you chronicled so well in <u>Stage Blood</u>), when Ace and young Kris were first introduced, it was so apparent that they walked on eggshells around each other. One could see the Sorenson fire in the young man.

Each of them had been through so much pain, loss, and confusion. I remember an altercation one night just before we docked in Naples. Ace had said something that Kris took as an insult to his father. As I recall, the exchange went like this:

Kris turned on his grandfather with anger and a surprising amount of force for a young lad. He shook his finger at the Captain, saying, "You will watch what you say, Sir. You forget to whom you are speaking. My adoptive family is of warrior and noble blood. I will have you imprisoned."

Typical Ace, he howled and came back on even more of an attack.

"You little wanker, you are about as close to bloody Bulgaria as you gonna get. Go ahead, Lad, give a yell. Send in the fuckin' troops. I'll talk as I like about my own flesh and blood. Royalty! Bollocks, ya baby blighter, you've got the blood of convicts coursing through ya veins as much as I do."

I tried to step in between the tempest and the little whirlwind, saying, "Captain, remember your temper. Please try to remain calm. He's only a...."

Ace stopped me with a gesture and continued, "No, Darana. He has been trodding my decks like a puffed-up bantam since we pulled up the anchor. He needs to understand what's going on here. I'll not have a grandson of mine...."

Kris slammed the table between them. The anger and blustering fire so present in the males of this family was now showing forth in this youngest generation.

"Grandson? Crap! Grandfather? Don't make me laugh, Old Man. Where were you, huh? Answer me that? Where? Were you there for my Father? You tossed his ass out! And my Grandmother? Tell me, old man, where the fuck were you?"

Ace, with clenched fists, rounded on the accusing boy. "You got balls judging me. Now you watch your mouth."

Ace raised his right hand but stopped. A storm of memory seemed to crash on the shores of his emotions. He had been at this impasse so many times when the boy's father... when Eric was growing up. In the fulminating air around them, I saw a younger Ace raging at a defiant fallen angel. Only, at that time, the disciplining hand held the strap.

Kris said nothing. He only locked defiant eyes with his Grandfather. It seemed that the motion of the universe had stopped for each of them. I don't think the young prince had ever received corporal punishment in his life.

Tears crested the boy's lower eyelids and streamed to the lower edges of his handsome face. His countenance was lit with anger from within as he wiped back the tears. Ace's fury began to abate. His hand shook.

We were interrupted by the quiet voice of the First Mate of the *Inala Princess.*

"Captian, we will be arriving in Valletta, Malta, in thirty minutes."

I stepped forward, took Ace by his raised hand, and said, "Thank you, Mr. Dickson." I turned Ace from the fight and drew him close. He and the boy started to cool. Kris backed up from his grandfather and went further up the ship to his cabin."

Later in our cabin, Ace said, "You bet your arse. It was like twenty years ago with his father, Darana. I am a doomed man, caught in a reoccurring dream of anger and resentment."

"Take it easy, Ace. You and he have been through so much these last couple of days. Remember, love, very few things are ever permanent. You and he will come to detanté, and then peace will have its day."

Two days later, when we made port in Naples, the two of them had little to say to each other as they parted. Kris was in a depression that was matched by his Grandfather. I remember thinking that a reconciliation would be difficult – such strong and stubborn personalities.

I thought they were tourists. Three couples. I will be honest. I was totally distracted by the ranch's activities that morning. Ace was getting ready to join the muster in the southeast, vaccinations against a new infection – something in the water.

The jackeroos, jilleroos, and ringers began the round with the Yulara River mob, yarding the cattle for their shots. The vets would accompany the rounders with the pharmaceuticals. The muster would last through mid-December.

Ace did not have to be there, as our crew was superb. He wanted to "troop the colors as the figurehead" of the entire Inala enterprise. "Spot flying," Ace called it, dropping out of the sky like some divine Grazier. He flew into each mob on one of the station's planes with Inala's cattle dogs, yapping and announcing the Boss's arrival.

I remember seeing the visitors talking in the front paddock with Mark and Rebecca after they alighted from their van. Alice was growling and kept positioning herself between the visitors and our Inala folks.

Then a shout. I went to the window and saw Mark knocked to the ground with a big goon on top of him, tying his wrists behind his back. One of the villains was taking aim at Alice, but Rebecca was on the attack. The other dogs ran to the rear of the house. I dashed to Ace's office and went for the gun cabinet.

"You seeing this, woman? What the bloody hell?" Ace took a firearm, and we both slammed cartridges into the weapons. We raced to the rescue. As we stepped out of the front of the house, Ace was blindsided and was knocked into the dirt. Rebecca was being held at gunpoint near a tied-up Mark. Alice leaped forward to sink her teeth into the calf of the largest, only to be kicked away. She only succeeded in puncturing his boot.

A gun to my temple, a woman asked me who else was in the house. "Servants, four. Three in the kitchen and the butler's pantry, one upstairs."

The six invaders hustled us into the front room and closed the thick sliding doors. The man who was the leader of the assassins said, "I am sorry to inform the four of you that you have come down with the measles. Make any arrangements you need to isolate the main house, business, social commitments, whatever. We will be taking over for the time being."

As Ace roared, one of the thugs knocked him out cold. In the end, Mark and Ace were bound and confined in the root cellar, and Rebecca and I became the kitchen maids for the invaders. The servants were dismissed. One member of the evil group supervised my shutting down communications from the office. She locked our cell phones in the office drawer.

We waited.

Chapter Forty-Six: Run

The car in the ditch was on fire.

No traffic in either direction. The abductors would come for him soon. The crash was not that far from where he had been held captive. *Where the fuck is this?*

No injuries to speak of. The fat ass in the back seat was like an airbag, taking most of the impact and the mangling of the crash. The driver was getting barbecued in the wreckage. *Poor one-eyed bastard.*

The boy remembered the smell of the raining petrol as he reached into the crushed front seat between the driver's legs. He dashed away from the wreck just as the explosion shot up and out, reaching for him like a chained demon.

The light from the burning wreck cast fearsome shadows across the surrounding landscape. The car had gone airborne, crashing over the guard rail and through a wire fence, and was on its back, blazing in the cool summer night. Grapes vines in rows chased each other up and over the hillside. Beyond were the mountains up against the moonlit sky.

He raised his hands over his head and slammed them down, bringing his elbows to his ribs. The movement was rapid and forceful. He cried out as the overwhelmed duct tape split against his wrists. He stooped to pick up the phone.

No fuckin' signal. No towers in this shit hole.

He looked around for the path that would be his roadway out. He grabbed a bunch of green grapes and crushed them to his mouth. The liquid and the sugar were what he needed. He felt the tears rise. He fought them.

Kris forced himself to think of something, anything--the athletic staff at the Lyceé. Soccer training gave him the strength and endurance for this shit, he thought. Yeah, and that defensive maneuvers course. His buds jokingly called it "Kidnapping 101." However, the combat trainers from CEPOL were excellent and focused students on how to escape from an abduction. Because of their blue-blood status, the students at the school were especially susceptible kidnapping targets.

He and Kaito had liked the big dude named István. He was playful and tough with both of them, seeming to sense the bond they shared as very close buds. The warrior had tossed each of them on their respective asses during training. Kris remembered how the big bruiser had found his way into his teenage dreams.

He missed Kaito and wanted to get back. He had to let Nick and Kayne know where he was and that he was OK. He realized that he was crying full force now as he backed away from the wreckage. He saw the headlights far down the highway.

He raced up the hill along the rows of grapevines. Once, he stopped, faced the burning car, raised both arms above his head, and screamed into the night.

"I AM MY FATHER'S SON!"

Kris ran into the darkness.

Chapter Forty-Seven: The Red Queen's Check

"If I understand you correctly, you are telling me that a fifteen-year-old boy overpowered two of your henchmen, killing them both and escaping. At this time, you have no idea where he is. Tell me, are you a total idiot?"

"Look, bitch, I never wanted you in this to begin with. This has been our deal from the start. You co-opted this operation because you wanted to get your greedy hands on the project. Tell me, how does being Reese Stephenson's whore get you all the *gravitas* you seem to think you have?"

"Bastard! You will respect me or leave my presence. I have the means to get this done on my own. It is through my generosity that I even allow you to be a part of this project. Caliban Ariel is for shit, as they say. If you want to survive, your only recourse is Parallax. And, me."

The man raised his voice, "Fine! I am prepared to do this on my own. Using the boy as a hostage is not my only move. He can rot in the mountains or wherever he is. Sorensen has a few other pressure points I have already begun to engage alternate strategies."

"It seems we each have our own accomplices, but you and your associates are incompetent and no rivals to us, I assure you. What matters most is that we get those flash drives."

The Grand Duchess turned and spoke to the men in the doorway. "Allow me to show you what else you do not have in this game. Bring him in."

A very dashing Prince Preslav and one of his men pulled a bound man into the room and tossed him to the center. He sprawled unconscious on the floor, face to the luxurious carpet. The Grand Duchess moved the head of Max Caliban with her boot. His face was bruised and his clothes torn, indicating the struggle that accompanied his capture.

"He is uninjured, merely sedated."

Konstantin Preslav said, "Mr. Lockwood, you will be interested to know that the SUV of the CEO of Caliban Ariel Energy was found crushed at the bottom of the Cranston Chasm up in the mountains. No corpse was found. The man was drinking copiously since the death of his lover, so driving while intoxicated will be suspected as the cause of the crash."

"Mr. Lockwood," said nothing. Now, they had captured his pawn and would willingly eliminate him.

Preslav took the hand of the Grand Duchess and kissed it lovingly. He stood behind her. His associate loomed over the subdued Max.

"So let's be clear on my strategy to win this game. Despite your idiocy at failing me like the complete amateur you seem to be, I will keep you in the game on the condition that you complete your arrangement for the recovery with the Sorensons. They are the 'pressure points' as you call them. I intend not to be directly involved with them unless I have to. Dr. Sorenson is expecting you to contact him with the terms of the exchange. We will leave it at that."

Lockwood said nothing, glancing from time to time at Max.

"I will give you instructions for the handoff. You will turn the materials over to us and thereby relinquish any and all interest in the project. When all is complete, I will release my prisoner unharmed. At least, I hope that I can. You see, my dear Lockwood, my beautiful Konstantin, like me, has a taste for very intense games. Do you not, my Prince?"

Preslav said nothing. He walked to the bowed-over Max and pulled his head up by the hair. The young man's eyes flickered with dull recognition as he looked at his tormentor with a stunned expression. The Chief of Security went down on one knee to caress the bruised and handsome face of the prisoner like a lover while stepping on his hand. Max's mouth opened in a silent scream as he slipped back into unconsciousness.

Lockwood spoke finally and without emotion. "It will be as you say. I will get it done quickly." He bowed and left the room.

The Prince signaled to his man, who roughly extracted Max from the room. He turned to embrace the Grand Duchess from behind and slid his tongue into her ear.

She gasped, "You are a beast, Your Highness. We are well-matched in sin, betrayal, and the torment of idiots. I give my permission to use our captive for your pleasure.

"Soon, we will have everything we need to take control. No one will stop us."

"Soon, you will be the Queen you were born to be, my Olga. An uncompromising ruler in wealth, power, and sin…"

He pressed against her, saying vulgar things into her ear. She turned, kissed him, and then stepped away.

"Lockwood has blood on his hands, the Indigenous ones, Nangala, Ariel, we will need him to kill the traitor Peris when the time is right. Have you no fear of the revenge of their ancient blood?"

The Prince responded, "I am fearless, my dear, as long as you are mine. You control this game, the most powerful and ruthless of the players. It excites the spirit as well as the body."

Before she was swept again into the arms of her young nobleman, she spoke into her cell phone. The door opened, and a somewhat ragged fifteen-year-old ran into the room, bowed to the two royals, and was engulfed in a child-like embrace with his Aunt.

***

"You are safe now, Prince Kristof. Mr. Stephenson has given us the run of his estate while he is away. Your Great Grandfather's Head of Security is arranging for your safe return to your school in Bulgaria. I accompanied him to Australia when we learned where you had been taken. You have no worries now, my dear."

Prince Preslav bowed to the young man and said, "Prince, please allow me to congratulate you on your resourceful and brave escape. The other men who abducted you are still being pursued by our government and our Australian friends in law enforcement. I have assigned one of my men to keep you under surveillance until we get you back to Sofia. It will not be long, but I hope we can rely on your patience. The Tsar must keep a distance from these affairs, you understand, but he will be happy for your return."

"My Uncle and Officer Sechi, where… well, I was sure that Great Grandfather would arrange for their help in rescuing me."

Olga Danilova replied, "Oh, my dear boy, it saddens me to tell you they were not interested in helping the Tsar. His Royal Highness received a very distressful response when he endeavored to contact them. They are, no doubt, somewhere in America where degenerates like them have the freedom to…. well, let us not discuss rude things at such a hopeful time for our family."

She nodded to Preslav, who said, "Come, Your Highness. I will introduce you to our guards. We will get you bathed and fed and provide you with some clean clothes."

He placed his hand on the shoulder of the boy, who was carefully scrutinizing the two faces of his Aunt and the Prince. Preslav turned the boy to the door, guiding him out of the room. Kris stopped, looked the Prince in the eye, and removed the man's hand from his shoulder.

He turned and bowed to the woman and said, "It would seem, Aunt, that you are in control of the board."

He exited with the bearing of a man.

Chapter Forty-Eight: Knight to QB2

Nick Sechi's Journal

The spotlight immobilized me. It was like my body was paralyzed, and my bare feet stuck to the floor. Joao approached and raised his fists.

"We have to finish this, Nick. I know it is what you want – what we both want."

He brought his rugged face close to mine. I felt like my body was thawing, and I could begin to move. My hands were encased in MMA gloves, and my teeth clenched a mouthguard. Kayne approached, stepping into the spotlight.

"Nick, we need to go. The game is on. It's your move."

I ducked a punch from Joao, who failed to stop his own momentum and sprawled on the canvas. Rather than stand up, he gestured for me to join him on the floor, which had changed into a giant chessboard.

My mother's voice outside the spotlight, in the darkness: "Nick baby, tell Kayne what you want. There is no time for delay right now."

I looked for Kayne, who pulled Max Caliban into the light and kissed him passionately. He looked back at me with a questioning expression that seemed to imply, "One for me and one for you." Reaching out to them, I heard two voices, Allira and Rebecca.

"Fight for him, Nick. He is the last knight left, and he is your spirit's song."

"Darling, I am so tired of waiting for you. Why are you so fearful?"

Again, I turned. A figure approached dressed in black-- shoes, pants, and a pulled-up hoodie. A large scorpion crawled up the specter's chest to the side of his neck. Kris' voice came from under the headcover, speaking as he slowly dematerialized.

"Nick, all this sucks, Dude. Find me, man."

Only Joao now, rising a few feet from me, taking his stance. His right leg came up with a high switch kick, powerful and whiplike.

I fell out of bed.

***

Kayne reached for me and for my chirping phone at the same time. "Are you OK, my love?"

"Yes. Stupid dream."

"Lost it. Unknown number. He'll call back. Gotta be Lockwood."

"Damn, the game must be on, Boss." I pulled in next to him in bed.

"Here's the thing. We have four of the chess pieces, and that's all Lockwood gets. We just take Kris and get the bloody hell out of where ever. This inaction thingo is maddening and is so at an end. I can see that clearly this morning."

We both looked at his silent phone. *Nada.*

He kissed me good morning as I leaned over him and looked at the display. "You were dreaming and talking in your sleep, calling for your hot fighter jock. Your morning tumescence confirms my conclusion of obsession. Not the Calvin Kline cologne but the psychological condition. It would appear I have a rival."

"You are my one and only obsession, Kayne, you tease. And you know it." I snuggled. "Did you sleep?"

"Alas, the sleep of the just continues to be withheld from me, my love. Sometime during the morning, I did drift off into a deep state, and I missed the phone call, I am afraid."

As he spoke, the call came again.

***

Allira stirred her coffee. "No location? Just a time."

Kayne chose a table far from the rest of the customers at the hotel's restaurant. He ordered only coffee. I was ravenously hungry.

He said, "Exchange at midnight. Location to be communicated sometime this morning. I suspect Heathcliff. There is much going on here that defies explanation. Max is hiding something. I am sure of it.

264

His behavior while we attended the funeral rites was that of a man in deep, soul-filled torment. A discomfiture that goes well beyond the death of Zach Ariel."

I swapped our four flash drives and exchanged them for five of Allira's. Spreading orange marmalade on my toast, I placed it on my bread plate and pushed it to Kayne, catching his gaze and raising my chin at him in a silent gesture that said, *Go ahead and eat this, Boss.*

"What would you guess is the connection?"

"I never guess, Professor."

OK, let's stop here for a moment and remember what the Nickster concluded last night. My man needed rough and red-hot sexin'-up to clear out his cognitive processes. The next morning, he is totally clear-thinking and in his Sherlock Holmes persona. E.g., "I never guess, Professor." Am I right, or am I right?

He is so gonna launch all cognitive at this point, so let's get back to our movie....

Kayne looked up from the table to organize his thoughts and explain. "The mysterious woman at the funeral reception at Heathcliff was the Grand Duchess Olga Danilova, niece to the Tsar and a notorious figure of scandalous intrigue. Bedroom politics seems to be her forté, according to my intel from our confederates in research.

"She has been suspected as one of the silent backers of a rightist movement in her own country, as well as in Romania. Last year, her connections to the armed insurrection in Ukraine were uncovered. She has denied any involvement in a plot to cause instability in that government. Since the Russian invasion of that country, she has visited her 'palace' in the Crimea quite a few times, hosting some important Russians and earning the appellation 'The Red Duchess' and sometimes 'The Red Queen.' Quite the web of intrigue."

He reached with his fork to my plate and helped himself.

"Politically, in her own country, she appears to be backing the aspirations of another member of the royal family, Grand Duke Michael Alexander. My informants have confirmed that they are actually estranged, and her backing is a sham. She is working to replace him as leader of the conservatives and, if she gets it, will become the next prime minister when the present government falls."

I moved my breakfast plate totally in front of him and said, "The Red Duchess becomes the Red Queen."

Kayne nodded and said, "Her lovers seem to be among the powerful and influential across the globe, and all have the same political mien -- ultra-right. There was a scandal two years ago that reached the Tsar's court involving the death of the wife of a prominent Brazilian politician. Danilova was romantically involved with the widower well before the mysterious demise of his unfortunate wife."

I signaled to our waiter that I wanted another round of the 'Hooligan Breakfast Plate.'"

"Our Bulgarian Circe is often seen in the company of a young Chinese, Xiu Ying, twenty-three years her junior. He is a rising star from Hong Kong and head of the conglomerate SinoTec. Xiu's company is predicted to soon outdistance Microsoft.

"A year ago, she was named in a suicide note penned by a woman who was head of a naval armaments consortium in Finland. Again, the connection was romantic. In addition, it would seem she has some powerful friends in this country, both men and women. She has worked behind the scenes to buy up stock in Caliban Ariel and agitated for a seat on the board of Parallax. Our girl tosses off these scandals with indifference and outrageous bravado."

Allira interrupted, "Kayne, I need to tell you something."

"From the way that you have twisted your napkin since I mentioned our villainess, I conclude you are about to tell me there is a connection between the Red Duchess and your work. She wants the project, yes?"

"We were introduced at an informal meeting with Reese Stephenson. She is quite a woman. One who definitely likes to give orders. She made clear that she was very interested in my father's work, but the project belonged in the hands of the developers and not the scientists. She implied that there was a lot of cash behind her interest. She advised me to carefully consider certain offers.

"I saw them at the funeral with Reese's lawyer, but they make my skin crawl, to be honest. In a somewhat drunken moment, Max confided in me that he wished they would leave. Apparently, they trouble him."

I watched Kayne continue to eat and elaborate on the intrigue behind this case.

"Allira, what of Max and Zach? Caliban Ariel? Elaborate, please."

"Preliminary discussions put them and Parallax at the top of the interested parties, together with a Chinese company from Shanghai. A lot of *yuan* there, my friends. The big cash offered by the energy industries is so tempting. Caliban Ariel is cash-poor, and the board blames Zach and Max — too much diversification too fast. They were barely able to survive a hostile takeover by Parallax.

"We know of Zach's desire to keep the Nangala project within the community through his proposed foundation, an idea only my team and I like. Parallax and even Caliban Ariel have no backing for Zach's dream, apparently. Cuts them out of some substantial profits.

"There was a pretty murderous blow-up at one point in a very public venue. C/A's board chair and Stephenson ripped into Zach, who came back with some pretty belligerent words. Max and even Earnshaw got into the mix – quite appalling."

Kayne grabbed his cell as the screen lit up with a text.

"Bendigo"

Chapter Forty-Nine: The White Knight's Gear
Rebecca Quinto's Notes

Nicky Darling, I swear the "Big Bads" this time are such dolts. This was a piece of cake. Dumb as dishwater, Darling.

First of all, keeping folks out of Inala, even in the case of quarantine, is virtually impossible. The Evil Quartet lying to visitors and inquirers — they were kidding themselves. They also did not count on the intricate design of the Nineteenth Century Victorian mansion that is the estate's main house. It's very much like the ranch house "Reata" in the movie "Giant," large and imposing, set in the middle of nowhere.

It has three floors with a tower, many secret rooms, and back stairways. Darana and I find it easy to get to places without their knowledge when not under close scrutiny. Quite simple to get to any of the many gun cabinets, but we decided to use the fabled "woman's weapon," poison.

It seems that the head chef for the ranch, in charge of feeding the vast estate staff and family, Phạm Khánh Minh, is a Vietnamese herbalist. The kitchen is his kingdom, along with the other cookhouses on the property that feed the ranchers. So, his stash of potions and remedies is located in none other than the very root cellar in which the invaders had locked Mark and Ace.

Under the pretext of bringing them food, Darana returned with a packet of just what we needed, *Lá ngón,* dried gelsemium. We added a bit of Cascara Senna to bring the enemy's bowels into play.

We knocked them out at dinner on the second day– talking dropped down to the dining room floor from off their chairs, kinda knockout. One of the big guys was slow to succumb, but I managed to help him along by kicking his chair out from under him in the middle of the *crème brûlée.*

We freed Mark and Ace, who were so pissed that we did not rumble with the villains. (*Sigh! Men, Darling... all that testosterone makes you boys crazy.*) They had the honor of toting the bodies to the root cellar and tying them up before the authorities arrived and took away "those bloody bastards," as Ace called them.

We decided to finish the excellent beef stew with a few bottles of a spicy Malbec. We gathered in the enormous kitchen as the staff returned to the house. Alice and her dog buddies, previously exiled to the barn, were overjoyed to have the run of the main house and yard again.

I will admit, Darling, I was thinking of you and Kayne and Lewis Carroll as we upended yet another bottle. Ace was holding court, and Mark was ravenous. I felt something come over me, Nick. I know I was a little tipsy with the wine and the thrill of our victory over those nasties, but it seemed like I was moving in a dream.

Around us, from the ceiling and wall shelves, hung a collection of kitchen pots, pans, baskets, bunches of herbs and vegetables, and implements, many of which were impossible to understand. The conglomeration reminded me of the White Knight's gear cluttered over his horse in the Sir John Tenniel illustrations for Through the Looking Glass.

Nick, I swear, Darling, there it was... about twelve inches tall, bright white, and high on a shelf. I asked my own knight to get it down.

Mark joked, "You just want to see my spectacular man ass up on that ladder, 'fess up, beautiful."

I hugged him and said, "Later, Studly, let's not offend the staff."

Mark retrieved the object of my interest, which I held before the Lord of Inala with a questioning look. Ace had been bragging about how he and Mark were working their way out of their bindings, ready to kick some arse when Darana opened the root cellar door and let them know that it was pretty much a done deal."

"Ace, what is this?"

"Busted pepper mill. Never did work. Came from a bloke who rented my house in Melbourne-- a thank-you gift, I suppose. Have no idea why I even kept it around."

"Nangala?"

"My girl, how did you know? I reckon you been hanging with my Kayne too long. His superpowers rubbing off?"

I worked the mechanism like you showed me and opened the head of the White King.

We have the fifth flash drive, Darling.

Thomas Paul Severino

Chapter Fifty: Bendigo

Nick Sechi's Journal

Kayne landed the "Firehawk" around 10:15 pm at the Bendigo airport, northeast of the city. Our final destination was the Olympic Paradise, an abandoned mine southwest of the center of town.

Gold had been discovered in the area during the Victorian Gold Rush of the 1850s, creating the boomtown of Bendigo from a former sheep station 93 miles from Melbourne. Once the gold in the surface soil had been depleted, mining companies dug deep into the underground deposits. Bendigo was the highest-producing goldfield in Australia in the Nineteenth Century and the site of the largest gold mining economy in eastern Australia. We passed through a town lit up in the night with a rich Victorian architectural heritage.

There were many abandoned mines in the rolling plains and low hills. We followed instructions to a solitary, two-story building that seemed to be shuttered up and quite dark. The large house had a broad porch encrusted with architectural gingerbread. There were warning signs notifying trespassers that the City Ordinance demanded that no one enter the premises. Peeling paint and missing floorboards gave way to a large double door. It was unlocked.

The old house was empty. We walked through dark rooms filled with cobwebs. A staircase swept up to the second floor. Using the flashlights on our cell phones, we followed footprints in the dust back through the dining room, through a butler's pantry. Mullioned cabinet doors with broken glass hung from busted hinges. A thick coat of dust covered every surface. Our trail led to the old kitchen of the house.

Below an opened cellar door in the kitchen, dim lights led the way down. The owners of this decrepit mansion had a private entrance to the underground Bendigo. We figured the floor below led to an opening in the Olympic Paradise Mine. As we halted before the cellar opening, a shadow in a kitchen corner came to life.

"Right on time, Gentlemen."

"Prince Preslav, I am not surprised to see you here."

273

His gun was trained on my chest, but the tall royal spoke to Kayne. "Come come, my dear Doctor. You must admit you had no idea of my affiliations in this affair. I have played out my role as the Tsar's devoted soldier with duplicitous precision."

"Not so, Your Highness. You have been far too clumsy in your attempt to gaslight Nick and me – a very juvenile attempt at a false depiction of reality. Putting you in the ranks of the militia of the Red Duchess was simple. You are, in fact, her team captain.

"When we met, you had two long brown hairs on your left shoulder, and you smelled faintly of *Guerlain Le Bouquet de la Mariee,* a scent preferred exclusively by Her Royal Highness. You, Sir, are her man and a traitor to the crown."

Kayne stepped in front of me so that the Prince's gun was now trained on him.

"I should kill you for your insolence, Sir...."

I tried to get to him, gun or no gun.

"You miserable crud." I challenged. "Put your gun up and fight like a real man. Show me how a blue-blood dominates, Turdo."

Preslav smiled like an engorged gargoyle. "My, my, my, so brash. You are true to your reputation, boy, a hot-headed degenerate like your daddy here? Are you his caretaker, or is he yours?"

Kayne stopped me from a very risky disarming of the Bulgarian.

"Let us not argue like kitchen girls, gentlemen. The Red Duchess awaits below." He motioned with the gun to the stairway.

A cluttered cellar opened at the rear to an ancient caged elevator. A swag of electric bulbs showed the way and snaked down into the pit. Every sixth one or so seemed to sputter. We entered the lift at gunpoint and descended what was to be a great distance. Before we finished our descent, a woman's voice came from below, dreamy and slurred.

"I do not climb, gentlemen, so I had the elevator repaired. It is one of many. The Olympus Paradise goes on forever in every direction. So far into the earth, the miners had to take precautions against the bends. There are twenty-three entrances to this mine. Most of them are closed up, and some shafts are caved in – accidents that resulted in many miners being buried and forgotten. In many places, it is a cemetery of avaricious men. One could quarter an army in the miles of vertical and horizontal shafts and caverns that remain."

We stepped off into the presence of the Red Duchess, Olga Danilova, seated regally amid a few armed men. One of her minions stood between her and us. The regal woman's head was thrown back in a dark ecstasy, her breathing deep and sensual. The attendant put away the implements of his mistress' deadly bliss, pulled down the Duchess' sleeve, and stepped away.

More naked bulbs illuminated her subterranean throne room, once a large management chamber for the Olympus mine. Narrow-gauge rails snaked in every direction, a vast underground railway serving this level with many connections to lifts connecting levels above and below. The naked rock around us was drill-scarred and fractured with veins of color.

I fought my fear of being in enclosed spaces by trying to focus on formulating exit strategies and calculating our chances of overcoming our opponents. Being so deep in the earth was a nightmare, but I needed to suppress the terror.

Regaining a bleary-eyed consciousness, the wicked woman waved her hand towards the intersecting entrances to the tunnels that ran off in many directions like the tubes in the New York Subway System. She spoke with mock gravity. "Olympus Paradise. Raped of her treasures and abandoned. Alas, Mother Earth, men have mistreated you as they have disparaged so many of your daughters."

She stepped up to me and took the backpack, handing it to her guard. "My, you are a beauty. Nick, is it?" I said nothing as he touched my sternum. "Alas, I had my fill of boys by age seventeen, and so now, I do not favor youngsters, so much training involved. However, one or two of my associates do." She smiled at Prince Preslav.

The deadly Olga now turned her attention to Kayne. "But this... this is a treat more to my liking. A magnificent male in the fullness of his manhood, yes, in all his glory and beauty." She ran a hand over his arms and upper torso. An exquisitely manicured finger touched his cheek and his lips. She moved his bang aside and traced the forehead scar.

The intensely beautiful woman, dripping evil, said in a husky voice, "I have invented an exceptional conversion therapy, Dr. Sorenson, for men of your... shall we say, ilk?" She grasped him by the hair and pulled him into a clinch, whispering into his ear and anointing him with her wet tongue. He firmly pushed her away with disgust.

Preslav slammed the gun barrel into the side of his head, knocking him to the ground. I leaped on the Prince's back but was caught by a bullet to the thigh from one of The Duchess' armed guards. I sank to the ground.

The Duchess leered wolf-like at the wreckage beneath her feet, delighted. She stepped closer to me, planted a boot against my wound, and stepped down hard. I struggled not to cry out but fought the blackness of unconsciousness that began to rise. I dug my heels into the dirt and kicked at the torment. She stepped away and hissed, "You bad boy. You have gotten blood on my boot. What a shame."

She turned and addressed the entire cavern space, "Shall we all come out now? The danger is passed. But I warn you, do not wander far, for the openings are treacherous, and the lights are not continuous."

Shadows moved, and figures emerged into the old concourse. I sat up, trying to staunch the flow of blood in a world of pain. Kayne was recovering on all fours from the pistol-whipping, shaking, and holding his head. As he came around, he stood and ripped most of his shirt into strips and tied them around my leg. He lowered himself next to me and pulled my reclining body into his arms. We watched the drama continue to unfold eight stories below ground.

Shadowy figures came together. "Mr. Lockwood, I believe the Red Queen has just brought about checkmate. I am sure you agree. I have tipped the White King into defeat in the traditional gesture."

She pointed to Kayne at her feet.

"And his pawn is as good as dead."

They emerged from opposite sides. First, Max Caliban. The angry man yelled, "Lockwood, you fucking black heart! You bloody shit! You despicable man, I hate your fuckin' guts. Father, you have killed me."

He drew out the last word like a banshee.

Earnshaw stared from the opposite side of the cavern. He pointed at his son. "You and your pederast were bent on the destruction of Caliban Energy, everything my father and I built." He struck Max with disgust, a firm bitch slap sending him to his knees. "You gave that bloody wog my company and made me a servant, his servant."

"A company from which you stole and in whose name you murdered and kidnapped a child. You deserve to rot in jail. I took you in when you had nowhere to go to escape indictment. I lied and covered up for you. Dr. Nangala, my beautiful Zach, the Sorenson Prince, the men on the Harbour Bridge. How many more will die? Now you have killed me!"

The Red Duchess spoke, "Oh, make that hysterical idiot stop. Silence him. Shoot him. He annoys me." A guard knocked the shouting Max Caliban back to the floor.

"Lockwood, our association is at an end. It is unfortunate that you and your son will have disappeared so suddenly. The young man's despondency over the death of his lover points to inevitable self-destruction, and no one will care much if a servant disappears."

She paused with a sudden moment of inspiration, laughing horribly as she spoke, "Oh my, suppose the servant made off with some of the family fortune. My Konstantine, I love it. Make this happen. It is genius."

"It shall be done, your Royal Highness."

Earnshaw stared as if hypnotized, confronted with the true face of evil, a paralyzed bird within reach of the cobra. She raked at his hair and said, "They will never find your bodies, David. So very sad."

"They are authentic, *Princessa*. The equations are definitely the quantum physics of matter-antimatter energy. They fit into the formulas we have been studying." The minion typed on a laptop mounted on a tall and ancient accounting desk. He seemed to be a bit worried.

Olga turned to her confederate, "For your sake, they had better be." She spread her arms wide. "This elaborate drama unfolds only once." She turned to Kayne and stepped towards him. "If you have tricked me, I still have one important pawn." She arched her head toward one of the darkened bays." A boy was allowed to enter.

Kris strode in with a regal bearing. "You will remove that gun from my presence. In fact, I do not wish to look at you at all." He addressed his words to Prince Preslav. He ran to Kayne and me. He touched the blood oozing down the back of his uncle's head.

He confronted the Red Duchess. "You, Aunt, will order your assistants to provide my family and me with emergency assistance as we are leaving your hell pit now."

Damn, this kid has balls.

Danilova smiled coldly, stepped forward, and then slapped her nephew with force. The boy staggered.

"Bastard Prince, you will not give orders but follow them. I am sick to death of your insolence. You are the son of a whore and a degenerate, a total insult to my family. She raised her hand to strike again, but Kris grabbed her wrist and stared into her cold gaze. "Be very careful, you bitch."

He dropped her arm.

I began to sag against Kayne– bleeding out. Funny, when you face the end... everything starts to slide into slow motion. The chamber closed in, shifted, slanting, growing blurry. I expected reinforcements... am I seeing Rebecca, Mark, Gints... riding in and saving the day? Dropping from the ceiling on rappelling ropes in black ninja outfits. Kayne was speaking to me, but his voice did not match the movement of his mouth... so far away...

Darkness.

Chapter Fifty-One: Endgame

So, Here It Is, Dudes and Dudettes – by The Kris

The first one embedded itself in the forehead of the goon dude standing next to my Aunt. The force of it split his face open from the skull to the upper lip. He crashed to the floor, inches away. The impact drove the curved metal deeper into his brain. Awesome.

The jerkwad Preslav jumped over bodies to stand next to my Aunt. I hit the floor like they taught us in school. Bullets rained through the chamber, people ducking and running. Those shit faces didn't know what hit them.

Preslav yelled to his men to stop firing, and three more boomerangs spiraled through the chamber from dark passages. They flipped into the cavern space, spinning and lofting like living things. The weapons either sliced into a bad guy or smashed into the wall with a loud clang. One swirled back out into the tunnel from which it came. *Stupid dudes, do you not know that you hit the ground during a weapons assault?*

Then, this weird music or chanting started coming from all around us. I saw this movie once where this green, evil witch runs around, screaming, "Seize them!" So that was the Grand Duchess, OK? Ordering her goons into the tunnels and shit. They never came back, Dude. Impact sounds … yells from guys falling… There were shouts down the mine tunnels in a language I had never heard – not English nor Bulgarian.

Big silence.

Max rushed to Kayne, and they started applying pressure to Nick's leg wound. Kayne switched to CPR, laying him out and doing mouth-to-mouth with a cardiac massage. I jumped at the nearest goon, the tech guy on the laptop, and we wrestled for his gun. I got the weapon and shot his computer as he backed up away from me, crawling on the floor. The geekazoid stopped when he was sitting against the wall, reaching for his shattered computer.

A black man and woman stepped into the chamber from opposite ends. Preslav, the fucker, leveled his gun on one of them as my Aunt scrambled for the lift closing the door behind her. She had snatched the backpack from the tech guy.

Kayne and Max were alternating with, "Come on, Nick. Hang in there, Kiddo. Breathe for me, Nick. Come on buddy... Nick, please." I was scared. The black woman tossed the war club so that it spun through the air and annihilated the head of the Prince. The bloody thing exploded like a shot melon, but not before he snagged the other woman ninja with two bullets.

The Earnshaw guy sprinted after the Duchess, waving a steel hatchet boomerang that had earlier felled one of the guards. She fastened the cage door closed and moved to the opposite side with the controls. The assembly began to rise.

Earnshaw scrambled up the chain link to the top of the lift and hacked at the cables as the entire enclosure rose out of sight. Then, in a moment, the cavern was filled with the screeching of ripped metal from the shaft above. The lights sputtered. The elevator crashed back down, disappearing below stories. I saw my panic-stricken Aunt imprisoned in her cage. The backpack and the manservant were attached to the wreckage. As it fell, it careened off the walls of the mine shaft. The entire shit mess wildly spiraled and fell into the lower depths of the elevator shaft.

My prisoner began to babble surrender phrases in Bulgarian. Our rescuers-- turns out there were five Aboriginal warriors in the group, rounded up to count casualties. I moved my prisoner over to where they were working on Nick.

Then somebody turned on some very bright lights.

The cavalry had arrived.

Chapter Fifty-One: Shaking the Red Queen

From the Case Notes of Kayne Sorenson, Ph.D

I shook her again and again. Her head bobbled back and forth. The terrible Red Queen with the face of Olga Danilova did not turn into a black kitten, as in Carroll's story. The chess piece which I pummeled up and down morphed into Nick. I was pounding on his chest again, and his eyes were without the glint of the living – flat, dull grey-green within the closeness of death.

"No! No! Nick, don't die... Please. NICK! Come back to me!"

I was screaming with a combination of mad fury and insane fear. I jumped up from the chair. Kris, who had fallen asleep on the floor with his head leaning against my leg, called out, "It's OK, Uncle Kayne, you were dreaming. It was just the dream." He soothed my shoulder and took my hand.

Mechanical breathing tube sounds and heart monitors... Nick was pale and deathlike on the hospital bed... a huge bandage covered his left leg. Hypovolemic shock brought on by class 4 hemorrhage... a bag of my blood drained into his arm... rare, AB negative. Kris, dirty, a bit scraped, and tired, attempted to bring me back from the torments of sleep.

I could make no coherent speech. I just blinked like some cock-eyed goldfish. Allira came into focus. She handed up containers. "Drink the tea, Kayne. Here you are, Kris. You gotta get your strength back if you are going to help these guys fight the bad guys."

Their voices came through like my ears were stuffed with cotton. I stared at the monitors, the blood and breathing tubes... the life support machines... the final option that seemed to be represented by the damn electric plugs.

Kris was saying, "I was totally in it, Allira. So fuckin' much going on. Oops, sorry, I cussed. You guys were like the Aboriginal Ninjas, Dude. So fuckin' fine."

"You cuss like your Uncle Nick, lad. Give us a hug and eat your burger and chips."

I looked at them and said, "Allira?"

"Kayne, you are still in shock. They are doing everything they can for Nick. He is showing REMs like crazy. Good sign, Mate."

I took Nick's hand. Warm. Nothing really mattered now. Nothing.

Kris set his burger aside and took me in a hug up. "Thank you for rescuing me, Kayne. Thank you a lot, you and Nick. Yeah, so don't worry. We got this, Kayne. He will make it."

Even though he was attempting to cheer me up, the lad's face was streaming with tears.

I heard Max come into the room behind me and speak softly to Allira. She shook her head and looked at the form on the bed.

"How is Ms. Renna? I heard she was hit in the mine battle."

"Ahhh, my amazing warrior. We are blessed that her wounds are superficial. Preslav was not accurate with his shots, thankfully."

Kris held me. I felt like the boy was keeping me from tipping into an abyss, dark and endless. After a bit, he eased up. His hold was replaced by a familiar grip, softly and gently taking hold of me. I heard a woman's voice speaking in her language, phrases I had heard before in a time long past.

"My son, my Kayne. Nick is in the Dreaming. See how his eyes move with the music and the songs. Your love songs. Behind the lids. See? Do you see my Son? He is journeying in the earth, the air, and the sky. He is not gone. He runs to you."

"No, my Mother, I want him here. I want him with me. WAKE UP, NICK! Please. Please." I held Kirra's arms around me.

Now, existence began to collapse. I saw things around me, elongated, as if in a tunnel, far away and slanting down. The body on the bed started to spasm. Machines began to make alarming sounds.

I sank to my knees and sobbed against his hand.

Chapter Fifty-Two: The White King's Court
Darana's Reflection

Despite the season of tragedy that surrounded us, Ace, as only Ace could do, decided to throw a party at Inala in anticipation of Kris's sixteenth birthday. Kick and Mitch had come from Colorado and were delighted with their nephew. Kris kept saying the superheroes in the family just keep adding up.

Gints and Scott from the Sorenson Research Team also came over. They are delightful men and, indeed, added class, skill, and humor to the family of crime fighters. Their first time in Australia– they were dazzled.

We were sitting beneath the rainbow gum trees at the back of the property in the warmth of the late afternoon. Ace had been touring the Tsar and his bodyguards in the open landrover and pulled into the paddock. The Lord of Inala and the Lord of the Bulgarians got along famously.

As I passed, Allira was explaining her team's rescue operations to a few listeners. "We decided to put our spiritual strength to work. The war clubs and other traditional weapons, the war chants – all of that, deep in the mines. We are a proud and ancient people and will never sit idly by while others attempt to destroy our loved ones or us." Allira and her comrades looked splendid in their party togs.

While I am on it, I need to stop here to describe how folks were turned out for the occasion. I know that my good friend Rebecca would be upset if I did not mention she was the most beautiful woman at Inala that day.

Ace arranged to rent a huge load of Nineteenth Century costumes from a theater group in Alice Springs. We all looked like a cross between a production of "The Thorn Birds" and "Downton Abbey" (transplanted to the Northern Territory, of course). Summer whites and beiges were everywhere – women in desert boots and parasols, long flowing skirts, and billowing blouses. The men were in straw boaters, braces, and collarless shirts above cream-colored riding breeches stuffed into tall riding boots or wide-cut, pleated slacks and kicks. The Inala serving staff completed the fantasy in period livery -- it was all there. Our Aboriginal friends and I wore richly colored fabrics with lovely art designs and patterns. Asian family members and friends were arrayed in 19th-century silks, cottons, and linens. The diversity was entirely Ace's vision of the world – whites, blacks, browns, and yellows, a glorious human family.

I continued passing through the assembly of guests and family in clusters of conversation that opened periodically to include other folks. Rebecca was recounting our adventures with the "Big Bads" at the main house. She explained how we turned up the final puzzle piece, the White King. "And Darlings, well, there it was. You know, just like the purloined letter in the Poe classic, it was hiding in plain sight." A soft breeze toyed with her pale rose summer shawl and beribboned straw hat, her long mahogany hair cascading down her back.

I mingled, listening and observing.

The birthday boy and his mate were in ivory knickers and matching argyle socks. Herringbone, tweed newsboy caps kept toppling from their heads as they roughhoused or used them to clobber each other with wide grins and much laughter. Braces held up their pants, and collarless white shirts with rolled sleeves completed the Nineteenth-century kit.

Earlier, Kris's Uncle Kick had tagged the lad and unbuttoned his shirt a bit, saying, "Let's show some of that muscle, kiddo. When I was sixteen, the men and the boys... well, never mind. Anyway, you have the Sorensen good looks, after all."

This led to a tickle fight that Kick won, but not without a lot of effort.

A somewhat grassed stained Kris to Kaito: "So those folks over there are the Special Agents for Australia. The old guy was in the service with my Sorenson Grandpa. The woman is also a special agent."

Kaito: "Very cool, Kris."

Kris: "Yeah. They are the folks that broke into the mine when the shit storm hit. They got Nick to the hospital as fast as they could."

He threw a few punches at his schoolmate, who defended and pulled Kris into a jock boys' hug.

Ace was introducing Robert Wilben and Joan Ross-Munroe to the Tsar, who graciously thanked them for their intervention in the rescue of his great-grandson.

Commotion!

Ace's sons from America with Gints and Scott, were doing athletics on the sunny lawn adjacent to the reception area. They had doffed their boaters and shirts. Magnificent, if slightly inappropriate, but the setting summer sun was still hot.

Mark was yelling as the squad came in for hydration. "It's touch football, you blockhead. American football – the one and only! None of this Aussie shit. Touch is no-tackle, Kick, you fucking shit-for-brains."

Kick grabbed Mark's braces and pulled him into a fierce wrestle at the feet of his father and his royal guest. Partygoers stepped carefully away, lifting skirts and tottering cocktails to allow the brawlers space. Mitch approached his husband from one side, and Rebecca hurried over, parting the crowd to reach the grappling men. Kick's rough-and-tumble antics were, as usual, suspect. The boy/man has such a crush on Rebecca's lover.

Ace bellowed, "Thomas Michael Sorenson, get ahold of yourself. You are giving our reputation a bad name, you Hoolie! Do up your bloody trousers, lad."

Poor Kick, his tail between his legs, stood up from whaling on Mark. He pulled in behind Mitch, who tried to placate the Captain. "All good, Da. It's just the sport. Boys being boys." He helped Kick and himself into their shirts, straightening their braces and pawing their hair into more suitable arrangements. Such delightful lads. Smiles and grins from the guests were hidden behind fans and boaters. The wild-arsed Sorensons were legendary in these parts.

Rebecca tidied up the flustered Mark, who stood and addressed the Tsar as he put on his white shirt. "Your Royal Highness, I apologize for my behavior as well as my rude language, Sir. And to you, Captain Sorenson, I extend a like apology."

Stefan II clapped the reporter on the shoulder and said, "I am an admirer of your work, Mr. Gadarn, and of your heroics. No need to apologize for your salty language. You cannot help yourself, Sir. You are, after all, an American."

The Tsar's eyes twinkled. Ace said, "He's a good lad, Stevie. And a good friend to my sons."

Only Thomas, "Ace" Sorenson could get away with calling Tsar Stefan Kadam Ferdinand Petar Saxe-Coburg-Gotha, titular sovereign of the Bulgarians, Prince of Tarnovo, Prince of Saxe-Coburg and Gotha and Duke of Saxony, "Stevie." The man is truly a wonder.

Mark brushed off Outback dirt with Rebecca's help, and the two of them engaged Ace and "Stevie" in quiet conversation.

Next, I overheard an interesting interchange. Kirra came up to the Sorenson brothers. "My sons, how is he doing?"

"Have no idea, Mother. You know Kayne. Even as a boy, he could close off from everyone – go into that private headspace of his."

Kick agreed with Mitch and added, "I tried to get him into the play, but he just blew us off."

Mitch said, "Did you get a chance to see the pictures of the house, Mother? Kayne intended on surprising Nick– a wedding present."

"Yes, beautiful. So big. I have heard much of this place, San Francisco. Your clear-eyed brother was thinking with his spirit. He has always been somewhat clumsy when allowing his heart to lead the way, I am afraid."

I moved forward toward the fringes of our crowd. Max and a few people talked over to the side near the food tables.

"So, the working title is the 'Zachary Warrun Ariel Foundation for the Advancement of Community.' My company will be a major contributor, but we are in negotiations for a significant funding source that will completely endow the organization."

I turned and saw Kayne walking in their direction, but I was stopped by the clinking of a glass and a barked call to attention by Ace.

"Oy, oy, oy, folks. Again, thank you for coming, and I hope you are having a good time and all of that. Shout out to my Grandson on his upcoming sixteenth birthday. Get up here, lad, and give us a hug, ya mug."

Kris bounded up to his two awesome relatives and hugged them both.

"Now, Stevie... ahhh, His Royal Highness here has agreed to join Kris and me in a ritual we are famous for here at Inala. Let's have all of our Aboriginal or Torre Islands Guests come forward? And I want my sons up here with me, also. Come on, you brogans, move your dodgy arses."

Kayne joined the family, and I accompanied Kirra, Allina, fellow scientists, and others of our people to the center of the gathering. Kris motioned Kaito to come and stand next to him.

The family members stooped, and each took up a fistful of Inala's dirt. Ace said in his voice-of-God tone, "This is Inala." The deep and lusty voices of the bothers shouted the traditional refrain. "Haroo! Haroo! Haroo! Long may she prosper! Inala! Inala! Haroo! Haroo! Haroo!"

The family held the dirt high in reverence. Guests cheered.

Ace continued by singing in his deep baritone. "We acknowledge the Traditional Owners of this land. We reverence our Mother on which we stand, on which we live, and from whom we draw forth our lives and our prosperity."

The Sorenson family bowed to my people. Ace continued. "We pay our respects to their Elders, past and present, and the Elders from other communities who may be here today, and we ask to be welcomed here."

Kayne, Mitch, and Kick yelled, "Hurahh! Hurahh! Hurahh!" The group cheered again.

Kirra, as the Elder, answered with arms extended, joining earth to sky.

"I ask the good spirits, the ancestors of the land, to watch over us and keep our guests safe while they're in our Country. And I proclaim to the spirits of their ancestors that we're looking after them here, and we will send them back safely to their Country."

The assembly cheered a third time.

Kayne left the group and wandered around to the front of the house. He sat on the porch steps, tossing pebbles down the walkway. I watched from the edge of the back lawn for a bit and then mounted the porch from the side, settling into a large rocker.

Livestock in the front paddock eyed the sad man but went back to grazing. Alice came up and settled at his feet. She pawed for a love scratching and finally dropped her head in his lap, carefully eyeing the hiker who approached along the long road to the manor house. Alice wagged her tail but remained next to the one whom she sensed needed her most.

I overheard the conversation.

"You look like your cat ran away. Why so blue?"

"Probably made a big mistake. I am so sorry."

"I just had to think about it, is all. Big step."

"Yes."

"Remember, I suck at this. Horrible track record. I made a mess of the last one. Well, you know that."

"Me too. Am a major fuck up the world over in this particular area."

They paused and looked at each other's faces as if to try and read an unspoken message or some hint on how to continue.

"So, I'm not sure...."

"I see, then. So, I guess I should...."

Kayne hiked a thumb toward the back of the house.

"Let me finish. I am trying to say... ahh... while I am not sure, Kayne, I know this for a certainty. I can't live without you. It seems, you see, that you are my everything. Whatever all of that is or may be.

He paused before adding, "It's just that... whatever it takes, I want to be with you always. So my answer is yes."

Kayne leaped into the air and shouted to the sky like his footie team had just won the championship, and he, himself, had scored the deciding goal. He ran around, throwing his arms out to embrace the expanse of Inala and the entire country, roaring, "He said YES! Whoo-hoo, hoo, hoo...."

The cattle in the paddock lifted their heads to see what all the excitement was about. Alice circled her two dads.

His fiancé smiled lovingly.

Kayne scooped Nick into his arms and kissed him like a crazy person as his brothers and family ran forward to lift them both into the air.

Thomas Paul Severino

Epilogue: Whose Dream Was It?

Nick Sechi's Journal

"We did it, Boss. Any regrets?"

"On the contrary, I am the happiest bloke in the whole universe. To quote the immortal chanteuse, Edith Piaf, *'Non, je ne regrette rien.'* I regret nothing, my love. You have made me very happy, Nick." He kissed me and settled into the chair next to me.

Alice and Chouko stirred and grunted in alternating rounds of snoring dog sleep. Lying at our feet, they were recovering from a day of high excitement and a thousand new smells and sights.

"Sorensons and Sechis – such a total 3-ring circus."

"I was afraid the Ace/Viola fracas over the reception menu was going to be the beginning of an international incident."

"Definitely, Boss. Food is a serious business among my people. Whenever Mama Sechi gets to the point when she says, 'No son of mine ...' you realize we are all at ground zero."

"At least my brother...."

"No, don't even say it, Kayne. Kick was over the top with my Italian cousins. Living up to Mitch's nickname for him– 'hot mess,' right?"

Kayne snorted a bit. "Yes, Mitch has his hands full with that one. And what about when Rebecca told him to lay off trying to play grab arse with sexy Mark? Again! Holy Hell!"

"Ohh shit, yeah. Right?" I imitated our lovely Justice of the Peace. "Stop thinking with your cock when it comes to my man, Darling, or set up a four-way-- just what we needed my Bronx aunts to overhear."

Kayne laughed.

"My family was impressed with our Rebecca her having a JP license. So cool that she married us."

"Rebecca is one impressive woman in many ways, my love."

I watched the star-filled sky over Pacific Heights. Clouds gathered on the horizon between a midnight sky and an ethereal sea. Around us, a few of the catering staff were doing the breakdown on the back lawn. One walked over to refresh our nightcaps. All of the guests were gone or asleep.

A somewhat rumpled Kris came over to us from the illuminated house behind us. He was eating a sandwich. He had goofy boy hair.

"Shouldn't you guys be doing the honeymoon sex-up? You know, the naked and the sweat and the…."

Kayne said, "Easy there, beast boy. How's my best man doing, lad?"

Before he could answer, I teased, "Boyo, I sure hope those grass stains on your knees are from sporting and not…."

"Yo, Dude, still gonna deliver on that promise to kick your arse, Uncle Nick. News Flash! I just replaced you as the family hotshot. Your sisters and cousins think this boy rocks, and you know what? Huh? Do ya? He *does*."

Kris did his very practiced killer smile, busted a few dance moves, and hit a young muscles pose in the remains of his white tux– pants with braces, tuxedo shirt, and patent leather shoes. *Gonna break a thousand hearts, this kid.*

With a kiss to my head and referring to his dirty knees, Kris said, "Mitch, Kick, and da Bronx cousins. Mark was trying again to teach the Aussies and the Euro boys American touch football."

I did an exaggerated "Whew! Won't tell ya… never mind."

Kris was a pro at abrupt conversation changes. "Yeah, so I'm gay, at least I think I am. Thought I was into girls there for a while, but definitely not. Like when I make out with a guy, it's so different and so hot… I think, anyway. Just thought I'd let ya know. Cool?"

Kayne pulled the boy across the arms of the Adirondack chair and into a hug. "Wherever your journey leads you, Kris, Nick, and I will always love you unconditionally."

"Be yourself, kid, and be fuckin' fabulous. You're rolling with the gay boys now, lad. Nothing like it."

"Thanks, Uncs. Not easy. All of this, I mean. A lot to deal with to say the truth. Kidnapped and shit... opps, I mean stuff... new school... and no Kaito/Batman crush anymore."

I said, "Guess that was pretty serious?"

"Dunno. Sorting it out a bit. We're just friends now. He has some issues with his family, coming out-wise. All good.

"And just so you know, I have been 'rolling with the gay boys,' as you say, for a while now. Just sayin'."

Kayne smiled, "Great, just what we need, another hyper-sexed Sorenson male."

I said, "Dude, you cool with the safe sex thing and all? Need any info on all of that?"

Kris reached up and pulled Kayne's head next to his, cheek to cheek. He pointed back and forth between him and his uncle. "See? Sorenson brains, Dude. Same. Most intelligent of the species. Unsafe is just stupid. This boy plays safe– wrappin' when tappin' or gettin' tapped. Ohhh, yeahhh. So good... so fine."

He jumped up, rubbed his hands together, and said, "Buncha rapid-fire questions. Ready, Dudes?"

"Go."

"Can I borrow the car tomorrow?"

"Too easy, Lad. No. Next question."

"But Nick."

"No license. No drive. You know how that works. Use public."

"Yeah, the appointment for the driver's test is this week, so that's cool. Sleepovers? Rules?"

Kayne took that one. He sat up and said, "Crikey, Lad. Already? You just got to San Francisco." Kris gave a sheepish shrug.

"Just an irresistible jock prince, I guess." He grinned, did a Timberlake bulge grab, and spun around. Earlier on the dance floor, he and my brother-in-law, "the Kickster," as Kris called him, were hot magic in motion.

"Well, resist a bit more, Ego Boy. A lot can be said for playing hard to get."

Kris's expression was easy to read. *Yo, seriously?*

Kayne started to continue but stopped. He looked at me and then said, "Ummm... I need to talk this sleepover thing over with your Uncle Nick. Still kinda blown away that you are sexually active at fifteen. We'll get back to you ASAP."

I guffawed, "Husband of mine– you know we were both horny males in high school. And, as you mentioned, the boy is a Sorenson, after all."

Kayne gave a fake wince and a finger-to-the-lips sign, which meant *Shush. Do not tell secrets.*

"Sixteen in two days. OK. Number next: Will Grandpa be very upset if I pass on Notre Dame and say 'yes' to the University of San Francisco?"

I asked, "A free ride also? Soccer scholarship?"

"Yep. I'll show you the letter."

Kayne said, "It's not what Ace wants, Kiddo. But, you're the man on this decision. How's the new high school?"

"Yeah, so, Gonzaga Academy is, um... interesting. Only one year, and it's nice not to have to board. Living with you dudes is dope."

Kayne asked Kris. "You comfortable with diversity and acceptance issues at the school, lad?"

"Too early to tell. So, I will get back to you on that."

I joked, "They're Jesuits. It's not like their Catholics or anything."

Kris didn't get it, but Kayne did. He laughed at my touch of blasphemy.

"You guys OK with taking Uncle Kick and Uncle Mitch up on skiing in Colorado during Christmas vacation? The Aerie Valley sounds amazing."

"Nick and I agree on the need for conditions, Kris. School reports have to be exemplary, Lad, and you missed quite a bit. Dazzle us with the grades, and then you get to go."

I added, "And we need to talk more about how to survive your Uncle Kick. He is so thirty-five going on fifteen."

"Tell me about it. Dude is fuckin' legendary. Did you see him do the flip over the wedding cake? Thought your Mom was gonna stroke out, Nick."

"Please do not remind me. I thought any moment Viola was going to gently lecture Kick on his behavior."

The boy counted off on his fingers. "OK, lessee... safe sexin', choice of college, sexin' up at home, driving, high school, me being a gay boy, winter break... yeah, think that covers it for now. You are probably eager to hit the sheets doing the whole consummating the union thing, so I'll just ...."

I threw a martini olive at him. He laughed.

"I'm gonna do some reading and turn in. Got to be up for practice early."

"Don't wake the guests, Lad."

He started to dash back to the house and stopped.

"Thanks for everything, Uncs. I love my room, the house, and San Francisco. I am so lucky."

He gave each of us a good night kiss and resumed his jog up to the house.

I reached across and took my husband's hand, looking at the stars behind his handsome face.

Soft, ambient light, scattering across our clifftop lawn, seemed to catch in his dark hair, caress his high cheekbones, and tickle his impossibly long eyelashes. He said, "How's your leg, my love?"

"Hurts some but not all that bad. The therapist is doing some good. Still a bit of trouble with range of motion, but I'm getting there."

Thomas Paul Severino

"Married with children-- all moving too fast?"

"Hell no, Boss. You're my deal, now and forever." He stood up and gently pulled me into his strong embrace.

When our lips parted. We walked hand-and-hand up to and into the house as the staff turned out lights one by one. I pulled him close to me as we passed the gigantic mirror at the top of the second-floor landing.

We stared at the newlyweds who stared back at the newlyweds who stared back at the newlyweds... one blue-eyed with dark luxuriant hair dusted with the highlights of an Australian Outback midnight sky... one a ginger muscled boy who was showing a bit worn out and tattered at the edges. Looking glass Kayne had his forehead scar on the right side. My noggin's hard part was on the left.

I pressed his hand to my lips and looked past our reflections to see if I could glimpse the sleeping Red King snoring on the settee behind us.

I heard my own voice ask, "Kayne, will the dreaming stop? The nightmares, I mean?"

"Yes, my love. For now, I have you."

The End

Acknowledgments

Again, I am indebted to my husband, Tony Wallner, for his support and guidance in creating this story. To quote a lyric from a classic Barry White song, he is "my first, my last, my everything." Other friends who guided the story are Joanne Mena, Keith Hickman, Michael Varga, and Merrie Meyers.

I am also grateful to our friends, Daniel Proh and Matt Nimbs, for checking that the story rings true with its memorable characters and settings in the amazingly breathtaking country of Australia. Daniel served as our host and guide when Tony and I visited some years back. Daniel and Matt helped me with the authenticity of this story.

I am thankful to my dear friend, Gretchen Cassini, for her careful and comprehensive manuscript editing. This skilled and warm-hearted professional's loving corrections and literary insight made the story so much better.

For this book, I am again indebted to Rob Lalonde for his generous time and artistry in creating the cover from Joseph Lycett's *Aborigines Resting by a Camp Fire near the Mouth of the Hunter River,* Newcastle, NSW, courtesy National Library of Australia.

The continuing saga of the Sorensons, the Sechis, and their friends has at the heart of it the enduring love of family, with all of its wonder and calamities. It is love that strengthens us and allows us to become stewards of the earth and generative members of the wider human family. It grounds us, gives us life, and enables us to move forward. In my life, I am blessed with the timeless love and support of my brothers and sisters. Love makes a family, and for that, I am humbly grateful.

Afterword

Thank you for reading <u>Ancient Blood</u>, book four of the Kayne Sorenson Mysteries. I hope you found it enjoyable.

Kayne and Nick will be back soon. The cases are piling up, and our boys easily grow restless for action. Wedded bliss will quickly give way to more exciting mystery and adventure.

In the meantime, what's up with Rebecca, folks? The intrigue and suspense continue.

Here's a sample from the first book in her series ...

Thomas Paul Severino

The Frozen Diva

The Amazing Adventures of Rebecca Quinto

Thomas Paul Severino

Thomas Paul Severino

Prologue

Obersalzberg, the Bavarian Alps, 1935

The young woman pulled the thick woolen shawl tighter around her shoulders.

The chilly spring air in the Austrian-German border mountains was filled with the awakening calls of larks, barn swallows, and swifts amid the soft rustle of pines – miles and miles of pine trees. Off in the distance, a cowbell sounded as a peasant boy led his herd from barn to hillside. Lights blinked off in the towns across the vista in the promise of a bright morning.

The view from the newly constructed terrace was indeed breathtaking. New greenery shimmered in the valleys below. Rugged mountains, still clothed in snow, towered in the distance along the misty horizon. White and tan houses with soft brown roofs clung to the slopes of the hills and pasture lands. Spiraling roads wound through the panorama. She marveled at how the ivory-colored motor trails, encrusted with low buildings and running wooden fences, climbed the heights and dipped down into the dales.

From where she stood, she could see the first construction workers arriving to continue the renovation of the mountain chalet. They toiled their way upward with tools over their shoulders.

Angela, the housekeeper, and her daughter, Geli, supervised the sweeping of the terrace. Servants entered and retreated into the house, stepping around the scaffolds and setting the tables for breakfast. The Chancellor and his guests would enjoy their morning repast on the broad overlook under the colorful umbrellas despite the chill and the surrounding clamor of the workers. He loved to talk about the construction project and was fond of explaining the design details. The Leader was passionate about the future, its challenges, and opportunities.

"I trust you slept well, *Fräulein*."

"Yes, thank you, Frau Hammitzsch. I was concerned that the cold air here would affect my voice, but the house is warm. Will I have the opportunity to exercise this morning?"

"Of course, the *Reichsminister* had the piano brought up the mountain and installed in the music room last week. The tuner was here yesterday. You will be asked to perform this weekend, no doubt."

"I will do my best."

A dark-haired man in a blue-grey suit stepped from the house and lit a cigarette, blowing smoke in the direction of the mountains.

"Please excuse me, *Fräulein*, I must have Geli get the Doctor's coffee. And I will have her bring your tea. *Ja*?" She hurried away.

"*Guten Morgen*, I trust you are well, *Fräulein*. Have you come to a decision on our Peter Pan Project?"

These Germans, she thought, *a minimum of the niceties and straight to the point* ...

"I am still undecided, to be honest, Herr Doctor."

"That is unfortunate, my dear, as the *Reichsminister* will be sorely disappointed. You see, he was planning this ..." He waved his hand in her direction, taking in her physical form like a magician. "... as a birthday gift for the Chancellor, in April."

The young woman said nothing.

The Doctor took her hand and led her to the low stone wall that served as the parapet for the overlook. They sat and took in the view for a while. Overhead, an eagle swooped, searching the rocky open spaces between the trees in search of food.

"Decide judiciously, *Fräulein*. You know that the Minister is in love with you, my dear. He talks as if he was struck by a thunderbolt that night at the *Staatsoper*."

Again, nothing.

She considered the consequences of her self-exile in Germany. Now, the world's eyes were on the new government leading the country out of the ashes of the Great War. *If I am to reach my potential as an artist, is this the way the fates are leading me? And at what cost?*

She attempted to change the subject.

"What are they building up there on the tor above the chalet? The surveyors are such early arrivals there on the summit."

"It is to be the site of a government meeting hall commissioned by the Chancellor. He enjoys receiving foreign dignitaries here. His birthplace is not far over those mountains in Austria."

The eagle was joined by its mate, and they soared up the mountainside as the German and the Italian were served their coffee and tea, respectively. The Doctor stood and walked a few steps with his cup but returned to the young woman. He lowered his gaze and sat back down next to her. His tone was insistent.

"You must understand what this will mean to your future, my dear. At Nuremberg, the Chancellor has declared this to be a thousand-year Reich. There will be much wealth and glory for all of us who give him what he wants and an eternity in which to enjoy it."

The ingénue stared at the older man as if she were succumbing to a spell. From inside the house, the first guests were finding their way onto the terrace.

She met his persistent gaze and slowly nodded in resignation. He understood her decision was made, and she would cooperate.

"Capital, my dear. The *Reichsminister* will be delighted."

The Doctor stood, clicked his heels, bowed, and turned to the new arrivals. They exchanged morning greetings as servants circled, showing guests to places at crisp, clean tables and bringing heaping platters and steaming pots of Bavarian breakfast fare. All heads turned as the Chancellor and the Reichsminister stepped through the doorway into the brightening day. They were smiling.

Above them, the eagle rose against the first rays of the sun with its prey dangling from its deadly talons. Its mate seemed to screech in victory, a sound that echoed across the pristine Alpine vales like a scream.

Thomas Paul Severino

The diva pulled her shawl even closer.